They left [illegible] with night falling. Three stones' pitch away from the last tent, the mesa fell away, and the land became vertical. They made a fireless camp near a trail that wound down the mesa's edge in a zig-zag of switchbacks, leading finally to the dark at the bottom of the canyon. In the starlight, the river at the bottom of the gulch appeared a long, gray scar.

"Makindi Trench," Nissa said. "Our way lies there, unfortunately."

Sorin and Anowon sat with their backs propped against the boles of the few young Jaddi able to eke out a living at the edge of the mesa where the soil was exposed and infertile. Far down the trench a fire lit the canyon. Sorin blew into his hands and stamped his cold feet. Nissa gnawed on a square of hard waybread wondering what creature Anowon had eaten last, and which would be next.

Walk the Blind Eternities . . .

Discover the planeswalkers in their travels across the endless planes of the Multiverse . . .

AGENTS OF ARTIFICE BY ARI MARMELL

Jace Beleren, a powerful sorcerer and planeswalker whose rare telepathic ability opens doors that many would prefer remain closed, is at a crossroads: the decisions he makes now will forever affect his path.

THE PURIFYING FIRE BY LAURA RESNICK

The young and impulsive Chandra Nalaar—planeswalker, pyromancer—begins her crash course in the art of boom. When her volatile nature draws the attention of megalomaniacal forces, she will have to learn to control her power before her powers control her.

ALARA UNBROKEN BY DOUG BEYER

The fierce leonine planeswalker Ajani Goldmane unwittingly uncovers the nefarious agency behind the splintered planes of Alara and their realignment. Meanwhile, fellow planeswalker Elspeth Tirel struggles to preserve the nobility of the first plane she has ever wanted to call home. And the dragon-shaman Sarkhan Vol finds the embodiment of power he has always sought.

And revisit these five classic planeswalker tales, repackaged in two volumes

ARTIFACTS CYCLE I

THE THRAN BY J. ROBERT KING

THE BROTHERS' WAR BY JEFF GRUBB

ARTIFACTS CYCLE II

PLANESWALKER BY LYNN ABBEY

BLOODLINES BY LOREN L. COLEMAN

TIME STREAMS BY J. ROBERT KING

IN THE TEETH OF AKOUM

ROBERT B. WINTERMUTE

Magic: The Gathering
Zendikar:
In the Teeth of Akoum

Published by Wizards of the Coast LLC

MAGIC: THE GATHERING, WIZARDS OF THE COAST, and their respective logos are trademarks of Wizards of the Coast LLC in the U.S.A. and other countries.

Printed in the U.S.A.

Cover art by Jaime Jones

First Printing: April 2010

9 8 7 6 5 4 3 2 1

ISBN: 978-0-7869-5476-6
620-25353000-001-EN

U.S., CANADA,
ASIA, PACIFIC, & LATIN AMERICA
Wizards of the Coast LLC
P.O. Box 707
Renton, WA 98057-0707
+1-800-324-6496

EUROPEAN HEADQUARTERS
Hasbro UK Ltd
Caswell Way
Newport, Gwent NP9 0YH
GREAT BRITAIN
Save this address for your records.

Visit our web site at www.wizards.com

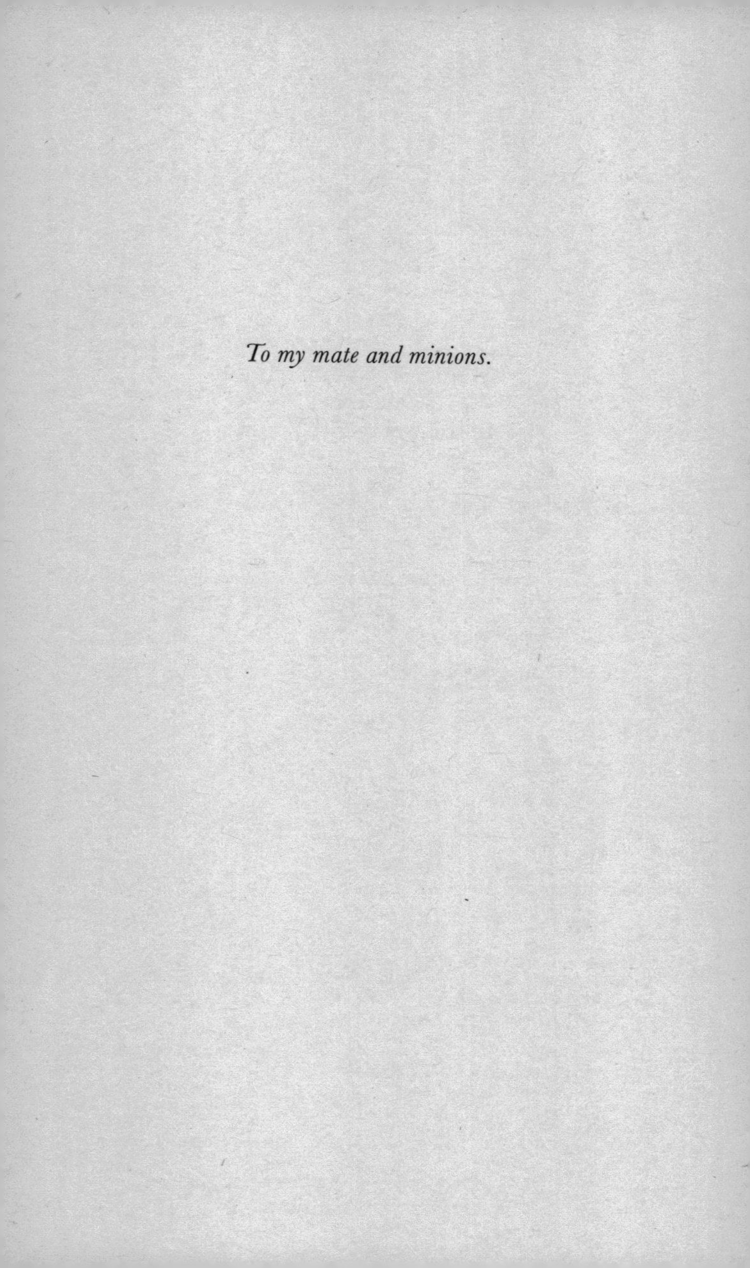

To my mate and minions.

CHAPTER 1

Nissa Revine heard a rustle and a snap, and she knew Hiba was running toward her through the undergrowth. She moved carefully as an accipiter beetle perched on her hand, keeping a wary eye on its venom-tipped spike. As she watched, the insect unfolded its hairy, purple wings.

"Come quick," Hiba said, bursting out of the foliage.

Nissa looked up and saw him freeze, his eyes on the fist-sized beetle. He took a step back, but it was too late. Sensing him, the beetle suddenly shot at his face. Hiba ducked and stumbled backward as the bug whizzed past his ear and away through the trees. Nissa watched it go.

"Stealthy as always," she said, her eyes on the gap in the branches the beetle had flown through. A breeze rustled the leaves, and Nissa sighed.

"One day," Hiba said. "You'll stop saying that."

She watched as he brushed himself off. In the heat of the forest floor, the smells of moss, sweaty leather, and jurworrel-tree sap wafted off him.

"We Tajuru don't spend our days sneaking around down here," he said, also glancing in the direction the beetle had flown. "Doing whatever it is you do down here."

Nissa smiled inwardly as she took his measure. Like most Tajuru, Hiba was lightly armed and well tethered. Only a short sword dangled from his belt, clanking against his climbing hooks and rope. His torso and thighs were crisscrossed with complex waist-harness loops and shoulder slings of warthog leather and turntimber bark, the latter nearly indestructible. His arms were saddled with long muscles capable of sudden feats of quick strength. He could, in half the blink of an eye, find a grip on a sheer cliff face, and support three other elves with one finger. She'd seen him do it more than once. He had saved her life in Teetering Stone Canyon when she'd missed a toe hold. Unlike the Tajuru, her own Joraga elves weren't much good at climbing—a failing more than made up for by their stealth, summoning ability, and combat prowess.

She shrugged the strap of the long staff slung over her shoulder back into place and followed Hiba.

The way back to the home tree took them shimming up a towering, corkscrew turntimber trunk and along moss-carpeted branchways wide enough for ten elves to walk shoulder to shoulder. They soon found the rope bridge hidden among the hanging lichens that always reminded Nissa of snakes moving in the breeze. *Snakes,* she thought, swallowing hard. Snakes teemed everywhere on Ondu—in fact, there was one wrapped around the rope handrail as she approached. *Snakes*. Nissa tried not to shiver as she passed by the handrail. *Only vampires are more disgusting than snakes.* Hiba noticed her grimace. The young elf smiled as they walked.

"Still afraid of snakes," he said, more of a statement than a question.

"I think you meant, 'still afraid of snakes,' *Captain*

Leaf Talker?" she corrected, using her official Tajuru ranger designation. "Is that what you meant?"

"That is exactly what I meant, Captain Leaf Talker," Hiba said. He was teasing her she knew, but she did not mind too much. Hiba was as near to a friend as she had in this place among the weaker elves.

They were very near the tree—she could tell by the smell of fires. But the tree was so well camouflaged that the forest seemed to extend in unbroken stillness until they were virtually at its trunk. Only the continuous creaking of the turntimber trees filled the close silence.

Silence was yet another odd aspect of the tribe that had adopted her. She did not understand their need for quiet. Her old home in Bala Ged had been a noisy place. But she certainly could not go back to the Joraga elves there. Not until she'd completed her appointment with the Tajuru. It was something all great leaders of the Joraga did; to live abroad with another tribe for a time. But Nissa had done so much more. She'd traveled out past the blind eternities to flat lands of endless of grass, to lands of alloy and fire, even to endless cities where people stood on each other's heads. But none of those planes were her place, and no plane had more mana or beauty than Zendikar, so she soon felt drawn back.

Nissa snapped out of her thoughts. Hiba had stopped walking and was standing stock still in the middle of the bridge, a long ear cocked upward. Far below she could hear air passing over the wings of a bird of prey circling the floor's duff. Above, the green tangle of corkscrew branches held strangely still. Then she heard it: a rhythmic scraping somewhere ahead and up. She knew better than to make any noise as she very carefully freed her staff from the strap slung over her shoulder.

It could be many things. The Turntimber was full of dangerous predators; simm cats that kicked with their sharp back claws; forest trolls with their swords made of chipped stone. Perhaps it was even the undead Tajuru from the kor tales that wandered the forest floor at night, waiting to suck the brains of the living out through their eye sockets.

Or it could be something else. Lately there had been whispers of a new threat in the forest. *Something* had been seen.

The scraping sound continued; the sound of long claws sharpened across the hard wood of a turntimber branch. *Onduan baloth,* her mind suddenly screamed. She'd seen one, many times the size of an elf, hop casually from one trunk to another—a jump of nearly fifty body lengths—and swipe a Tajuru in half with its thick claws. They fought casually, and could eat whole families.

Nissa and Hiba stayed still and listened to the scraping and the creak of the trees until Hiba smiled and took a hook from his belt. He very carefully drew it across the nearest branch as a pass sign. Soon a whistle echoed through the boughs, and Hiba clipped the hook back on his belt and walked forward.

Two sentinels were perched above a ladder in a nest of moss. They were so well camouflaged that Nissa had to look at the nest for some seconds before the outlines of the elves revealed themselves. One nodded as they passed. The branch behind the two was wrought by clever enchantment into a long horn that could be blown to alert the home tree.

She had to give credit to the Tajuru architects as the full view of the home tree settlement opened before her. She'd lived here only a month, and the sight still made the hairs on her arms stand up. Thousands of brightly colored wood-and-moss, hedron-shaped huts clung to huge belts of woven bark girded around the branches and trunk of a vast turntimber. Complex strut works of wood, rope suspension bridges, and planked walkways festooned the tree in arcing loops. The fact that the turntimber tree healed over any attempts to penetrate its bark only heightened her amazement—the clever tribe had been able to make the marvel without even one nail.

The rope bridge joined into one of the plankways, and with creaking steps, Hiba led the way to the longhouse atop a massive branch. Other Tajuru were walking together in the same direction. Many were talking in whispers among themselves, and were fully outfitted in ornate harness systems and slender bladed weapons. None of the tall, fine Tajuru looked like the Joraga, who, ever-hard in Nissa's memory, hissed vows as they smeared the blood of fallen enemies along scars they'd received in battle.

The longhouse was full to capacity when they arrived. Aggressively casual, some Tajuru were even sitting on the white jaddi wood windowsills and passing small bags of dried wolf berries back and forth. In the center of the room, standing on a slightly raised platform, Nissa saw two elves she's never seen before. She could tell by the hushed tones in the hall that the visitors were important.

Hiba leaned close to her ear.

"Speaker Sutina," he said.

She had seen a couple of messengers and important visitors stop by the home tree in her time with the tribe. But even the tribe's large size didn't seem to constitute such visitors as the two that stood on the platform. Nissa looked carefully at the female that stood in the center of the room. Speaker Sutina was wearing a jerkin of simple green leather, and her advisor was similarly dressed: no ropes, no harnesses. Neither Sutina nor her assistant seemed to be armed in the least. Their lack of gear alone should have alerted Nissa to their stature. But the Tajuru didn't think in terms of importance and stature, and she had already started adopting their ways of seeing the world.

Nissa forgot about what Sutina was wearing when she put her arms out and started to speak.

"Friends," Speaker Sutina said. The word seemed to hang shimmering in the air above their heads. Nobody spoke. One of the Tajuru dropped his bag of wolf berries on the wood floor. With the smallest trace of a smile, the Speaker's eyes cast around the room. When they met Nissa's eyes, her smile faded. "Friends," she repeated in a voice suddenly louder. "I won't mix words now that I have traveled so far to visit you. We have come to Ondu to alert others to a great rot in the roots of the forest."

Sutina's eyes fluttered for a moment. When she spoke her lips were dashed with green phosphorescence, and the words that came out of her mouth were guttural, rasping, and filled with chirps. Her eyes fluttered open, and the smile flitted across her lips again. "This is the language of the infection traveling in the forest right now. Do any of you recognize this talk?"

Nissa didn't bother to look at the faces around her. She knew the language belonged to nothing from their plane . . . It sounded like flint chips knocking together. Even mountain trolls spoke more pleasantly.

Sutina's eyes fluttered and went to their whites again as she channeled something else. "What is that?" a concerned male Tajuru's voice echoed out of her throat. "What are those holes? Stina, Rawli, give that thing a volley."

"But the wind," this time a female voice. "The wind."

A silence lasting nearly thirty heartbeats followed.

Nissa watched the muscles in Sutina's cheeks and around her eyes twitch and spasm. Her chin jerked side to side and up and down, and Nissa knew she was reliving the last moments of each of the scouting party's lives. Then the whites of Sutina's eyes blinked back into place, and she smiled. All around her the Tajuru had grown quiet. All the elves had bowed their heads. Their lips had all become slightly green, she noticed with a bit of unease. The elves did that sometimes at meetings.

A Joraga would never share consciousness with her tribesmen—it would be a shameful action. But the Tajuru seemed to want to do it when even the smallest thing went wrong. Nissa waited. Through the windows of the longhouse she could see patches of sky through the trees.

"Stina is my sister's name," a Tajuru said from the crowd. "We haven't heard from her in a week."

Another spoke up. "That was Leaf Talker Gloui's voice."

"He patrolled the far west," someone else said, almost in a whisper.

Wind, Nissa thought. *Where was there wind in a forest?* Breeze, yes, but never wind. She still didn't know the topography of the Tajuru's lands as well as she would like, but she did know that wind would be something of a rarity in a forest.

Hiba leaned over. His lips weren't green, Nissa noticed. "The Binding Circle," he whispered. "It's on a plateau."

Just then, in response to his thought, someone across the room said, "The Binding Circle is in the west."

"The Binding Circle," other elves repeated, almost in unison.

Nissa hated when they did that, speaking together like the undead.

Nissa, Speaker Sutina's voice said, suddenly speaking in her head. The Speaker's eyes were on her, and then she spoke aloud, "You will take a force of Tajuru and your own significant abilities to find and eliminate this threat."

Nissa nodded. She'd been a Leaf Talker for the Tajuru ever since her arrival in the Turntimber. The Tajuru always gave her the most difficult assignments. Many at the home tree were impressed with her abilities, she could tell; and many others thought she was a threat—the first step to a Joraga invasion. But for whatever reason, Nissa liked taking the dangerous assignments. What was she leaving anyway? A cold room in the home tree with a slug oil lantern and the distrustful stares of the Tajuru.

Nissa looked around the longhouse. Most of the Tajuru were filing out of the hall. She walked toward the door with Hiba following close behind.

The other Tajuru edged away from her as she passed. That was as it should be, she figured. It wouldn't do for them to get too friendly with a Joraga. Hiba was different. He appreciated her Joraga ways of disciplined magic and combat. When she'd first come to the home tree, some Tajuru had refused to sit at the same dinner table with her. She couldn't blame them. The experiences they'd had with the Joraga had not been pleasant. Nothing about the Joraga was particularly pleasant, unless your idea of pleasant involved training all day, leading raiding parties all night, and sleeping on the hard ground in between. Except for their distrust of scholarship, Nissa liked the Joraga lifestyle. She had the fetid jungles of Bala Ged in her blood, but she couldn't go back yet. And so she was leading a scouting party to defend the land of elves who distrusted her.

As Nissa walked out of the hall, she recounted what she'd heard about Speaker Sutina. The leader lived far away in the Tumbled Palace—an ancient structure crumbling to pieces on the cliffs of Sunder Bay. It sat clutched in the boughs of an ancient jurworrel tree which was slowly walking its way to the edge. Rumor had it that the Speaker partnered with the Moon Kraken once a month when that creature made its disastrous rise from the depths of sea.

Hiba's hand closed around Nissa's shoulder, stopping her mid-step. She turned. Tajuru in rustling silks and dyed leathers walked quietly around them. Her lieutenant's long ear was cocked to the sky, and his large jaw was slack, listening. That ear was his best asset in many ways, and it alone made him useful to have around. He could hear an owl preening from three tall timbers away, and that was impressive even for an elf. And from their scouting expeditions together she'd come to know his facial expressions very well. She could tell what creature lurked by how his lip curled and where his eyelids sat on his eyes. But the expression he showed just then, standing on the boardwalk outside the longhouse, was new to her.

A moment later the warning horns began to moan through the undergrowth. The Tajuru on the boardwalk stopped walking and stared down at the forest floor. Nissa fell to a crouch, and her hand went to grasp the staff strapped to her back. Before she could get to it, however, Hiba grabbed her wrist and pulled her off the edge of the branch. The ground rushed up as Hiba snatched a hook off his belt and threw it away, catching the crevice of an old tree. The rope jerked hard when it caught, and Nissa felt her teeth snap shut, but then they swung in a long arc away from the tree.

As Hiba let go of the rope, Nissa caught a spinning, blurred look at the branch they were hurling toward, gauged the distance, and executed a tight flip that plunked her feet squarely into the branch's mossy duff. She grabbed Hiba's arm and pulled him in as the larger Tajuru teetered on the narrow branch. Somewhere far off an eeka bird cried. A brace of giant hedron stones floated in the tree canopy above their heads, knocking unceremoniously together. It was a sight so common she barely took notice, but today their movements seemed more patterned than normal. They listened for the sounds of battle but heard nothing; neither horn, nor the sizzle of magic coursing through the air; not even the clash of steel. For a moment Nissa thought she heard a far-off scream, but when she asked Hiba, who was listening hard, he shook his head.

A moment passed, and then another, until suddenly Hiba jerked his head. "They are coming," he said. He seized the short sword clipped onto his belt, and Nissa held her staff firmly in both hands. She heard a low whistle and moved her staff at the last moment to deflect the dart, or some such thing, away into the greenery. And then, whatever it was in the trees was jetting toward them, chirping as it flew.

She got almost no look at it—gray with many arms—before she and Hiba were knocked off the branch and falling through the air. Nissa heard Hiba slice at the air with his sword, before they hit the forest floor and rolled off in opposite directions.

Nissa hopped to her feet and held her staff in both hands while she whispered the incantations she knew so well. As always, her staff felt burning hot as the lines of energy rippled through her body to spin around her head and away. She felt her mana lines stiffen and intensify until they were like glowing veins running straight from the jungles of Bala Ged. And in a moment, the four Joraga warriors she had summoned from the æther were standing in loose formation around her, blinking in the dim light of the forest floor, and smelling like spicy jungle orchids. Their eyes were sharp. They snatched small bows from their backs, nocked arrows, and drew back in one fluid motion. The arrows flew to the two beings squatting in the trees looking down at them.

Black and gray with highlights of vivid color, and covered with geometric plates of chitinous material, each of the creatures' arms was split into two; their legs were shiny tentacles. They had no heads—only bumps on their shoulders. And their bodies were covered with lidless blue eyes that stared down without expression as their thin arms knocked the arrows away. From behind, Nissa heard a titter and chirp, and she turned to see four more creatures swinging silently on branches. The Joraga released more arrows, but most were knocked away by the creatures. One arrow did find its target, catching the thing in the upper torso, and the creature gave a strange moan, pitched foreword, and fell spinning to the ground. The remaining creatures jumped with surprising fluidity and found their way to the forest floor to surround the one that had fallen, touching it all over with their tentacles.

The Joraga nocked their arrows and shot another creature as it stood over its fallen comrade. The remaining four turned slowly. It was their eyes that caused Nissa to pause—those blue, expressionless eyes that covered their bodies. There was no anger or sadness in those eyes, no evil or good. She had the unsettling feeling that they saw her the way she might see a zeem beast—as prey.

The Joraga shot a third creature and the three remaining beasts broke into a smooth charge on their powerful tentacles. One seized the Joraga next to Nissa with its thick arms and pulled him to meat. With a muttered incantation, Nissa took up her staff and thrust a blow into the chest of the nearest creature. The thing stepped back, and its blue eyes looked at the green glowing dent in its hard flesh. Suddenly a stalk and a leaf popped out of the impression.

Nissa had seeded adversaries in the past, of course, but never had one reacted so. She had once seen a petra giant yank the plant out. When he had taken hold and pulled, the root had popped out of his chest clutching his pumping gray heart. But this tentacled creature watched as the plant grew, shimmering and stretching, until it was taller than the monster itself, at which point a bud appeared and opened to reveal a mouth that snapped shut around the creature's head.

Something whizzed by Nissa, and the monster that had been poised behind her fell with Hiba's short sword sticking out of its chest. Its tentacles kneaded the handle of the sword as it lay in the rotting leaves on the forest floor.

The last creature knocked away the arrows the remaining Joraga fired. Nissa struck her staff into the earth and took a deep breath, feeling the energy pulse up through the soles of her feet and along her spine, and shimmer all around. She ran and jumped into the air, swinging her staff so that it connected with a dull thump on the top of the creature's head. It stood still for a moment in the dappled light coming through the trees, and then crumpled to the ground.

Nissa landed, turned, and walked back to the creature. She bent down for a closer look at its body. To her surprise, the plants trapped under its body had turned brown and died. She would have liked to investigate further, but Hiba was already running back to the home tree. Nissa took one last look at the creature on the ground before following him with the two remaining Joraga keeping in step.

Hiba stopped at the base of the gigantic home tree—so thick it would have taken one hundred elves holding wrists to encircle it. But instead of elves, twenty of the tentacled creatures lay still around it. Some were festooned with arrows, and one was strangled with vines. All had fallen from above. Hiba wasted no time in hopping onto the tree and climbing. Nissa and her Joraga followed.

There were at least twenty more of the dead creatures scattered on the platforms of the settlement, some of which were still writhing. Small groups of Tajuru were walking from creature to creature with long knives clutched in their pale hands. Nissa watched as an elf shoved the blade of his knife deep into one of the creatures, stilling it forever.

"Here," Hiba said. He was running to the longhouse. He stopped outside the door of the house, near a small crowd. The elves in the crowd were bending down and lifting something.

"It isn't her," Nissa said to herself as she ran.

But by the time she arrived, they had already lifted the body of Speaker Sutina. She was still wearing the same smile on her lips, but the elf leader's leather jerkin was torn and bloody. Her arm flopped free and something rolled out from her dead grasp. The object bounced twice, rolled over a plank, and came to rest in a crack. Nissa glanced at the other elves. None seemed to have noticed. Without thinking, she bent down and plucked the smooth object, which appeared to be a large pearl.

As the body of the Speaker was borne away, a small group of Tajuru around the door of the longhouse did not help hoist the body, but watched the procession leave. When it was gone they turned and looked at her, each with a less-than-friendly expression. Nissa glanced at the two remaining Joraga leaning against the side of the longhouse. *Wonderful.* Had they *all* seen her take the pearl? She hoped not.

Nissa turned her back to the other elves and had a closer look at what the Speaker was holding when she died. A pearl the size of a human's eye rolled in the palm of Nissa's hand. She had never seen one so smooth and round. A strange, squiggled script was etched into its blue opalescence. She could feel the mana emanating from the script. *Where had Sutina gotten such an object, and why was it in her hand when she died?* It didn't bear thinking about. She looked back at where the Speaker had fallen. Two creatures lay crumpled on the stairs nearby. She bent over one.

"What are you doing?" Hiba said.

Nissa ignored him. She knelt. The creature's tentacles were not moving. She carefully looked the thing over from tentacle to tip, moving its appendages. She found one curious thing. Under the creature's right arm, a proboscis-like tube extended four feet. The tube was fleshy and very thin, and looped so that it did not dangle down.

"Strange. They have no mouths," she said, glancing up. The small group of Tajuru watched her silently from the door of the longhouse.

"So they have no mouths?" Hiba said. He glanced at the group.

"How do they eat?" she said, poking at the spongy tentacles. She could almost hear Hiba's shrug, but she didn't look up. "Why were they here if not to eat?"

"Maybe they don't like Joraga?" Hiba said. The comment was meant for her, but she ignored it.

Hiba walked over to the group standing around the door. Nissa could hear them muttering, but couldn't make out any words. Instead she looked more closely at the creature.

It was like nothing she had ever seen on Zendikar. It had tentacles, yet no webbing between its digits, and no gills. Its lidless eyes and ridged skin spoke of a subterranean life, but how could something without a mouth live underground? There were no weapons and no clothing. And the creature smelled somehow clean and tangy, like she imagined a snake would. She curled her lip in disgust.

Still, something about the creatures was familiar. She had felt it the second she had seen them squatting on the branch. While she considered that, Hiba came down the stairs and stood.

"Do they look familiar?" she said, standing.

"Like something from a children's story," he said.

That was it! They looked like the monsters in the old stories she'd heard from the kor troubadours. *Those that lurk.*

"Do 'those that lurk' have tentacles?" she asked.

"We did not call them that," Hiba said. "And I do not think ours have tentacles. Ours have horns."

She nodded. Still, there was something about them.

Hiba jerked his chin at the Tajuru at the door of the longhouse. "One of them just stumbled in from MossCrack. These creatures attacked there before they attacked here."

MossCrack was the next settlement, just down the forested gully through which the WhiteShag coursed.

"What else did he say?" Nissa asked.

"That he does not care for Joraga," Hiba said. He gave her a grim little smile.

"That he does not care for Joraga," Nissa repeated. "That is comical." She thought for a couple of seconds before deciding. "Alright," she said. "We'll take the zip. Collect those in the doorway and any others Tajuru who care to make a trip to MossCrack." She started walking down the boardwalk, then stopped. "Or they can cower here and let the Joraga deal with this menace."

"The zip, Leaf Talker?" Hiba yelled after her.

"The zip," she confirmed.

By the time Hiba arrived at the zip-line platform he had twenty elves, grimly outfitted and smeared with their combat colors. Some wore red circles around their eyes; others had blue lips. Each configuration represented the elf's personal totem. "Very pretty," she muttered to herself. "But can they fight?" She was painted in the fashion of a Joraga: black bars that came in from all sides of the face and pointed at the eyes. It meant she was Joraga. It meant she trusted only her own. *The heart of another is a dark forest,* the Joraga saying went.

They all squeezed into the topless gondola made of woven vines. It was attached to the zip-line by a curved vine and two jaddi-wood pulleys housed in a turntimber-bark sleeve. The bark-twilled zip led away into the greenery.

The compartment bobbed and swayed as Nissa stepped on. She'd ridden it once before, and despite its appearance she knew it worked well enough. Those were the contraptions that the Tajuru excelled at. Still,

Nissa could not totally blot out the realization that working well or not, the gondolas made good targets.

Hiba was at the front. With a foot pedal he could slow their speed, but he didn't seem to know that, Nissa thought, as they hurled at greater and greater speed through the forest. Branches slapped at the sides of the car, and the wind sang through the gaps between its vines. Soon she could see the WhiteShag far below, smashing down through the rocks. Her breath caught in her throat for a moment when a lean Onduan baloth stood on its hind legs next to the river and watched them intently. But even a baloth couldn't catch them in the zip.

She knew they were near MossCrack when the Tajuru began unhitching bows from their back and fixing arrows. Nissa closed her eyes and felt the wind whistling over the tips of her ears. She breathed in the forest, and felt the sap in the trees rising in her blood, and she felt the great raw lump of the ground far below pulse as though it was rising to meet her.

Soon MossCrack's home tree rose before them above even the tallest turntimber. Hiba had not slowed their speed, so Nissa reached out and allowed her hand gather the energy that writhed up and around every tree in the Turntimber. She let a moment pass to bond with the invisible mana that permeated the entire forest. The trees all grew around these spikes of mana in their characteristic twisted way. By bonding to to the mana, Nissa was able to slow the car's progress, and she eventually pulled it to an easy stop. When she opened her eyes the elves were all looking at her.

"Did you think we would march right into the midst of them?" she said. "I know you're not the best warriors in the forest, but try to keep up." She could feel them bristle at that, but instead of looking back she peered over the edge. The forest floor was far below, mostly obscured by undergrowth and tree branches. "Ready," she said. Without waiting for a response—this wasn't a tribal council meeting, there would be no handholding—she hopped out of the gondola and landed softly on the nearest branch. After a moment, they grudgingly followed. When they were all on the branch, she turned to them. In the dappled light, her black and white camouflage blended perfectly. "Now," she whispered. "You are all honorary Joraga. As Joraga, we are going to fall upon our enemies unawares and destroy them, whatever they are."

She turned back and led them down the branch and to the next, and over many more until they neared the home tree. Nissa stopped frequently. But, strangely, she heard nothing. Then Hiba stopped and flicked the tip of his long ear and pointed off to the left. Soon she heard it too: a particular cracking sound and the swish of branches. They crept closer, and the sounds grew louder until they saw movement through the trees.

Her Joraga stopped and took out small, dried scute-bug shells. As the Tajuru watched, her Joraga carefully dipped the points of their arrows in the shells before quivering them again. Then they held the bug shells out for the Tajuru to clumsily dip their own arrow heads in.

"Distillate of bloodbrier," Nissa hissed. "Shoot for the neck . . . if they have one." She motioned to Hiba, and they got down on their hands and knees, crept to the edge of the branch, and carefully parted the leaves.

Hiba was the first to get a good look. Nissa heard his sharp intake of breath. And in a moment, she understood why. The creatures were there, at least one hundred of them. But it wasn't their numbers that shocked her. It was the sun. There was sun on the forest floor. With turntimber trees around there was never full sun on the forest floor. But the creatures had managed to do what Nissa had not thought could be done. They'd felled a small turntimber. They'd dug large holes and were in the process of stripping the leaves off the fallen tree, hauling them to the holes, and stuffing them in. And the creatures were not all the kind they'd fought earlier. Some flew and were only masses of floating tentacles with thin and vile arms extending out. Some were tentacled and crawled on the ground with round, white heads that appeared to be made of solid bone and lacked even the slightest face. Some were huge . . . the size of a stomper and just as thick. Others were the height of three elves, and as she watched one grunted and stood, towering over all the rest. "That one must have killed the tree by pushing it over," Nissa muttered. "It goes first."

Some among them had no tentacles. They were white-skinned even as a corpse might be and they were bound at the shoulders and elbows with what looked like leather straps. Some of those pale beings were stripping the leaves off the trees. Others were bent over the Tajuru strewn over the ground, sucking their blood from their bodies.

"They have vampire slaves," Hiba hissed.

As Nissa watched, one of the tentacled creatures casually seized a vampire by the neck. It wasn't done cruelly, exactly. More like an elf might seize a wild fig off the branch. The tentacled creature searched until it found the tube under its right armpit, and it jabbed it into the vampire's chest. Then the creature squatted and stared down at the ground, while the vampire stood stock still, growing whiter and whiter.

"What is it doing?" Hiba whispered.

"Prepare the attack," Nissa said. She pulled her eyes away from the grisly scene. "Right now."

The words were not fully out of her mouth when a branch snapped in the forest behind them, and the tentacled ones were upon them. The climbing kind they'd met at the home tree, perhaps thirty of them. They charged from branch to branch.

Nissa brought her staff sweeping from the right, pulling energy from the branch she was standing on and directing it in a wide swath out the tip of the staff. The mana touched the trees, and they animated and pulled in together, forming a wall of branches and vines that reached out for the beasts. The elves began shooting between the branches at the creatures, two of which fell as Nissa watched. The other creatures threw themselves at the wall, thrashing against it as the elves shot them dead.

Nissa heard a swish behind her and turned to see a squad of twenty flying creatures rushing at them. On the ground, more creatures converged on the tree they were in. The giant one lumbered on tentacles twice as wide as her waist. *This could be the end,* Nissa thought.

She screamed a warning, and some of the elves turned, but not before the flying creatures crashed through the foliage. One of the beasts bashed into the Tajuru standing next to Nissa, and she knew by the impact that the elf was lost. Another came at her, but she whispered the secret name of her favorite flower, the dendrite, and with that spell delivered a blow with her staff that sent the creature shooting backward off the branch. Other elves had turned and shot many of the flying creatures before they reached their ranks. And the climbing creatures on the other side of the grasping wall of branches and vines, Nissa noticed with a quick glance, were much diminished.

Then she felt the turntimber under their feet jerk hard to the right. She regained her footing, but the tree shifted again. She looked down and saw the huge creature through a gap in the leaves, pushing against the trunk of the turntimber.

One of the flying creatures slammed against her, and they fell crashing through the leaves. She silently mouthed words that pushed mana ahead of her like a pillow, and in a moment she was falling slowly, eventually landing next to the creature that had fallen with her, its body still.

And then they were on her again: two of the creatures with blue eyes, and the giant one the size of two forest trolls. The giant had lowered its shoulder against the tree and was pushing, its tentacles churning up the soft earth as it struggled for purchase. She focused her mind and felt the mana boiling, making her hands glow green. She twisted her staff and pulled out her stem sword—a long, thin green shoot hidden inside its wooden sheath—just as the first creature lowered its head and charged. She stepped to the side and pivoted hard to her right leg. As the beast barreled past she inserted the rigid stem neatly into its side, just where its heart ought to have been if it had one. She pushed the sword all the way to its wooden handle before yanking it out. With a whispered word, the bloody stem became flexible. She snapped it like a whip, and the stem lashed out and took off the arm of the behemoth pushing on the tree. It turned its body and regarded her calmly, as pale blood bubbled out of its arm stump. *No scream, no anger,* she thought. *Not even a sneer.* The creature simply planted its other shoulder against the trunk and kept pushing.

She was about to take the behemoth's other arm off when the second creature charged hard into her side. But as she fell, she kicked away and turned, whipping half its tentacles off with a puff of emerald-colored mana.

She landed just as the tree shifted to the right. Its flat root ball heaved up and out of the ground, slapping Nissa violently against the giant creature. She clambered up its back and onto its shoulders, and wrapped her stem sword around what should have been its neck. As she pulled and twisted, the creature's hundreds of blue eyes blinked and turned to look at her, but still the creature did not stop pushing. She'd seen single-minded animals in her life, but never anything like the giant. She pulled hard for some minutes, and began to fear that the creature had some enchantment about it, but eventually she heard a crack and the creature went slack and fell forward into the trunk.

They must have a spine, Nissa thought. She looked around as she sheathed her stem sword in her staff once again.

The tree had settled into its new position, pitched off to the north. She followed its trunk with her eyes, hoping to catch a glimpse of her squad through the branches. But she heard neither the twangs of their bows nor their battle cries. She walked away from the trunk. A loud grinding sound echoed somewhere through the canopy. A common sound of two floating hedrons rubbing against each other in the sky above the trees came to her.

She walked to the clearing, ducking under the white-barked boughs of a young jaddi tree.

A narrow draw extended to her right, and farther down it, the pound of the WhiteShag thundering through its deep ravine echoed off the still trunks. The sunlight shone through the trees ahead and she walked toward it as if in a dream.

Nissa stopped at the edge of the forest. Once her eyes had become accustomed to the sunshine, she saw the swath of land dotted with what forest plants the creatures had not stripped and stuffed in their holes, dug in irregular intervals throughout the cleared land. The bodies of MossCrack's Tajuru were strewn about between the holes. The nearest was only thirty paces away, lying on its side with a crushed skull. A handful of vampires on hands and knees were bent over the corpses almost tenderly. They were wearing rags, and their matted hair was dull in the bright sun. She wasn't sure if the rank smell was the dead Tajuru or the vampires. Or was it the tentacled creatures standing behind each vampire, sucking vampire ichor through the proboscuses under their armpits? Nissa swallowed the lump rising in her throat.

Suddenly, there was a chirping sound behind her, and Nissa turned with her staff at the ready. She expected to see the Tajuru and Hiba running toward her with a handful of creatures following. She closed her eyes and felt the nearly inexhaustible power of the forests of Zendikar rise in her blood and pull in from the vines around and the soil under her feet. She would show the beasts, those killers of trees, how the Joraga of Bala Ged dealt with interlopers, with *barong* outsiders. And it would not be pampering, Tajuru justice—but the savagery of the jungle meted out with plenty of hate.

She opened her eyes and nearly dropped her staff in shock. Where were her rangers? Where was Hiba? Instead, at least two hundred creatures of different sizes and shapes stood at the tree line they had created, staring at her. They were alike in only one way: they all had tentacles. One had a harnessed, growling vampire on a long lead.

But none, not even the four or five specimens larger than the one she'd killed in the forest, seemed angry with her. They simply stared at her. One cocked its head as it studied her. Some were spattered with blood, she noticed with a pang of regret, and many were festooned with short Tajuru arrows. She knew at that moment that her squad and Hiba were dead. She looked down to see her scarred hands, white and shaking, as they squeezed her staff.

The creatures ambled forward, their tentacles writhing and touching one another as they moved. When they were about forty feet away one stopped, and they all stopped. There was no speaking; there were no hand signs—only squirming tentacles. Where had she seen that behavior? It was like some insect. Like . . . Ants!

There were close to two hundred creatures grimly arrayed before her. The odds were not good. Her eyes wandered to the blue sky above the approaching host. A gentle breeze stirred her hair. Far away a lone stele floated over a high mesa. Beyond that, dark storm clouds promised a good rain by nightfall. It was a beautiful day.

Nissa twisted her staff. The stem sword she had gained the day of her coming-of-age-reckoning back home in Bala Ged slid easily out of its scabbard. She held the rigid green shaft before her eyes.

Where had her life left her? She was standing in a clearing in the Turntimber Forest, outnumbered and about to perish. Yes, she had traveled to a couple of filthy planes that had neither the beauty, nor the power of Zendikar, and were full of big-nosed humans and beings as nasty as any she could imagine. She glanced at the creatures ambling forward. "Beings like those outlanders," she said to herself.

She could planeswalk away, at that moment, and nobody would be the wiser for it. Her squad was dead—Hiba included. But if she ran, she would be running for the rest of her life, alone and wandering—a shadow out of the jungles of Bala Ged. Nissa drew a deep breath and released it slowly. She was a Joraga, and she would die as such. She scanned the ranks of the creatures, close enough for her to smell their mushroomy skin. She could take perhaps forty of them with her. She raised her sword and prepared to charge.

Suddenly, something caught the creatures' attention, and they all turned to the right to look. Nissa turned as well.

A lone figure stepped out of the forest: a human, by his height, dressed in black leathers, with shiny silver plates on his shoulder and a small silver breast plate. His hair was white and brushed back long off his forehead. A great sword on his belt clattered as he walked forward and clapped his hands together.

"What have we here," the stranger said in an accent that she'd never heard before. *Yet another barong,* Nissa thought.

"Have you all slipped your chains already?" the strange man asked as he walked. "I am lost and looking for the Eye of Ugin."

The creatures stood stock still, only their tentacles writhed back and forth between Nissa and the strange new addition. The man walked toward their side and flank. She could sense the creatures' dilemma. What they didn't want was to be flanked. *I'd attack if I were them*, Nissa thought. *Attack.*

And they did. With no obvious signal, the creatures began to charge. Nissa looked at the man. He raised his arms, and in a moment she could feel the air rushing past her ears, drawn toward him. Rivulets of dim energy condensed on the orbs suddenly blooming around each of his hands. And then he began to speak in the most booming, deep voice she had ever heard, but in a language she had *never* heard. The air between the stranger and the charging horde refracted and bent, and then each of the creatures fell to the ground in a lump, simply falling into a rotted mass.

As amazing as that spell was—and it was one of the most amazing and disturbing things Nissa had ever seen—still more startling was the reaction by the remaining creatures. Perhaps six of them were, apparently, out of the range of the man's spell. With their compatriots lying at their feet, the creatures continued charging at the dark-clad man. He said a few more grim words, and the remaining creatures fell.

Nissa wasted no time. She turned and started running back into the forest . . . to the tree. Once there, she glanced up and confirmed her worst fear. She climbed the trunk in seconds.

Her wall of vines was still in one piece, and it was with no small amount of pride that she counted nineteen dead creatures hanging from it, with arrows bristling out of them. But when she looked behind the wall, her heart caught in her throat. Some of the bodies of her raiding party were still there, torn into parts in the dappled light. Naarl flies the size of Nissa's fingers buzzed over the bright red meat. More parts were thrown into the branches around her. The buzz of the flies was suddenly too loud in her ears. When she turned to leave, the face of a decapitated elf was lodged in the crotch of a branch, looking out at her with fixed eyes.

She found him on the forest floor. His right arm was crushed flat, and both his legs too, but he was breathing. His left hand still held the grip of his bow, and she could not pry it free from his fingers, no matter what she did.

"Hiba," she whispered in his ear. "Hiba, I thought you were dead. Take a deep breath." She put her arms under his neck and under his buttocks and brought him, screaming, into the clearing. She put him down as carefully as she could.

The stranger was walking among the dead creatures shaking his head. He turned when Nissa approached and he watched her put the stricken elf down. The way he stared made her uneasy, but she busied herself by making Hiba as comfortable as she could. She tried to forget the spell she'd just seen the stranger cast as she cupped her hands around her mouth and turned to him.

"Do you have water?" she yelled. She made the drinking gesture. "Water?"

He walked over to where she sat. Up close he was taller than she'd thought and his gold-flecked eyes gave his pale face a curious intensity. He took only a casual glance at Hiba. His eyes sat on her.

"This one will die shortly," he said without looking down at Hiba, in a voice that echoed from deep in his throat. "This one is already dead."

She couldn't be absolutely sure if the stranger was talking about Hiba, or one of the creatures on the ground.

"Who are you?" she asked.

He looked out over the clearing. "I am called Sorin."

Sorin turned back and settled his golden eyes on Nissa again. Hiba moaned.

"And you are a Joraga elf, I should think," he said.

"Nissa Revane," she said, placing her right hand on her heart and bowing slightly, as was the elf custom.

Something moved in the middle of the clearing. An arm flopped. Sorin followed her eyes. "A vampire slave apparently lives," he said.

"Vampires," Nissa said. She had not meant to, but her lip curled.

The strangers watched her for an extra second before a slow smile stretched his pale lips. "Yes," he said. "Quite."

Sorin turned and walked to the middle of the clearing. He bent down and seized the vampire and lifted him by the wrist as easily as he might lift a water skin. He dragged the creature back to where Nissa was standing and dumped him unceremoniously next to Hiba. Nissa inadvertently took a step back.

Sorin chuckled. "Your home of Bala Ged is near Guul Draz. Is it not?"

"It is," she said. "And we fight to keep these from our borders."

The creature at her feet was different from the other vampires she'd fought. His hair was not in his eyes, for one. It was pulled into a tight, long braid. His skin was just as pale and bluish, however; and he was painted: a red line extended up his bare chest to his chin, then continued from his forehead to the top of his head through a shaved channel. He had the same vestigial horns extending in black curls from his shoulders and elbows.

"Where's his *bampha*?" she asked.

Sorin's face remained blank. "Oh," he said. "You mean its weapon. The brood lineage took it, I suspect."

Bampha. Nissa shuddered at the thought of their long, two-handed weapons of sharpened bone. Long elegant weapons left long elegant slashes. She had the scars to prove it.

"What did you call these things?" Nissa asked, toeing a dead creature's tentacle.

"These are brood lineage."

"Brood lineage," she said, licking her lips. "Lineage of what?"

Her words hung in the air.

"They have been slumbering all these years," the slave vampire said suddenly. "Abed in the stones of Akoum."

A bellowing growl echoed across the clearing. Sorin seemed not to notice the sound. He was looking down at the vampire, who was looking up at him with wide, unblinking eyes. *Those eyes,* Nissa thought. *Those black, iridescent eyes.*

"How do you know of the lineage?" Sorin barked.

Sorin's voice had a certain sharpness to it. The slave vampire winced with each word as he struggled up and carefully stood. There were numerous metal cylinders dangling from his belt. His hair braid, as thick as a man's forearm, reached almost to the ground. He wasn't nearly as tall as Sorin, but just as slim and lithe. He felt for each of the metal cylinders before continuing.

"I was present for their release," the vampire said. "In the Teeth of Akoum."

"Is that so," Sorin said. "At the Eye of Ugin?"

"The same."

Another growl, louder that time, cut through the trees. Nissa bent down and put her arms under Hiba. "We must go," she said. "If that brace of baloth should catch us in the open like this . . ."

But Sorin seemed not to hear. His eyes were on the vampire. "Who are you?" he asked.

"Anowon," he said. "Formerly of Family Ghet. I was taken prisoner at the eye."

"Well," Sorin said. "Do you know where I am now, Anowon, formerly of Family Ghet?"

The vampire's eyes fell on Nissa as she hoisted Hiba. "Somewhere in the Turntimber," he said. When Sorin said nothing, Anowon continued. "On Ondu." Still Sorin said nothing. "Zendikar?" Anowon ventured.

"And I don't suppose you know the way to the Eye of Ugin?" Sorin asked.

"It's on Akoum," Anowon said.

Sorin chuckled. "That's not what I asked. And if you want to bandy cute words, I will tear your heart out of your chest and have the elf eat it."

Nissa shifted uncomfortably from one leg to the other.

"I know the way to Akoum," Nissa said, glancing casually at the dead brood laid out in the clearing. "At least I can start you on the way." *Anything to get you out of my forest.*

"Excellent," Sorin said. "Finally, a bit of good news. You know this land. You will be our guide, yes. You will show us the way." He turned to Nissa. "That," he pointed at Hiba, "is dead. You are guiding us through this morass to Akoum. I knew the way once, you see. But I cast a forgetting spell on the place so it might be lost for all time. A forgotten blight."

"Why would I help you," Nissa asked, "when I could go back to into the turntimber and leave you two to be shredded by those baloth howling in the forest?"

"Because, dear savage," Sorin said, "what you saw here is just the vanguard of the true army. The rest are bearing down on this and every other location on this backwards plane even as we speak. If you want to have any hope of saving your people, you will assist me in containing this sickness, and in putting these broodlings back into their prison, which will not be easy. But it seems to fall to me to accomplish."

Nissa looked down at Hiba and felt a lump rising in her throat. He was dead. She swallowed and started to speak.

But Sorin continued. "Only I can cast the Eldrazi back into the crypt from whence they came. Only I can send them back into their forever sleep."

Nissa seemed to consider his words before speaking. "These are my terms: You both will help me bury my friend in the forest," she said. "And I will not travel with an unbound vampire. He must be bound and gagged, or you will have to navigate the teetering stones without me."

Anowon's mouth went to a sneer. "Joraga moon slug," he said. "I would not deign to touch lips to the likes of you. Your people taste of dirt and moss. Mushroom eaters."

Nissa smiled, despite herself. She hadn't heard that insult in quite some time. Strangely, it reminded her of home. Part of the reckoning ritual involved eating cut fungus. Invariably the young warrior died from it. Most lay dead for some minutes before blinking awake and sitting up gasping. If you survived, you survived. If you died, then you weren't meant to be a Joraga warrior, and your body was tossed into the Great Hollow Tree.

"Bound," Nissa said. "Or not at all."

As if in answer, another baloth howl drifted slowly through the trees, and Nissa started to walk.

CHAPTER 2

They walked once again into the deep forest, and buried the fallen elf Hiba near a young jaddi tree. While Nissa kept watch, Anowon dug a hole with a length of turntimber bark. With a face that betrayed neither thought nor emotion, Sorin watched the vampire sweat in the humid air. When the shallow grave was dug, Nissa dropped down from her high perch and placed a green paphian flower—picked from a clump she'd found growing in the crotch of a jurworrel tree—in Hiba's gnashed fingers.

An hour later they were traveling the branchways of the turntimber. Nissa, in the lead, was careful not to shy away from the serpents that hung like vines in that part of the forest, careful not to show her strange traveling companions any sort of weakness.

At sundown they stopped at a huge hedron stone, pointed at each end and broken in two enormous pieces, with a huge jurworrel growing out of the largest fissure.

"We dare not stop for too long." Nissa said. She wondered how long it would be before the Onduan baloth caught up. Before it tore them apart. A baloth was a creature that floated at the edge of every action in the turntimber—a pure predator that could cut through bone and muscle with the slightest slash of its claw, and which possessed an appetite large enough to devour a whole Tajuru squad. Those who lived there never left the safety of home without thinking, however briefly, about the likelihood of encountering one.

Sorin nodded once and looked back the way they had come. *Fool,* Nissa thought. *He has no idea.* She climbed to the top of the ruined hedron and cupped her hand to her long ear. "They are eating our scent even now."

Sorin yawned. He casually took a handkerchief from an inner fold of his black cloak and dabbed his brow. "*You* are the fool," he said. His voice was soft—so soft that Nissa found herself leaning in to hear him, unnerved that he had somehow read her thoughts. "You are a fool if you do not understand the true nature of the danger we are in. Do not trifle over *whatever* is following us. We must watch for the brood, and hope they haven't grown too powerful to counteract." He put the handkerchief back into the folds of his cloak and cupped his hands around his mouth. "Ghet!" he yelled.

Anowon looked up from where he had been peering at the hedron stone's inscription. Even though his wrists were bound, he had managed to pinch a small book between his thumb and first finger, and was copying the engraved symbols into the book with a bone pen.

"Find me food," Sorin commanded.

Nissa hopped down off the hedron. "I can bring you game."

But Sorin was looking ahead at the rising mesas in the distance. "The Ghet will acquire my food. I have special tastes."

Nissa looked from Sorin to Anowon, who was tucking his small black book into a little pack he'd rigged from vines strung through the leaf of a gourgi bush. The vampire walked over to Sorin, who untied his hands.

"How do we know he will not flee?" Nissa said. *Or waylay us to our doom,* she thought.

"He will not," Sorin said, looking at Anowon, who kept his eyes forward. "He is an archaeomancer; his interest lies in the magic of this ruined empire. He has no use of such things as ambushes or bold combat. Anyway, he wants to take us to the Eye of Ugin. Don't you, Ghet?" Sorin's voice raised in volume and pitch. "DON'T YOU?" he repeated.

For a moment, Nissa could feel the weight of Sorin's ominous words float in the air like a physical presence, and then they settled onto Anowon. The vampire's pupils dilated, Nissa noticed. He nodded once, then turned and walked under a branch and disappeared into the high grass.

Nissa looked at Sorin. *Why would a vampire do what a human ordered him to do?* she wondered.

"He will meet the baloth," she said. "And die."

"You don't know vampires," Sorin said.

And you do? Nissa thought. She moved her staff to her other hand. "You don't know baloth. A vampire bleeds like anything. I have proven that many times."

He raised an eyebrow. "Yes, but they have the rather unerring ability to sneak up on things. A bit like elves, I must say," Sorin said, laughing.

The shrill screech of a barutis bird rang out in the high canopy.

"Where do you want to travel?" Nissa said, once her pulse had calmed. The barutis's cry, so senseless and without reason, always shocked her.

"I have told you. Akoum . . . The Teeth of Akoum," Sorin said.

"But do you have a path in mind?"

"I believe it is called Graypelt now," Sorin said. He was looking into the west again, at the high mesas.

"Graypelt? Why travel through Graypelt? Graypelt is full of trappers and stinking humans," Nissa said as she looked down at the ground and cursed herself inwardly. "Of course there's nothing wrong with humans," she said. "Humans are fine."

"Humans?" Sorin said, drawn out of his own thoughts. "Oh yes, humans. They're wonderful. Such large noses!"

Soon the sun fell in the sky. The forest took life, and the crash and hiss of insects was so loud that Nissa's ears rang. Something loud but slow crashed through the forest to their right. Probably a fang deer, Nissa thought. *Or worse.* But it was no baloth—Nissa knew that from the sound. One did not *hear* baloth.

She gathered wood and stood it with the tips together over a small wad of special moss that had been soaked in flammable sap.

"No fire," Sorin said, suddenly loud in the total darkness. With her elf eyes she could see him sitting cross-legged. His lips were moving, but she could hear no sound. An incantation of some sort perhaps. She wondered if he could see her as well as she saw him.

"Baloth hate fire," she said.

"Brood lineage love it.

"Brood lineage love it," she repeated. "What are the brood lineage?"

Sorin's lips stopped moving. He turned to her in the darkness. "How can you not know? Have you not traveled?" he asked.

"Only a bit. I am from Bala Ged on the other side of the ocean," Nissa replied, sensing a trap. *Tell no one of your abilities.* It was more of a curse than anything else—this ability to planeswalk. It allowed her to lose her family and be exiled from her tribe and people. And to make matters worse, it wasn't worth it.

Sorin's lip curved up and to one side. "Only a bit," he said, his turn to repeat.

He knows. How can he know?

Sorin cleared his throat. "Do you know the Eldrazi?" he asked.

"A childhood fable—the ancient ones of Zendikar."

He nodded. "They are no fable," he said. "Believe me. These are their children, free at last."

"The Eldrazi are real?"

"Did we not bury your little friend in the forest?" he said. "Did you not interact with their brood today?"

Nissa felt the sweat on her forehead in the cooling night air. "And these *brood* dance in their crumbled palaces and eat sky mushrooms and steal children? Like the stories say?"

"They are both children and minions . . ."

"But what are they?" Nissa interrupted.

Sorin kept talking. ". . . and they will eat this plane."

"But how. Why?"

Sorin didn't reply. He was looking up at the star-spattered sky. Nissa waited. Soon a particular sound, a rustle, issued from the forest. She listened for a time, expecting against expectation a red-eyed baloth to come bounding out of the trees. Or a troupe of tree stalkers, the baloth's smaller relative. They were almost as bad as baloth. Some said they were worse, because their size allowed them to sneak better than a baloth. One thing was sure: they had all the ferocity and cunning of their larger cousin.

With baloth, and tree stalkers for that matter, it was wisest to be on the ground when they attacked. In the branches, an individual was vulnerable from all sides and from above and below. On the ground and with somewhere to put your back, you had only one area to guard.

Sorin took first watch.

Nissa kicked a depression in the moss on the forest floor for her hip and lay on her side with her back against the hedron stone. It gave off a curious heat.

In the dark she listened to the waja lizards tearing the bark of the trees while the screamer bugs split their shells in the high branches. The trees knocked together in the breeze, and in a moment Nissa fell asleep. She dreamt for a time that she was floating in the deep, black space above her head. She screamed down at the green forest below, but still she floated higher and higher.

Suddenly she started awake. Sorin was standing above her in the dark. As she watched, he bent down over her. Her staff was beside her, and she knew she could have her stem out in a split second. "What is it?" she said.

Sorin froze.

"It's your watch," he said, after a time.

She rose in the cold dark and stretched, feeling the kink in her back loosen. The stars overhead had the quality of the finest velvet and a certain depth that Nissa had always liked. Anowon was back. She could smell him sleeping someplace nearby and even hear his slow breaths. He must have been as stealthy to not have woken her. She pulled her cloak around her bare neck and drew her knees up. She sat with her arms holding her knees and her back to the hedron and listened.

Sorin was awake, she could hear. The breaths he drew were less even than Anowon's. He sat back against the hedron watching her. She imagined she could hear him scheming in the dark. *Who was he really?* She had intended to ask him, but the right time hadn't presented itself. Well, if he slept tonight, if he ever slept, she would know. It was all fine to creep into camp and breathe quietly, but nobody could be stealthier than a Joraga, and she intended to prove it. But first Sorin had to fall asleep.

And he did. But by the time his breathing became steady and long, the stars had moved in their nightly rotations past the jaddi tree's top branch, and the sky to the east was starting toward gray. She stood and stole as quietly as dust to where Sorin slept next to the hedron. She'd seen him draw his handkerchief out of an inner pocket of some sort. She carefully put her fingers to finding the pocket. But she couldn't. He was wearing a black leather jerkin with plates affixed to it. There were no pockets in his cloak that she could find. It seemed that no part of his attire involved pockets, but the one pocket she could find in his pants contained only a common gray stone..

Nissa crept back to her lookout. *No pockets. How no pockets?* A human appears in the Turntimber Forest, widely known on Zendikar as an extraordinarily dangerous place, with naught gear but a smooth gray stone? And he is lost. How did he find his way into the forest without knowing his way out? It is as though he appeared in the middle of the forest. *Strange, unless he is a planeswalker.* She backed against the warm rock and looked out at the dark shadows in the forest. When the hedron she was leaning against had fallen long ago, it crushed flat the trees that had been growing. Tajuru popular legend named the huge hedron the

sudkin, and many believed that one could hear the trees pushing and scratching underneath. And that the trees will try but never move the stone. There was even a saying about it: "That will happen when the sudkin moves." Meaning never.

A form moved in the darkness. Nissa blinked and leaned forward. She stared until her eyes went dry, and she had to blink again. Anowon and Sorin were asleep to her left. Their breathing was the only sound in the forest. The only sound. A stiffness began to radiate from the back of Nissa's neck, and her stomach turned suddenly. *The only sound.* The forest was never quiet, yet it was, and so suddenly. It had very recently been teeming with the sounds of spiral beetles foraging in the spent leaves on the floor . . . of snail, and the claw birds scrapping at the crotches of the turntimber and jaddi trees nearby, looking for bugs and frogs. But there was nothing anymore.

She rose quietly, holding her staff with both hands. Nothing moved in the shadows. She stood and watched, unmoving. She stood for so long that a snake slithered across her foot, and she looked down for a split second to see if it was poisonous. But it was only a nectar snake, with dark circles on its back. When she looked up again a shadow had moved. A normal eye would not have noticed it, but Nissa's eyes weren't normal. The change was slight: what looked like the shadow of leaf was curved ever so slightly, whereas previously it had been straight. Nissa bent and took hold of the jaddi nut that she'd placed next to her when she took watch. She brought the nut to her lips, whispering a spell, kissed it, and tossed it into the shadows. A green mottle arced up, following the nut's path as it flew through the air. *It is almost time to wake up anyway,* she thought.

The nut hit the ground with a sudden flash of light. The tree stalkers—three, in fact—were caught standing, blinking their eyes in the flare. One was young—probably the one that had moved enough for her to detect it—but even in the blinding light it did not move again. She had precious seconds. Unlike the baloth, the stalkers' fur was white. They were lean. Their teeth-crammed mouths hung open tasting the air, and as was their way, each was standing on its hind legs with its two over-sized front legs dangling so their purple claws almost touched the ground.

She had fought one soon after her rite of passage, of course . . . *but three.* The lead stalker groaned and leaned to the side before pouncing, and she stood and swung her staff, catching it on the chin. Its head jerked to the side, as it fell and rolled. Nissa whispered and reached out with her mind and a turntimber branch swung down on the stalker and pinned it to the duff.

The two remaining creatures jumped at Nissa. She felt movement next to her and smelled Sorin. Out of the corner of her eye she saw him jump forward, and for a moment the lead stalker shied as it flew through the air. With a word from Sorin the creature fell into a stinking pile on the ground, leaving one of its eyes bouncing away through the leafy duff.

The first creature's paws hit her, shoved her backward, and knocked her staff out of her hand. Suddenly the stalker was on her chest, digging in its claws and crushing the air from her lungs. She gasped and tried to roll out from under it, but the creature was four times her weight and bore down on her, opening its wide mouth to her face. She heard a high whine and felt the creature shudder, and something heavy cracked out of the stalker's chest. She could feel the heat from the object on her right cheek as the creature's legs buckled, and it fell with an audible thump on the ground next to her head. Nissa twisted as it started to fall, but the creature's head fell on her back, slamming her into the leaf mold.

Nissa lay on the forest floor looking up at the trees. It felt as if she were floating on a cloud of air. She was dimly aware of movements and sounds all around her, but she couldn't move her arms. Then she blinked and took a breath. She managed to tip the stalker's head off her. There was no sound except the rushing of blood in her ears, and no feeling except the pain in her chest. Soon the swish in her ears subsided, and she could hear the stalker trapped under the tree branch struggle and moan against the leaves.

She sat up and was immediately greeted with a jab of pain in her chest. Wincing, she stood. She went closer to the fallen creature and saw the ragged folds of the heart, where it had exploded under the body like a melon. In the raw dawn light, the stalker's fur seemed as soft as a blanket. Nissa reached out to touch it.

"Perhaps a cloak?"

Nissa turned. Sorin was standing against the hedron looking like he hadn't slept on the ground with his hip in a hole. Anowon was standing next to him with his hands bound in front, watching Nissa with an expression that she could not read.

"Why did you kill them?" she asked Sorin.

Sorin laughed. Anowon did not.

"You would have had it bite your face off?"

She turned back to the dead stalker where it lay sideways with its legs straight out. "My death would have been the way of things."

Sorin laughed again. "I have a sneaking suspicion there will be plenty of possibilities for you to lose your life." He put his shoulders back. "Now, which direction is it to Graypelt?

"You really don't know?" Nissa asked.

"How would I?"

"You seem to know a great deal about Zendikar. You know how to walk the branchways. You know to avoid the cut fungus. You knew to lunge at the tree stalker to make it shy before attacking."

Sorin watched her.

"Is that all?" he asked. "I hope I know more than that." He started to walk north toward Graypelt, and then he stopped and turned back.

"You fought well against those creatures, for an elf," Sorin said. "Not as well as me, of course, but perhaps you will be useful for more than scouting." He turned and began walking. Without a glance, Anowon followed.

If he knew the way to Graypelt, then why was she involved? Nissa wonderded. She walked over to where her staff had been flung and picked it up. The stalker under the branch struggled. Its red eyes followed her as she walked. She stopped. She swept her hand through the air, and the branch snapped up to where it had been. The creature sniffed the air, glanced at her, and bounded up the nearest turntimber and away.

Sorin watched it go. "We'll walk on the ground from here."

Once again he had the right of it, Nissa thought. From the edge of the great mesa, Graypelt was best reached on foot. Soon they would descend to the ladders and perhaps even the zip line the Tajuru had strung years before, when the treasure hunters that flocked to Graypelt were considered friends. They had since become *barong,* interlopers. She would not be surprised in the least to find the zip line broken by vandals.

They walked all day, ducking the branches and dense undergrowth that grew at the edge of the mesa. They passed abandoned camps, where signs of struggle were everywhere, but nothing else remained. Sometimes the remains of a site were no more than stones piled in a rough circle. Once they cut a wide arc around what had been a large camp, erected around the floating remains of a huge statue with tentacles for legs and symbols and words engraved into its crumbled base. A massive turntimber had grown up under the figure, and its trunk and branches had wrapped around the strange effigy. Patches of the tree's bark had been peeled away, and a broken box was strapped to each patch. Nissa stopped and spat into the loam. It took deleterious magic to keep the turntimber from healing itself.

"Blood suckers," she said, glancing at the boxes strapped to the trees. "Sucking the land's energy. The *barong* put quartz in those boxes to absorb the energy of the turntimber. They sell the stones to other fools in Graypelt who think it will cure their ills."

Sorin walked closer to the abandoned sap boxes. Anowon followed. Sorin looked at the box for a moment before inserting his hand into the back of it. A smile spread across his face.

"Yes," he said. "Yes. Very pure." He turned to Nissa. "Why would this place have been abandoned?"

She pointed to a place on the trunk above his head. A small scuff.

"An arrow hit there," she said. "Or I am much fooled."

"An elf arrow," Anowon said. He had been quiet for so long that both Sorin and Nissa turned when he spoke.

"Just so," Nissa said turning back to the tree. "This forest is stewarded by the Tajuru."

"But not you," Sorin said.

"I am Joraga."

"You are a fool to not utilize this power," he said, removing his hand from the box.

"All elves receive power from the land. We do not need to cut and hack and burn as humans do." She looked from Sorin to Anowon. "You are all, human and vampire, suckers of life. You are the same in our eyes."

"Are we?" Sorin asked, smiling and raising an eyebrow. "The same?"

"In a manner of speaking."

The smile stayed on Sorin's face. He started walking. "In that case, let us continue to Graypelt and see what we see."

"Why Graypelt?" Nissa asked, walking after him.

"Because it lies between us and our destination in the west."

"The Teeth of Akoum?"

"The Eye of Ugin."

She stopped and looked over her shoulder. Anowon stood next to a box strapped to the tree, watching as Sorin began walking the footpath that led west from the camp. His hands were bound, but still she stopped.

"He walks in front of me," she yelled to Sorin, keeping her eyes on Anowon.

"Ghet!" called Sorin.

Anowon started walking, keeping his eyes straight ahead. He passed Nissa, and she watched his long braid sway slightly as he walked.

They went one behind the other along the narrow path though the forest. The way was fraught with boulders and thick, rank growth. Eventually the trail ended completely, as if the beings that had once walked it had ceased to exist in mid step. Nissa backtracked on her hands and knees until she was able to locate a track in the ground that was not too old and pointed west to their destination. Since the trail itself ended, they would have to follow the faint reminders of past travellers and hope they led to Graypelt. They followed signs for the rest of the day: a broken twig, a torn patch of moss. The forest echoed all around them. A little past when the sun was highest in the sky, they crossed a small river, and Nissa searched for a sign on the other side. She found it.

"We are close," Nissa said. She could see that the toe digs and heel divots of varying creatures had previous converged on their small path. There were the toe claws of goblins and tracks of at least six different hobnailed humans, as well as a barefoot kor and an elf. The footfalls were clearly visible to the eye. On the breeze she smelled sweat and wood smoke . . . and something else she couldn't exactly place. The land had grown rockier, as she knew it was supposed to at the edge of the great mesa. "Just ahead somewhere," she said. "Prepare yourself."

CHAPTER 3

They encountered the first ragged tent when the sun was low in the west. Many of the tents were gray and of different sizes and materials, but some were fire-blackened and abandoned. Others were flattened, as if stepped upon. Past the tents the forest dropped away, and Nissa could see the sun setting blood red behind rows of jagged peaks capped with snow.

Sorin looked about him with a bemused smile on his face. "Graypelt."

"So named because of the Turntimber warthog tents."

Sorin appraised the destroyed tents hugging the end of the mesa. "Since when are warthog skins called 'pelts?' "

A sudden gust sent a piece of burnt tent flapping. The wind caused some of the cookfires in front of the tents to blaze to life. Somewhere a dog whined. At least, Nissa hoped it was a dog.

Above the nearest fire pit, a carcass was skewered over a pile of low coals. A human squatted back on his heels and turned the meat slowly. He looked up at them with crossed eyes. On his head he wore a helmet with the tip of a hedron affixed to the top.

Sorin pushed his jaw at the skewered meat. "What do you have there? Elf meat?"

The man spat and turned his eyes back to the fire.

"Warthog," Nissa said, her eyes scanning the tents. She found a tent larger than the rest and black in color and led them to it along the makeshift streets of mud. They passed two men standing on either side of a horse. Both were wearing heavy armor fixed with strings, and on each string was tied a stone. Climbing hooks curled off their elbow couters and the tips of their sabatons. They were busy lashing a folded green tent and long poles to their horse. With each movement the tiny stones tinked against their armor.

"Power sellers," Nissa whispered. "Each of those stones is imbued with a bit of the Turntimber's special raw mana. They sell them."

Sorin looked back where the men stood, watching them. "How much do they cost?"

"Less than that," Nissa replied.

Sorin looked where she pointed. A bright red drake the size of a large dog sat on a roost in front of a gray, scale-skinned tent. The creature's bright eyes watched them as they passed.

"They find those drakes in the Makindi Trench," Nissa said, approaching the black tent. She stopped and looked back the way they had come. Every eye in the camp was on them. She turned and said, "Keep your lips tight together, and don't look at it."

With a deep breath, Nissa pushed back the stiff hide hung over the hole and slipped into the tent. The others followed. It was almost totally dark inside. A strange smell filled their noses so that Sorin groaned and Nissa held her breath. Anowon shuffled his feet. Something was buzzing in the tent.

"Khalled?" Nissa said.

There was no sound except for the buzzing.

"Khalled?" Nissa repeated.

More buzzing. Then something stirred. "Yes?" called a voice.

"Khalled, it is Nissa."

"Nissa. Come closer, child." The voice sounded like it hadn't spoken for millennia.

She walked in the darkness, feeling ahead with her foot before each step. When she was nearer to the buzzing, a rough hand groped her face.

"Nissa Revane. My nectar."

She heard Sorin sniff.

"I am here with two friends."

"Friends? They don't smell like friends. Or rather, they smell like friends to each other but not to you."

"Nonetheless . . ."

"Have you seen the beautiful flowers outside, Nissa?"

Flowers? "I saw no flowers."

"What? No flowers?"

"I saw some destroyed tents, Khalled."

The hand left her face.

"Friends you say . . . Light!" Suddenly light from many tiny points filled the room. What was amazing to Nissa was not that Khalled had hundreds of light beetles tethered with string in the corner of the tent. What amazed her was that he'd been able, with an enchantment of his devising, to have the beetles light at his command.

The sides of Khalled's tent were bookshelves, and each and every space on the shelves was crammed with books, scrolls, and reed papers bound with string. Nissa even recognized writings from her people: flat pieces of pale nadi wood graven with pictographs.

Nissa noticed that Anowon's eyes were on the books, and for the first time since she had allowed him to travel with them, his eyes were fully open. As he stared, he brought his bound hands up and scratched the side of his nose. She turned.

Khalled was looking at each of them carefully. Half of his face had been torn to the bone by a kraken, and he wore no adornment except a cloak thrown over his right shoulder and a loin cloth. Nissa noticed that the merfolk had started unbinding his wrist and ankle fins, and their translucent blue shone in the tent.

"I dreamed of an angel with a halo running across its eye line," he said, his eyes moving between Anowon and Sorin. "With a pulsing, tentacled heart in its hand."

Sorin smiled uncertainly.

"Ahhh," Khalled said. He reached out and touched the vial of water he had given Nissa, which she kept on a lanyard around her neck. "You still possess this. Wonderful."

"It is always my companion," Nissa said.

"That one," Khalled said, pointing at Anowon, "is a vampire."

"He is bound, Khalled."

The ancient merfolk shuffled closer. "What do you have hanging from your belt?" he asked Anowon.

Anowon moved his eyes from the books to the merfolk. He looked down at the metal cylinders hanging from his belt.

"Are those text imprinters?" Khalled asked. "For clay?"

Anowon nodded. The merfolk leaned over and took one of the cylinders in his hand and looked closely at it. After a minute, he let the cylinder go, and it bounced against Anowon's thigh.

Khalled straightened and looked at Anowon. "An archaeophile?" Khalled asked with an inflection to his voice that said he approved. "How do you come here?"

"He was—" Sorin started.

"—I was not speaking to you, friend," Khalled said.

Sorin's smile disappeared.

Khalled put his iridescent green eyes back on Anowon.

"I was enslaved by the Eldrazi brood lineage," Anowon replied, "and brought on their forage raids into the Turntimber Forest."

Nissa spoke. "MossCrack is no more. The Tajuru home tree was attacked, and Speaker Sutina is buried."

Khalled blinked like he'd been slapped. He looked up at the ceiling of the tent where the bugs buzzed and tittered.

"They attacked here some days ago," he said. "Many have fled. Some were killed."

"Yet you stay?"

"The Turntimber is not yet mapped," Khalled said. "And with the increasing Roil, it becomes ever more difficult."

"But surely, my friend, you would rather travel back to Tazeem," Nissa pressed. "To your lighthouse?"

"Yes, I can see where you might think that. But no." Khalled said, sighing. "Speaker Sutina. She was an unusual elf. I've told you what I knew about her and that kraken?"

"Yes," Nissa said. "But Khalled, these two need to get to the Teeth of Akoum. It is found on—"

"I know where the Teeth of Akoum are, dear child."

"Would you have a map?"

"I might," Khalled said. He looked at Sorin for a while. "What is it worth to you, and why do you want to go to that place? It is dangerous, and these creatures, these brood as you call them, are everywhere. I have received a speaking hawk from The Lighthouse at Sea Gate telling news of great hordes in the lands to the west."

The news seemed to trouble Sorin. He pursed his lips. "I have my own reasons, old map maker," he said. "But maybe I can make it worth your time." He put his hand into his jerkin, and it came out holding something.

Nissa watched him open his hand. A small black ball, the size of an acorn, rolled in his palm.

How? Nissa thought, leaning closer for a better look. *That wasn't in his pockets when I went through them this morning. There was nothing in those pockets. Where did he get it?*

"What is that?" Khalled asked. One of the beetles landed on his hand. He stroked it gently, and it glowed brighter.

"It is magic from far away."

"How far away?"

"Far."

The Jah-creed merfolk eyed the ball in Sorin's palm.

Sorin pushed it toward him. "It *sees.* Would you like to see what it sees?"

"No," Khalled said, after a long pause. "This smells dark to me. And as much as I love the dark, it tends to have too large an allure for me."

Sorin's hand closed over the ball. His faced showed no emotion, but Nissa could smell his metallic embarrassment in the air.

Perhaps Khalled could too, for he shuffled forward. "These two will have their map, Nissa. But why do you help them?"

"Sorin saved my life," she said.

"Twice," Sorin said.

"Twice," Nissa said.

Khalled nodded and turned to Anowon. "You will make me copies of your books. That is payment for the map"—Khalled turned—"Raspin!" he called. "Oh Raspin?"

A young human boy poked his head into the tent.

"Would you fetch clay? You will find it in the supply tent in the box marked 'Glyphs.' "

The boy pulled his head out.

"And Raspin?"

The boy put his head back in.

"Check with Margen and find out if we've spotted the enemy today in the west."

Khalled turned back to the group. "We see them almost daily. But they seem to be passing around us. They are odd. First they seem brutes, but then sometimes they do things with extreme forethought. Like the ambushes they have caught us in."

Sorin said nothing, but Nissa knew he possessed secrets of the brood that he had yet to reveal. "They're like ants," Nissa said. "It's like they talk with their tentacles like ants do with their antennae."

Khalled nodded as he thought about this. Then nodded. His eyes turned to Anowon. "You say these are the Eldrazi of myth? These are the ones who build the palaces and places of power . . . the ones who were put down in the uprising?"

Anowon glanced at Sorin, who was smirking again.

"I am not sure," Anowon continued. "I know they came from the Eye of Ugin, which in some of the research I have done is associated with the last resting place of the ancient ones."

"What family do you hail from?" Khalled said.

Anowon looked at the merfolk for an extra heart beat before replying. "My family was Ghet. I have been formally cast out."

Khalled raised his eyebrows. He turned and walked to one of his packed and drooping bookshelves. He drew out a slim but wide book and opened it. As they all watched, he licked his finger and began turning pages. "Ah . . . Ghet." He was quiet as he read.

Sorin yawned.

"Yes," Khalled said as he read. "An old family, but of minor designation. Disciplined in past conflicts." Khalled looked up. "Your seat is not in Guul Draz?"

"Malakir."

"The most marginalized of the vampire families there."

Anowon said nothing.

The boy arrived with the clay. He threw aside the flap and walked in teetering under the weight of an entire block. He staggered over to a table and dumped the block on it. "The tentacle creatures have been seen massing at the northern gap," he reported.

Anowon began unwrapping the block with his bound hands. As Nissa watched, he tore a corner of the reddish clay off and began kneading it flat on the table. When it was smooth and of a thickness that seemed to be sufficient, he unclipped one of the metal cylinders from his belt. Carefully, with his hands pressing down, he rolled the metal over the sheet of clay and imprinted what the cylinder contained.

"What is written on these tablets?" Khalled said.

"These are all records of my research and findings. Mostly about the Eldrazi."

"What language are they written in?"

"Ancient Vampire," Anowon said. "But there are no maps."

"Alas, one makes do."

"Khalled, they will need provisions," Nissa said. "But I have decided that I will stay here in the

Turntimber. My promise was to bring them here. With your map they have no other use for me. Let them be gone."

The merfolk wasted no time. "Raspin," he said, "bring provisions and gear."

"We *do* have a use for you," Sorin said, a smirk on his long face as he glanced at Anowon. "The Ghet here is no scout. And his combat facility leaves something to be desired. Also, he smells like a beast."

Khalled watched Anowon make the next imprint. "I would warn Nissa about you, vampire, but I would be more worried for your well-being should you anger her."

Anowon said nothing. But as they watched, he made imprints of each of his cylinders and lay the tablets out on the table to dry. He was finishing the last when Raspin entered, staggering under the weight of a large pack with shoulder straps.

"Excellent, Raspin," Khalled said. He handed Nissa a horn stopped at each end with a tree-bark plug. "This map should get you to Akoum. This location of the Eye of Ugin is unknown to me. But the vampire book-maker says he knows the way."

Nissa turned and handed the map to Sorin, who accepted it with obvious misgivings. "And I will stay here, in the Turntimber," Nissa said. "The Tajuru borders have been defended, and my place is back at the Home Tree."

Khalled took Nissa's arm and led her a couple of steps away.

"Lately my dreams have been filled with ill tidings," Khalled said. "I have deep misgivings about this brood. The birds I have received bear strange news of whole towns destroyed, castles crushed. Many of the birds themselves arrive on the edge of death."

"There could be many explanations."

The merfolk was quiet for a time. "Quite." Khalled said at last. He pointed at a large, flat table top of rough rock standing in the corner. The table legs were the huge femur bones of some extinct creature.

"Let me show you my fear," Khalled said. He snapped his fingers, and wisps of what looked like blue smoke wafted around the top of the table. Slowly the wisps formed into terrain and land features. Nissa recognized the continents of Ondu and Akoum separated by a great undulating sea. There was the Puzzle Tower, the Knuckle of Forgotten Ones, and the dense swath of the Turntimber Forest. The Makindi Trench gaped through the land like a wound begging for suture.

As Nissa watched, a pool of dark dots spread out of a mountain range she could only assume was the Teeth of Akoum. The dots spread in all directions and soon covered the land. Soon the blue wisps began to disappear, leaving only the black. As she watched, the Turntimber began to disappear in chunks, like the bites from a sopfruit, until the forest was no more.

"Have you seen the wild linnestrop?" Khalled asked.

Nissa felt her lip curl at the mention of the plant. "Of course."

"And where is it from, originally?"

"Not from the Turntimber," Nissa said. "Yet here it grows, choking out the plants that have lived within these green boundaries for time immemorial."

"And have you heard of the simeon plant? Do you hate it as much?"

"No. That plant lives together with the others. You can heal with it and—"

"Yet it is also not native to the Turntimber."

"You are right. It is a stranger."

"Like me," Khalled said. "Like you."

Nissa looked up from the terrain phantasm on the table top. "I suppose," she said.

"I have a strong fear in my hearts that these brood are of a sort with the linnestrop."

Nissa watched the merfolk snap his fingers again, and the wisps on the table dissipated.

"I believe the Turntimber and all Zendikar beg for help," Khalled said. "You, my sweet friend, are a leader of elves. The power of Zendikar is yours but I fear it will wither under the tentacles of this new addition."

Nissa nodded. She remembered the day she had first returned from her planeswalk to the faraway plane where densely packed beings had stepped on each other's feet and tried to kill each other. She had returned to the forest and sat for days watching the slow bloom of an incisor orchid's flower bud. It took three days for the bud to open, but when it finally did, its smell glowing purple stamens brought her to tears. The idea that such a flower would cease to be . . .

"You must travel with this menagerie," Khalled said as he swept his hand toward Sorin and Anowon. "To the Eye of Ugin. Zendikar begs you."

Sorin watched. He and Anowon were standing near the entrance to the tent. Anowon was strapping the pack Raspin had brought onto his own back.

Nissa looked around the tent and took a deep breath. Where was her tribe now? Either the Joraga or the Tajuru? Where were they to help her with this burden? No, she would not do it for either of her tribes. She would not embark on such trip for the tribe that had cast her out, or the one that hated her. She would make the journey for Zendikar. And for Nissa Revine.

"I will do as you suggest, my friend," Nissa said.

Khalled smiled, showing his strange, small teeth. "Well then, keep vigilant around that one."

"The book maker?"

"No, the other," Khalled said. "He is also . . ."

At that moment a horn blew outside. Nissa looked at Khalled. "Change of the guard. Nothing to be concerned with," Khalled said.

"Let this be our time to depart," Sorin said.

Nissa turned back to Khalled. The merfolk nodded. "Thank you," Nissa said to Khalled, placing her hand above her heart and bowing.

Khalled held a necklace out to her. "A pathway stone for your journey," he said. "Keep it well. It was cut off the Puzzle Tower itself."

"I thank you, my friend," Nissa replied.

"Remember what I said," Khalled said. "And remember that vampires live on blood."

CHAPTER 4

They left Graypelt with night falling. Three stones' pitch away from the last tent, the mesa fell away, and the land became vertical. They made a fireless camp near a trail that wound down the mesa's edge in a zig-zag of switchbacks, leading finally to the dark at the bottom of the canyon. In the starlight, the river at the bottom of the gulch appeared a long, gray scar.

"Makindi Trench," Nissa said. "Our way lies there, unfortunately."

Sorin and Anowon sat with their backs propped against the boles of the few young Jaddi able to eke out a living at the edge of the mesa where the soil was exposed and infertile. Watches were decided upon, and Nissa took a spot in the notch of a tree. A Gryphon screamed in the darkness over the trench as it hunted nighthawks. And then she was asleep.

Nissa heard the rain drumming long before it hit them, then the storm was on them with huge raindrops that hurt. Even the hood of her warthog cloak could not fend off the rain. She was soaked and shivering all night. But with morning the rain had ceased, and the giant drum toads croaked their booming dialect from the trench below.

Nissa woke the others when the first light tinged the night sky, and by dawn they were standing on the trail in the moist chill, blowing into their hands. The Makindi Trench was still dark below. Far down the trench a fire lit the canyon. Sorin blew into his hands and stamped his cold feet. Nissa gnawed on a square of hard waybread wondering what creature Anowon had eaten last, and which would be next. The archaeomancer hoisted the provisions pack onto his back and tied the waist and chest straps before offering his hands to be bound.

They made their way down a steep trail composed of wet stones. Twice Anowon lost his footing and slipped. Once he tripped and would have fallen forward if Nissa hadn't taken hold of his pack and swung him back.

At one point the trail became so steep that Nissa stopped and took rope from the pack. As she was taking it out, she glanced down at the charm Khalled gave her when she had first come to the Turntimber. It was a small vial of enchanted water taken from the ruins of Ior at the bottom of Glasspool. The only significant source of fresh water on Akoum was sacred to the kor.

As she watched, the water in the vial bubbled to life, a warning of what was to come. "Roil!" she yelled. "Hold on."

Still clutching the coil of rope, Nissa dashed for a small tree and just reached it when the first tremors began. She dove into the cage of exposed roots and fumbled her harness's belay line out, snapping its clamp onto the nearest root.

She watched Anowon scuttling for his own tree, and then the Roil hit in force, and Nissa could not see anything. She watched the trench below them buckle like a great rug, and the needles of the dwarfed pines writhe and whip. The ground began to jolt violently, and she was thrown against the roots. Nissa put her hands over her head, but the thrashing continued while the sudden wind howled and boulders crashed. She could hear the stone groaning and snapping all around her, and then the Roil stopped as suddenly as it had started. One moment the air was rushing; the next moment the stones that had been suspended in mid-air fell crashing down, and many of them rolled down the side of the mesa and into the trench.

Soon the rumbling stopped, and so did the ringing in her ears. Nissa unfastened herself and crawled out. The breeze smelled like raw sap. She peered around. The trees had grown. But the new growth was either snapped off or twisted into strange corkscrews that reminded her with a dark shudder of brood lineage tentacles.

Nissa had been through many Roils, but lately every one seemed worse than the last. That one had been fairly minor. Once in the Turntimber she'd found herself in the top canopy of a tree after the Roil.

But not this time. The trail was gone, and the rocks that had been stacked up in cairns to mark the switchbacks scattered. It took her a moment to understand what had happened: the Roil had torn a chunk out of the ground, and it floated high above the ground. Every so often a rock rolled off and came tumbling down.

The vampire and Sorin, she thought. They were nowhere to be seen. She looked around at the heaps of newly piled stones. *They're lost if they are under those.* She looked up at the floating land. They could be on that. She looked down. Far below she could see two black dots on the trench floor. She had to move fast.

Using her staff, she managed to scramble down the rest of the way to the bottom of the trench, but it still took the better part of an hour. It was fast work, yet still she was not the first to reach them. A creature with six legs was clambering over the rocks, its long curved tail tipped with a savage-looking stinger. It had pincer mouth parts and a curled proboscis tucked between the pincers. Crevice miners always seemed attracted to Roils. They were nothing more than scavengers, but still . . . She was lucky there were not more. She stepped closer to the two unconscious forms. The crevice miner stopped, its pincers, each half as long as her arm, opening and closing. One more step, and she would be forced into action. Crevice miners were some of the most succulent bush meat to be found. Many said they tasted like crab, but Nissa had never eaten crab, preferring to not to eat things that fed upon the dead and decaying.

Nissa twisted her staff and slid the stem sword into the daylight. The miner sensed her threat and rose up on its two back legs. It skittered forward a few steps, hoping to drive its spikelike pincers down on her, but Nissa sidestepped and let the pincers dive down on blank rock. The creature rose up and came down again, but Nissa stepped the other way, and its pincers crashed into the rock again. After three more tries the crevice miner turned and scurried away.

Nissa rushed over to where Sorin and Anowon were lying at the base of the scree. They were much bruised and covered with abrasions, but Anowon was awake. He watched her approach but did not try to move. She noticed with a start that his hands were unbound. Why was she helping these two? She could turn and go back home. There was nothing holding her.

"Are you hurt?" Nissa said.

Anowon's strange eyes regarded her coolly.

"Are you hurt?" she repeated.

"This one has not woken yet," Anowon said, regarding Sorin with the most casual of glances.

"Is he . . . ?" She could suddenly feel Hiba lying still in her arms.

"Dead? I don't think so."

Nissa approached, keeping one eye on the unbound vampire. She placed her hand over Sorin's mouth and felt a tiny puff of breath.

"He lives," she said. She raised her hand and brought it across Sorin's face with a loud slap. His eyes snapped open, and his upper lip drew back across his thin incisors. His eyes were narrowed, and Nissa took an involuntary step back. Then recognition spread over his face.

"An elf," he said. His gold-flecked pupils were wildly different in size, and the sweat was popping out on his forehead. When he turned his head, the knot above his ear was clearly visible. "Only an elf."

Nissa nodded. *Only the elf who saved your life.*

Sorin grabbed a handful of Nissa's sleeve and drew her to him. "I know about you," he said, slurring his words. "I can tell you have left this place before." He tapped his forehead. "I can tell."

Nissa yanked her sleeve out of his surprisingly strong grip. "I am sure I do not know what you mean," Nissa said. But she did. *Planeswalking.* She turned her head so Sorin could not see her face.

"Where is Lysene?" Sorin said.

"There is no Lysene here." Nissa said. She turned and eyed him critically. It would be hard to move him should he prove unable to walk. "Can you walk?" she asked.

Sorin looked blankly at her and blinked.

"Look," said Anowon in his reedy voice.

She turned. Four more crevice miners were mincing through the scree piles behind them. She knew that they would become more interested if she attacked them. And she could easily kill them, but more would be attracted by the blood.

"He must move," Nissa said. "I am not sure he should, but he must or we die here."

Anowon nodded. He casually took his long braid and brought it over his shoulder. The braid was as thick as Nissa's arm. Anowon parted some of the black hair and opened the small metal door of a box buried within. From the box he carefully pinched out something white and shiny with a symbol on it.

"Is that a tooth?" Nissa asked. The crevice miners were standing just out of a stone's throw's range, opening and closing their pincers.

"It is." Anowon said. "A molar imbued with a merfolk's phantasm." He made a fist around the tooth and threw it at Sorin. Immediately the outlander began to float. When his body reached shoulder height, Anowon took hold of him. "Without tethering, he will float away. And that would be such a shame."

Nissa shuddered at the thought of the tooth. One of the crevice miners stepped closer, and she had to throw a rock. It stepped back again.

"That will work once, maybe twice," Nissa said. She did not know if Khalled's map said they should walk down the Makindi Trench, but she did know that it was the only direction open to them. "Walk," she said. "Quickly and without turning. Miners are eaters of the dead; they like their meat bloated and tender. They do not favor attack, but the sight of wet eye balls can excite them into a frenzy. If they see us moving quickly, they may just give up and consider us too much work." Still, the crevice miners followed behind.

The floor of the trench was wide enough for one hundred to walk abreast, but boulders and large rocks of various sizes were strewn across it. The field of boulders created a maze of tight passages which Nissa led them through. She heard the crevice miners' carapaces clacking against each other as they struggled through. Soon the passages became so tight in places that even Nissa had to squeeze to pass. It was perhaps their only chance to out maneuver the beasts, and Nissa seized it.

"Run," she hissed.

The crevice miners heard the sudden movement, and sensing that their meal might be leaving, they surged forward. But the lead creature became trapped, and the others crammed against it in a desperate rush, entangling their long, hairy legs. Sensing their predicament the miners struggled and became utterly entwined and stuck in a space between the boulders.

Nissa and Anowon scrambled to the top of the boulders with Sorin in tow, and hopped from one to the other until they had put a good distance between the scavengers and themselves. But the effort was great. By the time Nissa stopped, her breath was coming out in rasps.

The miners were far behind, clattering their hard shells against one another and making a high keening cry that drove the hairs on the back of Nissa's neck rigid.

Some time later, the boulders gave way to sand and rocks, and eventually they were splashing through a small river of sluggish water meandering downhill. The sun had passed its zenith, and the darkness in the trench was almost total again. Nissa stopped to listen,

putting her hand on Anowon's chest to stop him. He looked down at her hand and then at Nissa.

"No frowning," Nissa whispered. She listened for scratching echoing from behind, and, hearing none, took her hand off Anowon's chest.

They walked in the shade of the trench. The swath of sky overhead was an overcast purple. Soon the first rumble of thunder tumbled down the canyon, and Sorin spoke.

"Ghet, you will lower me now," he said.

Anowon pulled Sorin down. When his feet were firmly on the sand, Sorin brushed off his sleeves and shiny shoulder plates before clipping his scabbard back onto his belt. He turned and marched ahead, and did not turn to look back at them. Anowon followed at a distance. Soon Nissa was walking next to Anowon.

"Where did you get those—?"

"Teeth?" Anowon said.

"Yes."

"They are from sacrifices at the Tal Terig," Anowon said. He waited a moment before continuing. "The Puzzle Tower."

Nissa knew of the place: a gigantic tower on Akoum assembled of dissimilar shapes. An ancient site. She could see it: the assembled vampires in a circle, all with their dirty hair blowing in their eyes and arms raised, watching a priest tearing a merfolk's teeth out. She felt the gorge rising in her throat.

Nissa cast a long look around as she walked. Ahead, Sorin's unusually loose gait had him weaving unsteadily as he walked. *At least he can be hurt like the rest of us,* she thought. She found herself not caring particularly if he went to sleep tonight and did not wake. She watched Sorin walk, strangely comforted by his obvious vulnerability, before turning back to Anowon.

"And these Eldrazi lived there?" she said.

Anowon nodded. "I have always studied them. Their monuments. Their writings. The Hagra Cistern where they generated their power from waste. The crumbled temple under the smooth water of Glasspool. Their remains were"—he looked up at the darkening clouds—"compelling."

"Were? What are they now?"

"You have met them."

Nissa frowned. How could the beings she fought have constructed the palaces she had seen? They seemed incapable even of picking up eating utensils.

Anowon glanced at Nissa's face before speaking. "Yes," he said. "How could *they* have made *that.*" He swept his hand forward in a grand gesture. Nissa had not noticed the thing ahead. It loomed large in the exposed strip of sky: a floating palace, mostly in pieces. As she stared, a jag of lightning traced the sky behind it, and a boom of thunder shook the canyon walls. She felt the fine hairs on her arms vibrate with the noise. A gust of wind swept down the trench.

"There must be something more to them," Anowon said.

And then the sky opened, and it started to rain.

Had it been a quick downpour, everything would have been fine. Nissa would have kept them walking and pulled up the hood of her warthog cloak. The rain would have soaked them through, and they could have made a fire to dry. They could have continued on their way with little or no disturbance. But this was Zendikar, Nissa was careful to remind herself as the fat raindrops fell in arcing sheets. Soon the rain obscured their vision, and the sand beneath their feet turned swampy.

"In what direction are we walking?" Sorin yelled over the hammering raindrops.

Nissa could not tell. She put her hands over her eyes, and through a tiny slot between her first and index finger she could see the barest image of the sky, which was still dark with rain that showed no sign of abating.

"This," Sorin shouted. He pointed up and around in an exasperated sweep. "And this."

She felt it too. The rain was falling hard. It drummed at her skull and made thinking all but impossible. It hurt. He head was numb with it. If the rain turned to hail they would be pummeled to death. Their time was fading. She put her hand over her eyes again and peered around. The shadow of the canyon wall was close, and slowly she made her way to it, sloshing through the rising water. The others followed.

There was no cave, only the steep incline of the canyon wall. Still, being so close to the wall of the canyon stopped some of the rain, and they hunched against it.

Nissa looked closely at the canyon wall. He eyes traced upward from between her fingers until she saw, some three heights up, a stunted tree clinging to the bare cliff face. A small rick of branches and dead grass had been swept into the bend of the tree's trunk. A small shelf jutted above the tree. Her eyes stayed on the small tree, and the wedge of plant material swept as if it was moving downward.

"Rope" she screamed at Anowon. "Hurry." The vampire shrugged off his pack and hurried to free the rope. The water in the trench was already up to their shins. If the torrent continued further up in the trench, there would soon be a wall of water pitched down their part of the rock chute. As Anowon worked, Nissa glanced up once again at the dwarfed tree, where the terrific force of the surging water had wedged what it carried between the rock and the trunk. As he uncoiled the rope, she fumbled through the bag. *It must be here,* she thought. *There must be one here.*

She found the grappling hook and would have yelled for joy if the rumbling hadn't started. It was low, but as she snatched the end of the rope from Anowon, the low growl increased in volume. Her numb fingers slipped the rope through the eyelet of the hook and fastened it with a quick hitch. In one fluid motion she stepped back and threw the hook with every bit of strength she had. The hook fell short of the shelf above the tree. She tried again, and the same thing happened. The sound from up the canyon was a roar now. *Not like this,* she thought. *Not this way.*

Anowon took the hook and leaned back and threw. It fell short.

When Sorin took it and threw, the hook traveled far up but tumbled back down not catching the rock. Nissa had to jump out of the way. On his second throw, the hook's tines caught a bit of rock, and they each scrambled up in turn.

Nissa was the last to climb the rope. When she was half way up, she stopped and turned. With the raindrops stinging her eyes,, she watched as a wall of green water crashed by, so high that for a moment it lapped around her ankles.

The wall of water was gone almost as soon as it had passed. They stayed on the shelf, and Nissa wondered if what she'd seen had been real. The rain was still falling hard. Perhaps she'd only imagined the water touching her feet.

Soon the downpour lessened, then stopped altogether.

Nissa waited until the cloudy sky above their head broke up and patches of pink sunset showed in the clouds of the swatch above their heads. Then she climbed back down.

"Well," said Sorin, once he was standing on the soggy sand. "I suspect we have heard the last of those scorpions. Surely they—" Sorin stopped in mid-sentence. He cocked his head to the side. "Do you hear that?"

Nissa listened. The faint sound of movement echoed off the canyon walls. She could hear something kicking rocks as it moved up the canyon. She glanced at the ledge.

Then the noise stopped. Nothing moved. The very canyon itself seemed to be holding its breath. Sorin sniffed. "Well," he said.

"Hush." Nissa said, putting up her hand.

After a time she swept her hand down, and they crept forward through the rocks. They moved quietly and passed around a boulder to the left and came face to face with a host of three hundred kor, their strange hooked weapons at the ready.

CHAPTER 5

The kor hookmaster was missing an eye. The socket wept yellow globules down the hookmaster's long and thin face, and he wiped the discharge away with the back of a slender hand. The fleshy barbels typical of the kor hung under his chin and almost to his belt. He was crisscrossed with harness works of pockets and loops. His clothes were tanned skins. And tethered with chains to various parts of his body were no fewer than four hooked and bladed climbing tools that Nissa was sure could double as weapons. In his left hand, he held a long, notched sword with a small hook dangling on a chain off its pommel.

All the other kor, males, females, and children, were similarly outfitted. None moved or spoke. In the silence, a rock skittered down the trench wall behind. A snail falcon cried overhead.

Nissa had seen kor fight before. They could be savage, if threatened. The Joraga had always been friendlier with the kor than other elf tribes—they respected the kor's avoidance of speech.

Nissa knew the kor to be nomadic, but from the packs they carried on their backs, they looked to be fleeing, their caravan reduced to the things they carried. She noted the signs of battle: Many were bandaged, and some were using jurworrel-wood branches for crutches. And some of their weapons were missing blades, or had only half a blade. They were tired, clearly. Some were stooped so badly with exhaustion that she feared they might fall. *How had they survived the flood?* she wondered.

Nissa opened her hands and put them palms up—the kor greeting.

The lead kor's eye moved from her to Sorin and then to Anowon, where it stayed for a longer time. The vampire stared back. Nissa could almost see him lick his lips. It occurred to her that she didn't know how long it had been since Anowon had fed.

"Well, savages?" Sorin said. "Going for a stroll?"

Nissa cringed inwardly. "They're refugees. Or are you blind as well as rude?"

Sorin said nothing.

Nissa kept her palms out. "May we speak?" she asked.

The old kor regarded her for a time. In the failing light of the canyon, the quietness of the kor was unnerving. Nissa found herself shifting her weight from foot to foot as she waited for the kor to decide whether or not they would speak.

Finally he nodded.

Nissa waited.

"Oh, this *is* thrilling," Sorin said.

She shot him a glance before turning back to the kor. "Please," she said. "From where do you come?"

When the kor spoke, his voice was unusually deep. It echoed off the near canyon wall. "We come from the west," the kor said.

"I'm glad we've figured that out," Sorin said. "Can we go now?"

Nissa ignored him.

"What have you found?"

"We have found those that have woken."

Nissa put her hand in front of her mouth and wiggled her fingers like tentacles.

The kor nodded.

"Brood lineage," Nissa said. "Is that why you are traveling?"

The kor leader looked back at the other kor and gave a signal to move on.

Nissa turned and caught Sorin yawning. Behind Sorin, Anowon stood staring at her. The vampire was always staring at her, she realized with a chill.

"The kor are the lost creatures of Zendikar," Anowon said, with a strange twist to his lips, as if his comment should remind her of other lost creatures. "They believe they are followed by the ghosts of their ancestors. Because of this they never stop moving. The mothers bear their young while suspended in a harness, and their fathers curse the ground nightly while imploring the sky. Both sexes use the bones of their ancestors in their daily rituals. Some go so far as to prop the dessicated corpses of their dead ancestors at the eating table. I like that last bit. A nice touch."

"Why are you telling *me* this?" asked Nissa.

"I am fascinated with the kor," Anowon hissed, moving closer. Nissa inched back. "I think you are fascinated with them, as well. Did you know they walk so much that the nursing mothers keep vessels of their milk on their hips, which are turned to cheese by week's end?"

Nissa stared at Anowon. He had never said so many words to her, and on such an odd topic. She was not sure she liked it. In fact, she was sure she did not.

The kor left as silently as they had come. The only sound as they walked was the muted clink of the hooks hanging from their shoulder harnesses.

When they were gone, Nissa began looking for a place to sleep. The light in the sky was gone, and already the damp of the trench's floor was turning to a fine fog. The sand was wet, and they spent an uncomfortable night on the ground.

Nissa watched Anowon as they stood shivering in the predawn gray. How was the vampire feeding? She'd been eating hardtack and dried warthog for the last two days.

Anowon caught her looking at him.

"What are you eating?" she asked.

The vampire stamped his feet and rubbed his hands together. His breath came out of his mouth in a puff. "I eat when I am hungry," he replied.

"He eats when I tell him," Sorin said, who also seemed well fed to Nissa. He stood in the cold as pink and as warm looking as if he'd been traveling in the jungles of Bala Ged.

They walked between boulders large and small. The sand was wet under their feet, and that made the walking harder still. The crested sedge that grew on the sunless canyon floor brushed against their hands as they passed. At one point they stopped to drink from a rock pool. A huge boulder stood at the far side.

The water appeared as crystal clear as one might expect in a Bala Ged oracle pool, Nissa thought. Sorin was the first to near it. When one of the stones at the bottom of the pool moved, Nissa looked closer. *Why was there a pool like this at the bottom of the trench?* Nissa wondered. *And after a flood.* "Stop," Nissa said.

Sorin turned with a scowl on his face.

"That is no pool," Nissa said. "Step back."

Sorin peered closely at the pool. Tiny fish were swimming in the clear water.

"Step back slowly."

After a couple of heartbeats Sorin did as Nissa told him. Nissa glanced at Anowon, who was watching the proceedings with an impassive face. But for just a second, Nissa thought she saw the side of his mouth rise in the barest glint of a smile at Sorin's predicament. Then it was gone, and Sorin was back by their side.

"Watch," Nissa said as she took a stick from the ground and tossed it into the pool. In a flash, a lip appeared from behind the boulder on the far side and snapped down over the entire pool with an audible snap that shook the ground slightly. Some black and green birds sitting in a nearby shrub took sudden flight.

"Ah, Zendikar," Sorin said, shaking his head. He turned back to the trail, chuckling. But Nissa saw he wasn't smiling.

They saw other groups of kor who passed without word or gesture in the day and night, looking like they had been resoundingly beaten by more than one enemy. The trench became deeper as they walked. The line of sky above grew more and more narrow. And as they walked, the rock changed. Where there had been red walls of crumbly sedimentary rock, there were sheer, sweeping walls of steel gray granite. Nissa did not like the look of it. *No toe holds,* she thought. *No boulders on the canyon floor to shelter behind.*

At midday they came to a fork in the trench. A massive statue, half the height of the canyon, was carved into the stone wall. It was a being Nissa had seen in statues in other parts of Zendikar, and although it was crumbled and missing limbs, she could tell what it had been: a creature with a large head, four arms, and tentacles that started at its waist—brood lineage. But who had carved the statue, and how long before? She thought of Anowon's words before the rainstorm that had created the flood: *There has to be something more to them.* As she looked up at the strange creature, she wondered if he wasn't right.

Nissa took the leather tube containing Khalled's map from her pack and consulted it. There were many lines extending from the trench. She found the tiny picture of the statue and realized they could follow the canyon branch that angled toward the sun, or the other which traveled but wound back in the same direction. She showed the map to Sorin, who eyed it suspiciously. He put one long, thin white finger on a landmass that lay on the other side of the sea.

"Akoum," he said. Both trench ways moved them in that direction. "If it wasn't for this plane's volatile energy, I would walk in the air and be there in seconds. I wouldn't need you or the Ghet." He waved a dismissive hand at them.

Nissa chose the left fork. The sun was half past midsky and the shadows were deep when Anowon stopped them. The canyon wall next to them was filled with images engraved into the smooth stone.

"Illuminated pictographs," Anowon said as he unscrewed one of his metal cylinders and slipped a piece of paper out of the hollow place within. He went to the pictographs and squatted before them. He consulted the piece of paper as he deciphered the writing.

"These are old," Anowon said. "It is unknown to me why they are written here in this wilderness." He kept reading, speaking as he did. "Perhaps this trench was not always as it appears now. Perhaps this trench was once an aqueduct used by the ancient Eldrazi for power creation. "

"Perhaps," Sorin said. His mocking smile visited his lips again.

"This main panel tells the story of the Mortifier," Anowon said, pointing.

Sorin stopped smiling.

"Who is that?" Nissa asked.

Anowon's fingers traced the image of a pictograph of a figure daubed with black. He used both of his fingers to trace the line. The figure daubed with black pigment stood with three huge, monsterlike creatures, but appeared to be a simple being. It did not have the tentacles of the other three. Before the figure were other beings, attached to it with long lines.

"These are ropes," Anowon said, tracing the lines. "These figures are vampires, and they are slaves to the Mortifier, who is one of these Eldrazi it appears.

"He is not," Sorin said, his voice a jot higher than Anowon's. "Does he look like those Eldrazi?"

Nissa considered the picture. "No," she agreed. "But those three Eldrazi don't look very much like the ones we've seen."

"These large Eldrazi are the ones that we see as statues around Zendikar," Anowon said. "Many scholars think they are deities."

"Gods with slaves?" Nissa said.

"Perhaps," Anowon said. "Why not? If this had been an aqueduct, then who dug it? Who built the fabulous palaces? And those slaves are not human."

"No?"

"They are vampires."

"Yes, Yes," Sorin said.

Nissa turned to Sorin. "Do you know about these Eldrazi?"

Sorin's eyes did not blink. "I know that Zendikar is at risk," he said.

Nissa turned to Anowon. "And why do you not question him further on this topic which so interests you?" she asked. "He is clearly hiding information."

Sorin kicked at a loose rock. "What I know is not for you or the vampire's ears. He knows not to overstep his place." Sorin said, staring at Nissa.

Nissa ignored Sorin's glare. "What force does he have over you?" Nissa asked Anowon.

Anowon looked up at the canyon wall.

Somewhere down the canyon a boulder crashed into rock.

Sorin coughed. "Can we keep moving before we are caught by another stinking troop of kor? I do not think my nose can handle another onslaught."

Anowon stood and rolled up his scroll. "As you wish," he said. As he was sliding the scroll back into its metal cylinder, Sorin came near Nissa.

"We must go now," he said.

"Bind the vampire and we'll go." she replied.

But he did not answer her. Instead Sorin started walking—leaving Nissa to it. They walked until they were stumbling in darkness, at which point they stopped next to what looked like a huge crumbled stone grate lying on its side and half buried in the sand.

Sorin insisted on a fire, and Nissa and Anowon were able to find some debris to make a small blaze. In the flickering firelight Anowon investigated the disintegrating grate, covered as it was with intricate line tracing and glyphs.

The fire was no more than coals when Nissa heard speaking echoing off the canyon walls behind them.

She had drawn first watch. She quickly stoked the fire and woke the others. They moved away and hid behind a boulder to see who came to the fire.

Soon a small group of goblins leading a female kor came around the corner. The goblins had small swords on their belts. One had a staff with a pathway stone floating at its tip.

The kor was strange looking and not at all like the refugees passing up the trench toward Graypelt and the Binding Circle. This kor's hair was wild and unkempt, and her clothes were nothing more than rags. Glass beads were knotted into her hair, and they flickered slightly in the firelight. She was wearing small bells somewhere, and they chimed lightly as she stumbled. As Nissa watched she tripped, and two goblins gently caught her and pushed her upright.

Most telling was that the creature wore no ropes or hooks, unlike all other kor. In fact, the only attribute that gave away her race was her long, thin skull and the pale skin stretched taught over it.

The kor's mouth was continually moving like some merfolk lull-mage engaged in his daily intonations. But when she saw the fire, she stopped cold. Then she saw the ancient grate and rushed to it, stamping one foot in the corner of the fire in her haste. The goblins rushed to catch up, but the kor paid them no mind. She fell to her knees before the grate and began chanting.

Anowon watched the kor intently as the goblins brushed her hair from her eyes and kneeled down next to her in the sand. They also began chanting.

Sorin drew his long sword from its dark sheath. To Nissa the sword seemed part of the dark. The coals did not reflect their red off it. It seemed to suck what light there was into it.

"I will slay the first goblin, and we can enslave the others," he said. The saliva in his mouth made his words slur.

Anowon nodded vigorously.

"No," Nissa said. "They are barely armed. We will not kill them now. Let us see what they know."

"But they are goblins," Sorin said.

Anowon nodded enthusiastically.

What is this all about? Nissa wondered. *Why are they so keen to enslave the goblins?* She stood from behind the rock and walked forward. "If you want to find your way to Akoum then stay your sword for the time being," she said. "Kor are some of the best guides."

The goblins did not sense Nissa until she was directly behind them, at which point they hissed and turned toward her. They struggled to yank out their small stone swords. One goblin ended up holding his dull blade and threatening her with the sword's wooden handle.

All the swords' handles were wood. With a word from Nissa the wood in the handles shot out roots and grew solidly into the sand.

The kor continued to chant—ignorant of the events around her. The goblins stood blinking, unsure of themselves in the firelight.

Sorin came out from behind the rock, his sword in his hand. Anowon stood.

"They should travel with us," Anowon said.

Sorin turned to the vampire, then back to Nissa.

"What is that kor babbling?" Sorin said.

"It is not kor," Anowon said. "But it is a language."

"I can tell that. What language?"

Anowon shook his head.

Sorin leaned forward to listen, cocking his ear to the chant. Before long a look of recognition spread across his face. Nissa squinted in the dim light. No sooner had she seen the look on his face than it was gone. Sorin stood up straight.

"This kor interests me," he pronounced. She and her entourage will come with me."

"You recognized the language," Nissa said.

"Yes I did."

Nissa waited. But it was Anowon who spoke first. "Well?" he said.

"As a matter of fact," Sorin said, "It is ancient Eldrazi the animal speaks."

Nissa felt herself blinking. She could not figure out what was stranger: that the kor was speaking ancient Eldrazi, or that Sorin recognized it as such.

"How could you know?" Anowon said, awed. "It has not been spoken in more than a thousand years."

Sorin sniffed and turned. "What does it have in its hand?" Sorin said, pointing to the kor.

Nissa looked. It was a rock as big as the kor's fist but longer. The creature passed it from one hand to the other as she chanted.

The goblins glanced at each other.

"A crystal," Anowon said.

Sorin leaned forward for a closer look. "She will be able to help us. Yes."

Nissa turned. "Why?"

Sorin shrugged.

"Who is this kor?" Nissa asked.

The kor stopped chanting suddenly, as if she had heard. She slowly turned. Her corneas were red. Nissa couldn't be sure if it was the fire's reflection.

The kor began chanting again.

"Take the goblins," Anowon said.

"Why do you want the goblins so very much?" Nissa said.

"Are you jealous?"

Nissa opened her mouth to reply, but Anowon stopped her words with a held up hand.

They listened to the kor chant.

"*Now* it is the old vampire tongue," Anowon said. "Or I am a fool."

Sorin leaned closer. "How can you tell?" he asked. "The words are so muddled."

"You know the ancient language of vampires, too?" asked Nissa.

Sorin smiled. "A person like me picks up many languages in his travels," he said.

It was Anowon's turn to smile knowingly. "I am sure," he said. "This language is one of those that is not spoken anymore, but lives only in books and is known only for the purposes of translation. A dead language."

"What is she saying?" Nissa asked.

Anowon listened to the chanting. "She's simply repeating 'The gift is in the loam' I believe."

" 'The gift is in the loam'?" Nissa said. "What could it mean?"

"We should leave this creature," Anowon said.

"And take the goblins," Nissa said. "I think you've already said that."

"Yes."

Nissa eyed the kor as she babbled. As she watched, a bug the size of Nissa's thumbnail ran out of the kor's hair.

"She will travel with us to the Teeth of Akoum?" Nissa said.

Both Sorin and Anowon were listening intently to the kor as she babbled. Again, she stopped speaking when she heard Nissa's words, and a moment later her body seized up tight. She stood straight with her arms at her sides, as her head began to wobble on her neck. Then she began to scream.

"What is happening?" Nissa said, above the kor's strange keening.

"A fit," Anowon said, without looking away from the kor. "But she is speaking."

The goblins rushed to the kor and began stroking her hands as they chanted.

Sorin was listening intently to the kor. "She says she is an Eldrazi, if you can believe that. She says, 'the key is requested.' And 'freedom is nigh.' " Sorin looked closely at the crystal clutched in the kor's white hand. "That could be the key she speaks of."

"Then seize and break it," Nissa said.

"She could gain us paths we cannot know," Sorin said. "She could allow us entry to the Eye."

The kor's screaming was hurting Nissa's ears. Something about the kor, perhaps her acidic smell, made Nissa extremely wary. "That is assuming she is telling the truth and not raving at the moon," Nissa said.

Sorin's eyes never left the kor as she screamed out her words. "Rather. But I do not think this one is fabricating . . . That crystal seems familiar somehow."

The goblins had been whispering among themselves. When Sorin mentioned the crystal, one of the goblins stepped forward. He was dressed in a much-used robe of thick worsted fabric, dyed red. "Crystal of the Ancients held by Smara, Chosen of the Ancients," it said.

"And that is Smara?" Nissa said, pointing at the kor.

The goblin bowed its head.

"And are you all allowed to speak?"

The goblin shook its head.

"Only now, me," the goblin said. "And I stop speaking now. Here I am stopping. I have stopped."

Nissa watched the goblin purse its gray lips together, trying not to speak. The other goblins watched with clear admiration on their faces. *Did they admire his discipline or his ability to speak—many times a challenge for a goblin?* she wondered. The goblin stood before her with his chin up a bit. *His discipline,* Nissa decided. *They all want to speak but are terrified by something.*

"I have stopped speaking," the goblin whispered. "Now."

Smara suddenly lurched forward, kicking the sand as she jerked a step. She was repeating words as she turned and began stumbling forward in the darkness with the chants on her lips. The goblins were on her in a second. But instead of bringing her to the fire, as Nissa expected, they led her forward, continuing down the trench and away into the darkness.

Sorin watched them go, as did Anowon. The vampire's face told a tale of loss and sorrow that Nissa could not help but chuckle at.

"We must follow," Sorin said. He began walking after Smara. Anowon almost tripped in his haste to follow.

"Why must we follow?" Nissa said.

"That one is somehow channeling an Eldrazi ancient," Sorin said, over his shoulder. "We have in a strange way gained access to the enemy's camp."

Nissa looked up at the early evening as sling-tail nighthawks swept the skies clear of lion flies.

They trailed behind the goblins all that night and into the morning. It didn't matter if they wanted the kor and the goblins to travel with them or not. Smara was walking in the same direction they were; and the goblins, having no food that Nissa could see—no provisions of any sort in fact—kept close. They looked so forlorn that Nissa gave them hard tack biscuits.

But neither Anowon nor Sorin would eat her dry tack. They looked drawn in the early morning light. Nissa watched Anowon as he followed the goblins, who looked over their shoulders nervously at him.

They walked for the rest of the morning and stopped for a rest next to a spring. The sun was shining, and above the canyon large, dark birds circled. Then a roar split the air, and the attack was launched.

CHAPTER 6

One moment they were sitting on rocks around the spring, and the next moment the creature was upon them. It rushed forward with great simian lopes that shook the ground and knocked Nissa and Sorin back with the sweep of a powerful hand.

Nissa spun in the air and was up the moment she hit the ground, but Sorin had not been so quick—he landed and lay motionless, slumped against the canyon wall.

The goblins drew their few remaining stone swords and looked at the head goblin, who looked back at them and frowned. He raised his sword for a charge and then lowered it again.

The trench giant rose up to its full height. Not quite as large as a proper giant, it reached the span of five human men and the width of a sizable cave. Its skin was the exact hue of the rock and the same roughness. The skin around its eyes and on its eyelids looked exactly like gravel. As she watched, the giant seized a goblin in its boulder-sized fist and snapped its head off with a deft nip. The blood spurted for a moment, and the giant waved the spurt in a merry pantomime. Then it chewed calmly on the head. Nissa could hear the goblin's cranium crunching in the giant's mouth.

It was surely the ugliest trench giant Nissa had ever seen. Stunted trees grew out of the crags that ran along its back. There were petroglyphs carved in its thigh. And even from where she stood, its breath was a foul miasma. But giants left scat, and that meant they had yeast in their stomachs and other small life. Nissa knew what she could do.

She planted her staff in the sand and whispered into the knot of carved wood on the top of it. And with the words of power, the staff started to hum in her hand as tendrils of mana wove up its shaft.

The giant tossed the body of the goblin aside and settled its gaze on Nissa. The ground shook when it took its first step toward her, and then the next; and then it was running full speed.

Nissa yanked up the tip of her staff and drew it level with the charging giant. The giant stooped down as it ran and brought its hand sweeping in from the right in a wide arc. Nissa stepped forward, bent her knees, and hopped straight up, and the giant's hand rushed under her feet. Unbalanced with the lunge, it tripped and tumbled forward with a tremendous crash that brought down a small landslide at the edge of the canyon wall.

The speed with which the giant regained its feet surprised her. It hopped up, turned, and charged again. Nissa ran at the giant and leapt. She planted the tip of her staff on the giant's forehead and vaulted over the top of it. The tremendous creature stopped and stood. From where Nissa landed some feet away, she could see from the cast of its eyes that something was wrong with the giant. The spot where she had planted her staff glowed slightly. Once she saw the glow, Nissa concentrated the mana in her fingertips and reached toward the giant's stomach. She felt the millions of tiny creatures living there move at her suggestion. In her mind she sang them into excitement, and in a moment the giant's eyes went wide. Nissa tickled the flora in its stomach further, and the giant's eyes screwed down in pain as its hands went to its belly.

As she concentrated, a drop of sweat ran down Nissa's nose. She incited the small creatures in the giant's stomach and intestines into higher and higher states of animation, and the giant fell to its knees. When she felt the giant had had enough, she severed her connection to the wildlife in the creature's gut.

The giant slowly fell over with a tremendous thump.

Nissa turned, and was hit so hard that the world went suddenly black.

Then the colors filtered back into her eyes, the tips of her fingers and toes were tingling. She could not move her limbs. When the tingling receded and she felt in control of her body again, she sat up slowly. There was a bump on the back of her head the size of her fist.

Across the canyon Anowon was standing opposite a second giant, His hands still bound. As she watched, Sorin stumbled up from where he had been thrown. Nissa turned, looking for her staff. The first giant was still on the sand behind her holding its stomach.

Her staff was nowhere to be found.

Then she saw it pinched between the second giant's thumb and forefinger. She stood and took a step and didn't fall, so she took another. Soon she was ambling toward the giant. But Sorin was there first. He paused and took a deep breath and began to hum. The he started to chant the strange words she'd heard before, in the language with inflections like a wet fish flapping on a stream bank.

Nissa could see the effort tense Sorin's body, but the effect was almost instantaneous. The giant's body shuddered once, but did not fall. Sorin kept chanting, but the expression on his face told her that he was surprised by the giant's resilience.

With its attention thus diverted, Anowon snatched another tooth from the folds of his clothes. The vampire took a running start, jumped, and executed a series of flips that landed him in front of the giant. The giant lifted a foot and tried to stomp it down on Anowon, but the vampire rolled away.

Nissa stopped short. She surely did not want to run through Sorin's singing, but one look at his quivering legs, and Nissa knew he could not hold the song for much longer.

Anowon threw his tooth, and the giant's leg turned to white marble up to the knee. The giant tried to turn, but the marble leg was slow to move.

Then the giant did something that Nissa never would have expected. It pointed Nissa's own staff at her. *It will not function,* Nissa thought. *How can it?*

But the staff did work. The giant became calm, and a tendril of magical energy shot out from the tip of the staff. Nissa had to leap forward and roll to avoid what enchantment the giant had managed to weave.

Sorin stopped singing and fell onto the sand. Anowon went through his pockets again.

Nissa rolled out of her tumble and into a standing position, just in time for the giant to kick at her with its good leg. Nissa jumped back to avoid the stony toenail as big as a battle shield. The giant pressed its advantage and stomped down at her, dragging its heavy marble leg. Nissa rolled away, but the giant raised its foot for another go.

Then Anowon threw another tooth, and the giant's other leg whitened to marble.

The giant pulled and was able to drag one of its legs, and then another, but the effort of it was clearly too much to keep up.

"Give me my staff," Nissa yelled up at the giant. "Or he will turn the rest of you to white stone."

The giant brought Nissa's staff up. It turned its head to the side and looked closely at it. Then it spoke. "If you turn me to white stone, you will turn your staff as well," it said. The giant's rumbling voice sounded like boulders moving under water in a river.

"It is only a piece of wood," Nissa said. "I can make another."

"Then you will not mind if I use it as a toothpick?"

Nissa tried to keep her face impassive. "Why would I mind? Except if you put it in your mouth the same thing will happen as happened there." She hooked her thumb over her shoulder at the other giant, still curled on the ground. As they watched, the giant moaned and rolled over onto its other side.

"Free him," the giant said. "I will give you back your toothpick."

"Give me my staff first," Nissa replied. She knew better than to trust a giant. Any giant. They were known to be fickle and untrustworthy. Her eyes stopped on Anowon, still digging through his pockets. *Fickle,* she thought. *Not unlike vampires.*

Nissa heard Smara chanting from the other side of the canyon. The goblins clustered around the kor and watched the giant with faces like mushrooms.

"We are not here to bandy words with the likes of you," Sorin said, suddenly next to her. He snapped, and Nissa's staff jumped from between the giant's fingers and into Sorin's hand. He took it in both hands and closed his eyes. For a moment he held the staff, and then his smuggest smile bloomed on his face. He handed Nissa the staff before turning to the giant.

"I may let my elf use her toy staff on you, too," Sorin said. The giant on the ground moaned again.

"Soon the blood will come out from both ends," Nissa said, looking at the giant on the ground.

"To where do you travel?" the giant said.

Nissa caught herself before she said too much. Giants were also shameless sellers of information if food was in the bargain.

"West," Nissa said.

"In the Teeth," Smara screamed suddenly. "In the Teeth." The goblins standing around her were so shocked—by what Nissa was not entirely sure, they must surely be used to Smara's screams—that some dropped their stone swords. The head goblin barked an order in the goblin tongue, and they picked up their swords again.

The giant made a face like it had bitten down on something bitter. It looked from the goblins to Nissa.

"Then you are walking to your death," the giant said.

"What? Is your cooking kitchen ahead?" Sorin said.

The giant looked at Sorin curiously. Nissa had to stifle a laugh. *Do giants even cook?* she wondered.

"There is only the tentacled scourge in the trench ahead," the giant said. "They have killed many of my kind."

"Oh, not the tentacled scourge again?" Sorin said. "They're everywhere . . . like elves."

Nissa cocked her head for a look at Sorin. Perhaps he should be thrown against the canyon wall more often. It seemed to affect his mood for the better.

The giant bent its knees and lowered its voice. "I know a better way to travel to Zulaport," it said.

"Why does that not surprise me," Sorin said.

"Nobody said Zulaport," Nissa said.

The giant smiled, showing teeth like gray, chipped flint.

Nissa sighed. "How far is this path?"

"Very close."

"How does it pass through the land?

"My path moves through the Piston Mountains."

"That way has perils," Nissa said. And it did. She'd passed that way traveling to Ondu from Bala Ged. Four in her party had died, crushed between the mountains.

"You will not live if you do not change paths."

"So you say," Sorin said.

"Keep hushed your forked tongue," the giant said.

Sorin, wide eyed, looked from the giant to Nissa.

The Piston Mountains, Nissa thought. Even on their current path they could be expected to travel another week before they ascended out of the trench. Then they would skirt the Piston Mountains to Zulaport. The giant's way could cut their travel in half. Still, the Piston Mountains.

"I would avoid that path," Anowon yelled from where he squatted next to the moaning giant, copying the petrogyphs on its legs onto a scrap of paper.

"Lead the way," Nissa said to the giant.

"What?" Sorin said.

The giant turned and heaved its marble legs.

"I lead this expedition," Nissa said, walking after the giant.

"Strange." Sorin started to walk. "I thought I did."

"Then open your eyes," Nissa yelled over her shoulder.

The giant labored its heavy legs four steps then stopped and pointed at the canyon wall. "There," it said.

Nissa followed the giant's finger but saw nothing except sheer wall. She moved her head to the side in case there was an illusion in the rock. There wasn't. The canyon wall appeared as just that.

The giant hummed to itself, and the glyph lines on its legs burned to life. Suddenly the path in the canyon rock glowed with the same pink as the glyphs.

"Zendikar!" Sorin said. "It is either in your hand, or it is at your throat."

"Now," the giant said. "Release my legs."

"Do not do that," Sorin said. "Need I remind you that this is a giant? We already have the path. Let's be on our way."

Nissa regarded the giant. She reached out to the other giant's gut and soothed the creatures in it. The effect was almost instantaneous. The other giant sat up and turned.

Nissa did not like the menace she saw in its eyes.

The other giant pointed to its legs and gave a ghastly smile. Anowon found a tooth and threw it, and in a moment the giant's legs were back to normal.

"Well," Sorin said. "Now that we are all happy again, can we go?" He turned to Smara and her goblins. Unaccountably, the kor was standing on her head, and one of her goblins had its finger in the nose of the goblin next to it. Sorin shook his head and started walking.

The giants watched them as they carefully threaded their way between the boulders and walked to where the path glowed in the canyon wall. Even with the way glowing slightly, it took Nissa some careful examination to find its beginning. The rock steps were so deftly fit into the canyon wall that they left little shadow to contrast. The path's invisibility was due to exceptional design.

Who could have built this? Nissa wondered. She was looking up at the symmetrical switchbacks, which looked so much like sutures holding the canyon together.

Anowon was standing next to her. "The old stories say the giants were once great builders."

"Of what? Booby traps?" Sorin said. He squinted at the path. Fine droplets of sweat clung to his upper lip. He lifted one trembling hand to brush his hair back. *He's afraid of heights*, Nissa thought, filing that realization away for later use.

"Are we all ready?" Nissa said.

Sorin said nothing.

But Anowon stepped up and held out his bound wrists for Nissa to see. "I have done all you asked. I am a vampire, but not all vampires are like the ones you perhaps met in the jungles of your home."

Nissa studied the vampire before responding. "Just so," she said, and cut the rope from his wrists with a small eating knife she kept strapped to her inner forearm.

"I thank you," Anowon said, rubbing his wrists.

Nissa nodded.

They began to ascend the trail. It started steeply from the canyon floor and became progressively steeper, but Anowon talked as they walked. "Something had to build those monuments dotted over the landscape. It couldn't have been the vampires. We were personal slaves that were used for manual labor of certain sorts. But we lacked the raw strength to move the large blocks."

"And you think the creatures that built the huge statues and palaces were giants?" Nissa said.

"It is possible."

They were all quiet as they climbed. Far behind and below, Smara and her retinue of goblins followed the switchbacks in silence. Nissa wasn't sure she had ever heard the mad kor speechless, but it was a good thing she was. The trail had become so steep that the travelers were compelled to use their hands as they ascended.

"They used vampires, not giants." It was Sorin who spoke. Nobody else spoke for a moment, at which point Anowon asked the question hanging on Nissa's lips.

"How do you know that?" Anowon said.

"I know," said Sorin. He looked back down the way they had come and grimaced. He was even paler than before. The droplets of sweat that had dotted his lip and forehead had grown into full sweat trails running down through the dust on his face. As Nissa watched, he unhitched his sword belt and slipped it over his shoulder before pulling the belt buckle tight again. *No jokes now,* Nissa thought and turned her attention back to the canyon.

"This is madness," Sorin said. "We should be harnessed in for this kind of climb."

"This is nothing compared to what we will encounter in Akoum," Nissa said.

"I can hardly wait."

Anowon scrambled up the trail in front of Nissa without the least hesitation. She noticed with approval that he always kept three of his limbs attached to the rock as he climbed. Something about the way his limbs moved reminded her of the Tajuru Hiba who had been killed by the brood in MossCrack. She pushed him out of her mind and kept walking.

The trail's pitch was somewhere between steep and vertical. Not so steep that they needed rope works, but steep enough that one could easily peel off the face if one slipped. The way forward involved handholds, and they climbed until the sun fell in the sky.

Later the moon rose in the dark sky, and the trail showed a ghastly pale silver. From the dark shadows cast by the moonlight came the moaning of rock lizards hunched therein, and soon Nissa's feet were staggering under her, and her numb hands fumbled over the rocks.

"We must stop," she said.

Sorin's breath hissed out from between his teeth as he climbed. Nissa could hear the tightness in his voice when he spoke. "Stop where?" he replied.

She leaned against the canyon wall and looked up. Even with the moon as bright as it was, the rock outcroppings obscured her view of the trail ahead. Nissa always found it impossible to gauge the height of a high place while actually climbing on it. The Joraga kept boards they could hang and sleep in. What she wouldn't have done for one of those.

Smara and the goblins were the last to arrive, and they all climbed in almost utter silence. When they attained a small shelf, the goblins plopped down and began playing a game, it seemed, that involved slapping each other's hands and then the rock trail. As Nissa watched, Smara took the corner of her robe and almost daintily dabbed the sweat from behind her ears and temples. She did not mutter or roll her eyes.

"Climbing suits her," Nissa said, to nobody in particular.

"Do you see where the crystal resides?" Anowon said.

Nissa looked. The kor's odd crystal was tucked into the waistband that bound her rags to her body.

"It is not in her hand," Anowon said.

"Just so," Nissa said. "It is not directly contacting her skin."

A rock rolled down from above. Nissa followed its descent as it plummeted by them and far to the right.

"The trail might continue like this for a long time," Nissa said. She leaned against the cool wall. A warm breeze rustled her hair. If she could just close her eyes . . . Sleep was about to take her when Anowon coughed.

"We must continue," he said. She heard his metal cylinders clink off each other as he began climbing again. It took some effort, but Nissa leaned out from the wall and started climbing too. He was right. For one, they were as exposed as babies out here on the face. If a drake decided to sweep in for a snack, they would have little way to defend themselves. And the giants. Better to not wonder if the two giants were still shadowing them.

She listened for Sorin to begin climbing. Why had his destructive singing not worked on the giants?

She asked him.

"They must be composed," he said, breathing hard as he climbed. "Must be composed of stone. I am only able to rot the living."

Nissa turned back to climbing. *Rot the living,* she thought. She tried to speed up so Sorin was not so close behind her.

The first reddening of the sky found them still climbing, though slowly. Nissa found that if she stopped thinking about anything, her hands found their own handhold, and her progress was more satisfactory. Sorin must have found the same thing. The rhythm of his steps sounded more regular, and his breathing had steadied.

Farther down, the goblins followed behind Smara, pushing and heading her up the trail, making good progress. They lived in rocky crevices and could clearly move in high, precarious places easily.

They attained the lip of the mesa when the sun was low in the sky. Panting, Nissa clambered onto the grassy veldt. To the right, a river poured over the edge of the mesa and cascaded the heights into the dark mist of the canyon. Nissa crawled to the river and had a drink. Her hands were cut and raw, and she put them into the cold water and cried out with the sting. Soon Sorin and Anowon were at the river. Sorin put his whole head in. Anowon put only his lips in the clear water and sucked peacefully. After he was filled, he walked up the stream with his eyes on the stream bed as he walked.

"What are you looking for?" Nissa said.

"Signs."

As she watched, he fell to his knees next to the water and plunged his hands into the rocks and pebbles at the bottom of the stream. His hands came out holding something.

"What is that?" Nissa asked. Her soreness made kneeling difficult, but she did it anyway.

The palms of Anowon's hands were filled with many small pebbles and a couple of rocks. Something about the scratches on the rocks set her curiosity on edge, and she bent to look closer at a green one. Soon a brow became apparent. Then slit eyes. The rock was crudely carved into the likeness of a head with an expression of anger. She looked up at Anowon.

"Each is similarly carved," he said.

She looked still closer at the pebbles in his hands. He was right—each of them, no matter how small, was carved to look like an earless head. Some had tentacles for mouths and some did not.

She looked at Anowon again.

"I have heard of these streams near the Binding Circle," he said. "All the streams around are filled thusly."

Suddenly Nissa had the feeling she was being attacked . . . something was running toward her. But when she spun, the mesa behind her was covered only with dense grass that spread away into foothills. There was no enemy. Even in the slanted morning light she could see the gaps in the mountains where the ancient ones had sheared off the tops and put their magic in between so they rose and crashed down at irregular intervals. The foothills extended into blunt mountains capped with snow, and dark, purple rain clouds sat on the horizon. On either side of the stream, twin statues of grotesque, tentacled statues stood in massive repose. One was missing a head, and the other's body was floating slightly above its pedestal.

She turned back to Anowon, bewildered.

"I feel it too," he said. "We must be on guard."

She nodded.

"Did you see it?" asked Anowon.

"No," Nissa said.

Anowon pointed. It was no more than a dot at the base of the mountains: a palace. It was in a sunless lee of the mountains and clearly crumbled, but it had obviously once been huge.

"Is this the Binding Circle?" Nissa said to Anowon.

"I don't know," he replied.

The morning sun was bright and warm on her neck. Anowon went off to lie in the grass with the pebbles in his open palms. Sorin was already asleep, snoring loudly. As she watched, Smara clambered over the edge of the Mesa, pushed forward by her goblins. She was muttering again, with her crystal firmly clamped in her right hand. But as soon as the goblins had situated her in the grass, she clutched her crystal to her chest and quieted a bit.

Nissa stretched out in the grass and felt her muscles loosen. She believed that vampires liked to cut their prey before feeding. Their teeth were not overly sharp. Anowon had no bladed tool.

A low rumbling sound drifted somewhere far off in the mountains. The floating parts of the statues next to the river cast long shadows. And Nissa fell asleep, without setting a watch.

CHAPTER 7

Nissa awoke suddenly, shivering in the darkness, listening for whatever had woken her. But she was unable to hear anything except the gusting wind shaking the grass fronds around her. There were no stars or moon overhead, and Nissa could not hear Smara's incessant babbling. Her staff was by her side, and she very slowly reached out and put her hand around its smooth shaft. She waited and listened, but nothing came and she drifted off again.

She next opened her eyes to bright daylight. Her staff was still clutched in her hand. She sat up. Smara was speaking somewhere, and the wind had disappeared, but not the feeling of foreboding. Anowon was sitting in the grass watching her, with his bound hands wrapped around his legs. Sorin was standing with his back to her, looking at the mountains. The goblins and Smara were grouped together near the river.

"Are you ready?" Sorin asked, turning. He looked surprisingly fit. His face was full as he smiled. "Anowon wanted to feed on you but I kept him from it . . ."

Nissa stood.

"But you have something in your blood, he tells me," Sorin finished.

Nissa turned and adjusted the climbing harness she always wore.

"I take the Joraga tincture," Nissa said. "Once a month." She took Khalled's map from the tube strapped to her belt.

"Where do you get *that*?" Sorin said. "Are you not a Tajuru, after all?"

Nissa stopped. *What did he say?* she thought. She bristled at the taunt. "Watch your tongue, human."

Sorin laughed.

Still, Anowon watched her.

"I have fought many vampires in my time," Nissa said. "And our tincture makes our blood poison to one. Now, if you are done?" She unrolled the map and considered its ink lines. *What had gotten into Sorin and Anowon? she wondered.*

"Did you sleep well?" Sorin asked.

She looked up from the map.

"One of Smara's goblins is gone." Sorin said.

She looked over at the group of goblins surrounding Smara. One, two, three . . . yes, there were only nine.

"Yes, and?" she said.

"We are wondering what happened to it," Sorin said, a smug smile on his face as he turned to Anowon. "Aren't we?"

She looked up in surprise. "Why would I have knowledge of this?"

Anowon didn't move.

Nissa looked from one to the other of them. A smile tickled the corners of her lips as the joke dawned on her.

"I ate it," Nissa said. "You have discovered me, human." She looked back at the map. "More like the vampire did. He seems in a stupor."

The lines of the map were clear enough showing the jagged run of the trench. The problem came in finding just what part of the trench they had been in when the giants had found them and, thus, where they had climbed out of the canyon. She could see the shaded area marked "Piston Mountains." There was no sign of a palace on the map. A palace of that size should surely be there. Nissa looked up at the structure that had been sitting at the base of the mountains when they first topped the mesa.

But it was gone. From her distance, all that was evident was a huge crater where the palace had been. She located it far to the right floating in the air with the divot of earth it had been sitting on still underneath it. Even from far away she could see lines extending from the ground to the palace. This was Zendikar, and Nissa had seen plenty of floating objects in her life, including a whole lake suspended above the ground leaving a dry bed full of flopping fish. She'd seen fields of hedrons numbering in the hundreds floating and banging together. But the palace was different. And judging from the lines of ropes, there were living things in that castle.

"Something is wrong," she said.

"You are coming to that realization just now?" Sorin said.

"She's right," said Anowon. He had come up behind her so silently that she jumped when he spoke. "The flood, the refugee kor, and now the Palace of Zemgora floating loose in the air." Anowon's voice was soft, as always, and Nissa found herself leaning in to hear more. "Did you notice how fresh the scars on those giants in the trench were? They were recently in a fight I fear they got the worst of."

"That is true," Nissa found herself saying. "The Roils lately have become more severe. That last one near Graypelt was so sudden that my spirit-water vial barely boiled."

"It is the brood lineage," Sorin said. "They are wroth and throwing Zendikar out of balance. They must be put back into the earth."

Smara looked up from where she had been sitting. She rushed over to Sorin.

"The gift is in the loam," she said. "The gift is in the loam." Then she began talking in another language and soon was repeating the same words.

Anowon watched Smara closely, as did Sorin. At one point Anowon quickly drew a slip of parchment and a thin piece of charcoal out of an inner pocket and wrote something down on the slip.

Sorin smiled uncertainly as the kor's words degraded into raving. Then he glanced at Nissa to see what she thought of Smara's words. Nissa pretended not to notice Sorin's look. *What is that one hiding?* she wondered, turning her attention back to the floating palace. *What is the 'gift is in the loam?'*

"What did she say?" she asked finally.

"Some of it was classical Vampire," Anowon said. "The rest . . ." He looked at Sorin.

"It was Eldrazi, but spattered with vampire," Sorin said. "Look."

Nissa looked where Sorin pointed. The piece of earth the palace was perched atop moved slowly, pulling its tethers tight. Many tiny things were flying around the palace. As she watched, one of the ropes fell.

Suddenly there was a small tremor in the earth and a sharp creaking, and the fluid in the vial hanging from the leather thong around Nissa's neck began to boil so that she felt its heat all the way through her jerkin.

"Roil!" she yelled.

Nissa twisted her staff in two and drew the flexible stem blade from its sheath. With a snap of her wrist the blade stiffened enough for Nissa to jab it into the ground. She felt the green blade shoot roots out and anchor in the black dirt. And in the next moment the Roil was on them.

Before the shaking became too violent, Nissa was able to catch a glimpse of a grass bloom—a wild and rapid groth of stalks that sometimes came with the Roil. A patch of earth jutted and tore out of the ground. Dirt sprayed, and Nissa closed her eyes and held onto the handle of the stem sword. The ground buckled and shook, and dirt sprayed down on her. Soon there was a massive tearing sound, and the ground heaved up and to the side. Nissa put her left hand over her eye, and through the slit between her fingers was able to see that the ground she was lying on was floating. *If I roll off, I'll be at the mercy of the Roil,* she thought. But staying would mean potentially floating high in the sky.

Nissa made the stem rigid, pulled it from the earth, and rolled off the ground she was on. She barely felt the fall. As soon as she hit the ground, the Roil bounced her back into the air, and she came down in a crater of some sort. She scrambled up, not wanting to sit in a low space if whatever had come out of the space slammed back in.

She was almost out of the crater when the Roil stopped abruptly. A shadow fell over Nissa. The land that had come from the crater was falling. She brought the stem sword back, and the blade lengthened and turned flexible as she snapped it out and wrapped it around a boulder that had not been there before the Roil.

Nissa was glad it was there. She pulled herself out of the crater and looked up, expecting the ground to slam back into the hole. But it stayed aloft.

The air seemed to shimmer after the Roil. She wiped the dirt from her eyes and looked around. The breath caught in her throat. Where there had been a plain of grass only moments before, there was an expanse filled with floating islands of ground. Nissa quickly counted seventeen of the islands, but more dotted the landscape. And the palace was not one of them. *Where is the palace?* she wondered.

She located the palace near the base of the mountains, lying on its side, perhaps a day's walk away if she judged the distance correctly. She heard a sound and turned. Anowon was standing near, looking out at the floating land. Smara was next to him somehow, talking to herself; or was she talking to Anowon? The vampire's face was impossible to read.

Behind them, Sorin was floating unconscious in the air, with his long white hair floating all around him like a shroud. As Nissa watched, he woke with a violent lurch that knocked him out of the air, and he fell with a grunt.

Sorin lay on the grass, which had shrunk again to the length of normal grass in the wake of the Roil. Many elves worshipped blooms, when plants and trees grew suddenly huge. And when the plants shrank back to their normal size after the fact, they saw that as divine as well. Not Nissa. Plant blooms did not seem natural. For the bloom to be holy, then the Roil would have to be holy, and that was something Nissa could not believe. Nothing holy could be that devastating.

After a moment, Sorin stirred and rolled over. He put his hand to his forehead.

"I'm beginning to like Zendikar," Sorin said, sitting up. "I really am. It feels like I've been here for years, when it's been more like weeks."

When Sorin saw the floating islands of grassland, he shrugged.

Anowon was with Smara at the edge of the mesa, peering over the edge. He looked up at Nissa and showed his teeth. She walked over to where they stood. Anowon pointed down at the canyon floor far below. "How are your eyes?" he asked.

She detected the movement on the canyon floor almost immediately.

Nissa doublechecked before speaking. "Brood," she said finally.

"What are they doing?" Sorin said, standing next to her.

"It's hard to tell, but some of them seem to be eating the ground."

Nobody said anything for a time.

"Eating it?" Anowon finally said.

"There are some large ones with tentacles for back legs and long muzzles . . ."

Sorin moaned. "Are their muzzles blue?" he asked.

"I can't tell," Nissa said. "But, yes, it is possible, now that you put words to it."

"Trackers," Sorin said.

"But why would they—"

"They are probably tracking the kor refugees," Sorin said. "But they will find us in the process if we don't move."

"How do you know these things?" Nissa said. "The 'blue muzzles'?" The words were out of her mouth before she knew it.

Sorin said nothing, but looked over the edge and squinted. For a moment Nissa wished he'd just step right off the edge. Then the feeling left her, and she wondered what his weak human eyes could see.

"There must be four hundred of them," he said. "The floor of the trench is covered with them. Wonderful."

Nissa looked over the edge.

"The giants were right," Anowon said.

"The giants are down there," Sorin said. "Their bodies are being dismembered right now." He was quiet for a moment. "Rather interesting entrails."

Nissa turned. "They will find our sign and ascend to us by day's end."

"Oh, undoubtedly," Sorin said.

"But we will not be here," Nissa said. She began walking toward the mountains, along the trail on Khalled's map. The trail would take them past the tipped castle. "We should run."

And they did. They ran, holding what gear they had against themselves to keep it from bouncing. The goblins managed to carry Smara. One held each limb, and a fifth ran in the middle, while others scampered behind.

Nissa felt the mana from the grass course around her ankles as she ran. With this mana she spun a camouflage spell around the whole party, hoping to make them appear as a patch of grass on the expanse to any prying eyes that might be watching. Nissa dropped back a bit and squinted at her companions. But it was hard to tell if her spell had worked. She was too close to gauge its effectiveness. Nissa sped up.

The party ran through the shadows of the floating islands of land, which dropped clods of dirt from bare roots as they passed. Nissa saw a small rodent poke its head out of a hole and almost plummet the distance into the massive crater where the other side of its hole continued.

The wind picked up and began to blow in their faces as they ran. Soon they were sweating with exertion. Nissa couldn't help but think about how the wind in their faces would help spread their scent for the brood tracking them. She ran faster, and the others picked up their speed as well.

The sun was half-past zenith when they fell to the ground panting. Nissa laid her face down and breathed the rich smell of dirt and grass. Her tongue was swollen, and her cracked lips hurt. She needed water.

"There might be water at that palace," she said.

The palace was closer, but it still lay tipped with its many tethers strewn around it. Nissa had watched for movement as they approached, but she had not seen any. It must have been inhabited by humans. They had begun to pass fields of grain, but what huts there were had been abandoned long ago. She was no judge of crops, but the stunted plants in the ground did not look like the most prosperous bounty she had ever seen.

After a bit of rest and hard tack, Nissa stood and began running again. Sorin was on his feet in an instant and following her at an alarming pace. He had passed her easily as they ran earlier, and she had the distinct feeling that he was slowing his pace so the rest of them could keep up. Nissa sped up to keep ahead of Sorin. It is the poor food I am eating that is allowing the human to run faster, she thought as she pumped her legs. *But what is* he *eating?* she wondered again. *How is his body functioning without food?*

Anowon, on the other hand, was not having as easy a time. Vampires were capable of alarming feats of

physical prowess. They were naturally stronger than most elves Nissa had met. In the jungles of Bala Ged, Nissa had seen a vampire literally run up the trunk of a tree. They could jump better than most elves, but Nissa had never seen a vampire freefall off a tree, spin in midair, and catch itself on a branch. Still, a vampire should be able to run at least as fast as an elf.

Anowon was not running as fast. In fact, the vampire was midway between Nissa and the goblins that were, after all, carrying a mad kor. She had little doubt that it had been Anowon who had disposed of one of Smara's goblins. If that were the case, then Anowon should be quite fit and able to run. Nissa found it strange.

They ran past more huts hunched next to the fallow fields, then topped a low rise. The palace loomed ahead. In its course it had floated away and then back again to its original crater, only to fall hugely canted to the right. There were three lines of smoke rising sideways from the ground around the palace.

Then Nissa saw the first hole. Soon she saw more dotting the landscape ahead. She stopped running. Each was about a man's length across and just as deep. Many of the holes were stuffed with what looked like crops. Others were empty. *Brood holes,* she muttered.

When Nissa saw a hole with a pair of bare legs jutting straight out, she jumped behind a nearby hut and crouched. When Sorin and Anowon joined her, she leaned over.

"Brood," Sorin said before she could even open her mouth.

Anowon nodded.

Ahead the ground was flat and grassy with small undulating ridges. The huts were more common along the foot-trod path they had been following. Each hut was made of thatch and turf bricks, and as

Nissa crouched behind one, she could smell cooking grease from within. A gust of wind blew her hair in her eyes, and with the hooked finger of her right hand she pushed it behind her long ear.

"There were people cooking in this one earlier today," she said.

The brood holes that dotted the landscape were fresh, and as she looked, Nissa saw plenty more legs sticking out of them.

"Why do they stuff the corpses in the holes?" Nissa said.

Sorin and Anowon said nothing, but Nissa had the distinct impression that one or both of them knew why.

"What's that?" Anowon whispered. He pointed.

A large column of dust far to the right in the grassland. The point from which it emanated was hidden behind one of the rises.

"That, friends, is the dust thrown up by a great host," Sorin said. He stood and began walking forward to a high point occupied by another hut.

When he reached the hut, he stopped and stared down. Nissa stared too. It was a group of something walking along the ridge between the grassland and the mountains.

"Sizable," Sorin said.

"The tentacled scourge," Nissa said. She could not make out the individual forms, but she could see that some were taller than others, and that some of them moved in strange ways.

"I suppose we should count ourselves lucky to be seeing their backs," Sorin said as he turned and began walking toward the palace.

Nissa had never seen anything like it. The populations of Zendikar did not have the discipline to form ranks. Plus, there was never enough of anyone, other than the wild creatures and trees, to form any kind of organized fighting force. And even though the brood were not formed in anything like ranks, they were traveling in a group. *Where had they learned to walk together in lines? she wondered.* She did not know enough about the brood to answer the question. But she would find out, she promised herself.

Behind the brood, the grasslands swept up in a smooth transition to the Piston Mountains. As she watched, the top of one mountain came hammering down on the base, and the ground shook.

"If we are very lucky," Sorin yelled over his shoulder as he walked, "The brood that did this"—he kicked at a leg poking out of one of the holes—"will meet and join forces with the brood advancing on us even now from behind."

Nissa looked back the way they had come. There, far away, was a smaller dust cloud.

"Should not be long now," Sorin said.

CHAPTER 8

The holes became more common as they neared the palace, which, itself, had bodies hanging from their riggings—heavy humans, dead in their armor with strange fighting devices strapped to their arms. Plumes of smoke spiraled from within somewhere. The huge tethers Nissa had seen from across the plain lay strewn on the grass, as thick as a man's torso.

Soon they were past the last hut and near the roots of the mountains. Ahead, a huge rock stood on its end, balanced precariously next to the trail. Nissa stopped and took out her map. The trail wound into the foothills and then skirted to the right. They would be moving parallel to the brood lineage that were beating their way around the base of the mountains. *Will they cut into the mountains when they find our path?* she asked herself as she rolled up the maps.

The stone balancing next to the trail appeared to wobble in the gusting wind. Nissa had seen other "teetering stones," as they were called. She had never known one to fall. On the other hand, she had never known creatures to kill whole villages and stuff the corpses in holes.

They passed around the teetering stone and kept running along the path.

Nissa stopped suddenly and crouched, putting her finger into a small depression. She always ran looking at the ground, watching for signs.

"An odd track," she said. "I have never seen it before."

Sorin and Anowon stopped for a look. Nissa traced the deep divots and deep knuckle grooves; it was as if something had dragged itself across the ground, but uphill. Nissa looked up at the treeless mountains ahead. There were small boulders and low clumps of grass, but nothing that appeared large enough for even a goblin to hide behind. And whatever had made the sign was larger than a goblin, by plenty. Each finger groove was longer than her shin.

"Well?" Sorin said.

Nissa shrugged. "It is large," she replied. "But I do not see any indication of tentacles."

From behind, a drum boomed over the plains. Anowon and Nissa looked back. The dust plume from the brood that had come up out of the trench was nearly at the palace.

"They have become musical," Sorin said. "Perhaps I will sing them a song of my own when we meet."

Nissa did not feel as confident. With each passing league they drifted farther away from the forest. She took a deep breath. The grasslands were rich with a different kind of energy, a kind she did not know how to utilize very well. If she had the proper rest, she could recuperate and draw mana from the land . . . But there was no rest to be had.

Sorin turned away from his view of the grasslands below and cast a wary eye at the tracks in the rocky dirt of the trail ahead. "So, we are being advanced

upon from the rear by a prevailing force"—he made a sweeping gesture with one hand—"and something of unknown potency is waiting in ambush somewhere ahead?"

After some moments Nissa nodded.

Sorin unbuckled the belt that held his great sword in place over his right shoulder. He moved the belt to his waist and cinched it tight again. "It is good to know these things," he said.

Nissa watched Anowon investigate the tracks in the dirt. He pushed his fingers around the deep indentations, nodding some secret confirmation.

Soon they were walking higher and higher into the foothills with the sun low in the western sky.

The first face they found was half buried in the sandy soil. Nissa knew such stone heads were called *Faduun*, and that one in particular was huge. It was so large, in fact, that Nissa suspected that fifty elves holding wrists could barely encircle it. Its nose was large, and its stern brow and angry eyes were set in a spiteful scowl. It was exactly the same face as she'd seen carved in the river pebbles that Anowon had found.

They found a smaller face an hour later, cut into the side of an outcropping. Each of the eye sockets had something shoved inside it. Nissa reached for whatever was in the right one.

"Do you really want to know what is in there?" Sorin said.

Nissa put her hand in and took out . . . a wad of cloth. She looked from Sorin to Anowon. The vampire shrugged.

"The Faduun are old," he said. "Do you see those?" He pointed to some writing above the right eye, scratched into the granite in tiny script.

Nissa leaned close. "Eldrazi?"

"No," Anowon said. "It is older than Eldrazi script, and yet it bears a certain resemblance. Those designs under the chin are remarkably similar to what we see at many Eldrazi sites all across Zendikar."

"These are not found in other areas?" Nissa said.

Anowon shook his head. "Only on Ondu. And nobody knows why."

"I know why," Nissa said. *At least I think I do,* she thought. "They are the first Eldrazi," she said. Nissa was not sure why she knew it, but having said it, she knew it to be true.

Anowon nodded once. "So it is said by some," he said. "But how can they not be there. How can the plane have no sign of their writing or design one year, and then they are present the next? Cultures take time to develop."

"Perhaps they are from somewhere . . . else." Nissa felt strange saying that.

But Sorin turned his eyes to her. "A good deduction, elf," he said. "Have you any proof?"

Nissa's pulse jumped. "What proof could there be?" she said, backtracking. "Such an idea is impossible, naturally."

Sorin looked at her for longer than was normal. "Naturally," he said.

Nissa looked back down at the foothills they had traveled. Past those, the dust plume had reached well past the palace. "We had better keep moving," she said.

The trail and hills were the smoothest rock Nissa had ever seen—red rock utterly barren of vegetation. She was curious to see what could live on the barren hills leading into the mountains, and she walked ahead paying no mind to where she was stepping.

They had dipped into a wet swale through which a slow stream gurgled. The trail passed between some low shrubs with wide, thick leaves that were two-times Sorin's height in width. The plants in the low spot intrigued Nissa. They reminded her of the jungles of Bala Ged, and she ran ahead, heedlessly. Despite the wetness in the low spot next to the river, the plants were wilted. Nissa found something about their color disgusting. Their leaves appeared green, but with an undertone of red, somehow, as if blood beat through the leaves' cells. But that was impossible. She stopped running, sniffed, and covered her nose. What was not impossible was their smell. "There must be something dead here," she said. But she kept walking to the small stream, her mouth already tasting its cool waters. Nissa knew they would be as clear as the becks of Bala Ged.

She stopped. One of the plants seemed to have perked up, its leaves a bit stiffer. Nissa turned, and just as she did so, she caught the sudden sound of movement—a branch stirred, and she instinctively ducked and shoved her staff forward. The impact that followed knocked her backward, and her staff flew out of her hand. She lay still where she fell.

Nissa was on her back, but slowly she pushed herself with her heels until she was looking up at the frowning Anowon. She stood. The plant was slowly drawing one long vine back into itself. Her staff was off to the side next to another plant. She could see a cleft in the staff's side that went almost all the way through. Anowon pointed off to the right.

A shape lay half-concealed under one of the plants. Its head lay on its side not far away, severed cleanly by the looks of it. The body was badly decayed, but Nissa recognized the form of a small drake.

Nissa recovered her voice. "Snap ferns," she said. "I was not paying enough attention."

Anowon nodded. "Something similar exists in Guul Draz. But ours shoot canes up through the water impaling the unsuspecting. *Siffleeb* we call them."

Hearing the guttural vampire-speak made the hairs on the back of Nissa's neck stand up. Or perhaps the feeling was caused by her almost dying a moment before.

Anowon was looking at her strangely.

Sorin inexplicably had her staff when she turned. He was smiling again and handed it to her. She took it and ran her palm along its smooth wood. The cut from the vorpal weed was higher than she had thought and went almost all the way through the shaft . . . exactly at neck height. She passed her hand over the cut, and the wood knitted together and the cut was no more. She whipped the staff over her shoulder, strapped it in place and started to walk up into the mountains.

They followed the trail all the rest of the day until the light fell and the small robber birds began to follow them, landing in the dusty soil to turn their heads and regard them through cocked eyes.

Soon the dark of the mountains was on them, and there was no moon again that night. The cold wind intensified as they walked through the foothills, and the rocks took on a grayer, more sand-whipped texture.

The rocks where they stopped did not radiate anything like heat. But soon Nissa found an indentation in the lea side of a boulder, and they all hunched there, mostly out of the wind. Fire was impossible, she knew. But Anowon took out one of his teeth and dropped it on a bare spot, and it began glowing and giving off heat. They encircled it and bent close.

"How many of those do you have?" Sorin asked. "How many toothless humans have you made?"

Anowon looked up at the rock they were crouching against. "They are not only merfolk teeth." The vampire stood and took a step back and looked again. A smile curled one corner of his mouth, showing just the edge of an incisor. "Look."

They were sheltering against a huge Faduun head, in the space created under its nose. Anowon stood staring at the face with the wind blowing his long braid almost sideways. His torn robes snapped in the wind.

"The merfolk speak of three gods," he said. "And I have realized something." He looked down at them huddled against the Faduun's lips. "There are three kinds of brood. Have you noticed?"

Nissa had noticed. There were the large ones with all the eyes and tentacles for rear legs, those that were all tentacles and could sometimes fly, and those possessing a thick bony skull without a face.

"Perhaps it is no coincidence," Anowon said. "That the mermen have three gods. Their stories are not as old as, say, the kor's. So, maybe the Eldrazi have only been here since those merfolk stories? The kor would never admit it, but their gods are the same gods by different names."

"But the brood are many," Nissa said. "The merfolk and kor gods are only three."

"Perhaps the brood have gods as well."

"Are they real?" Nissa said.

Anowon's brow dropped in confusion. "What a question."

But he said nothing more, and the wind howled around the stone.

Sorin sniffed.

Nissa glanced over her shoulder into the darkness where she knew the plains stretched thousands of feet below. When she turned back, Anowon was looking across the glowing light at Sorin.

"Are they evil? The brood?" she asked.

Sorin spoke quickly, which surprised her. "They are consumers. Neither good nor evil. They eat."

"And why do they put things in those holes?"

He shook his head. "I am sure I have no idea," he replied. "But I do know they devour pure mana. Their methods must have something to do with that."

Nissa nodded. It seemed the wind was blowing harder.

The goblins tightened their circle around Smara, who had been mostly quiet that day. As Nissa looked, the kor rocked back and forth with her crystal held against her small bosom. Her lips were moving, but no sound came out. Nissa watched her rock back and forth, and soon her own eyelids started drooping.

When Nissa opened her eyes, the tooth's glow had dimmed greatly, but she could still see the bare shadows of the others asleep. The wind had lessened a bit, but a deep cold had swept in on the breeze, and Nissa's teeth knocked together as she sat with her knees drawn up to her chest. She chuckled to herself. *Imagine perishing up here of cold after traveling through such danger,* she thought. But Nissa knew the cold on the mountain was not severe enough to kill her, as long as she stayed out of the wind. The Piston Mountains were a very long but very thin range, and not the tallest mountains on Zendikar—those were on Akoum. According to the map, they would crest and be on the other side of the mountains by the morrow. But that realization did not help the fact that for the moment, she was cold.

She stood up and stamped her feet. Then she took a couple of steps and heard a particular sound over the breeze. It sounded like a gargling gag combined with a sort of growl. The sound raised the hairs on the back of her arms. She saw a form in the shadows hunched over another form. She heard slurping.

As quietly as she could she turned and padded back to the circle. Her stomach, as empty as it was, fluttered, and for a moment she thought she might be sick. It was not the sound that had caused her such nausea, it was the smell. Blood had its own sweet smell, and arterial blood was the sweetest of all. She knelt on the ground and wrapped her cloak around herself and, surprisingly, she slept.

When she woke, the sun was just rising in the gray sky. She could see her breath in the cold air. The tooth's glow was gone. As Nissa suspected, one of Smara's goblins was gone as well. She looked again. Two of the goblins were gone. Anowon was staring at her from across the circle with his knees drawn up to his chin. Sorin was asleep next to him with his long head laid sideways on his own knees.

Nissa knew a vampire had to feed. She understood the natural order of that, mostly. Still, to see the feeding happening . . . Nissa glanced at the sleeping Smara and then back to Anowon. "Who is she?" Nissa said.

Anowon lifted his head. "I do not know."

"What is that crystal she has?"

He looked at the kor. "It has power," he said. "Can you feel it?"

Nissa nodded. She had felt its power the first time Smara and the goblins had rounded the corner in the canyon. But many objects radiated raw energy on Zendikar—it was not uncommon. Even the seed pods of the turntimber trees could make a goblin's pathway stone twist and jerk, which was why outsiders had such trouble navigating the turntimber forest.

But Smara's crystal radiated a different kind of energy. There was something about the crystal and the way the kor coveted it that Nissa did not like. As she watched, its surface seemed to ripple and swell darkly in the early morning light.

"I have been listening," Anowon said, shifting his eyes from the disturbing crystal to Nissa. "To her. When she thinks she is alone."

Nissa leaned in to hear what he would say next. Anowon's eyes were as large as saucers as he spoke.

"It is a strange mix she speaks to that crystal."

"Of what? Is it what Sorin said?" Nissa said.

"Yes and no. Sometimes it is kor. Sometimes Eldrazi or vampire."

"Yes?"

The vampire hesitated before speaking again. "Sometimes it is other languages that I have never heard spoken on Zendikar."

Nissa looked at him.

"And I believe I have heard or seen written every tongue," he said, looking again at Smara sleeping in the middle of the goblins. "It is good we have forgotten some tongues. Certain cultures should never have been."

Like vampire cultures, Nissa thought. But instead she said, "Well, maybe the Eldrazi had different languages. They did build amazing structures for a long time."

"On the backs of my people," Anowon hissed. "Lubricated with our blood." His lips pulled back suddenly into a fierce snarl.

Nissa found her hand reaching for her staff. By the time she had it up, Anowon had a faint smile on his lips. "You Joraga," he said, making a flourish with his hand. "Always ready."

Nissa lowered her staff, slightly.

"Anyway," Anowon said. "I have been listening to the kor, as I said. She talks to the crystal. She talks, and"—he put his hand to his ear, imitating himself listening—"I think it replies."

"What?"

"Do you know what a witch vessel is?"

Nissa shook her head.

"It is a being who is possessed by a ghost," Anowon said.

"A ghost," Nissa said, looking at Smara asleep on her back. As Nissa watched, the kor's eyes snapped opened and she spoke a word.

"Blood," Anowon translated. "She said the word 'blood' in middle Vampire."

Suddenly, Nissa could feel her own blood beating at her temples. The kor closed her eyes again, and Nissa turned to Anowon. "Are you saying she is possessed by an Eldrazi ghost?" Nissa asked. "If you are then we should put her in the earth."

"For the good of Zendikar?"

"The brood must be stopped. Otherwise they will do what they did at MossCrack. They must be put back in their crypt in the Teeth of Akoum."

"Oh, I agree they must be stopped," Anowon said. "They must be stopped by casting them off Zendikar."

Nissa felt her pulse skip "What do you mean?" she said. *Is he going to talk about other planes?* she wondered. *How can he know about planeswalking?*

The vampire looked up at the sky. "From my reading, I know they are not from this place," he said. "Which means they must have come from somewhere else, and they should go back to that place. I have read accounts of beings that claimed to have traveled from other places they said, not on Zendikar. There have been writings."

"And you believe them?"

Anowon shrugged.

Sorin stirred. After a moment he lifted his head and regarded them through slit eyes. "What are you discussing?" he asked, pushing his white hair out of his eyes.

"What indeed?" Anowon replied. "What indeed."

CHAPTER 9

The day progressed. Nissa knew they were in the mountains proper when she felt the ground under her feet shake. Most of the mountain tops in the range had had their tops sheared off and put back by with some magical process that allowed the tops to rise and fall, which they did without pattern. Every time the mountain crashed down upon itself, the rock dust and pebbles were rearranged, hiding the path further. It made keeping to the trail almost impossible.

They walked on, following the creases in the mountain upward until they were at the very top of the crest. The cap was up when they arrived, leaving a space between it and the mountain just large enough for any of them to pass through. Nissa bent down. The seam of light on the other side was not too far away, no further than a bow could shoot its arrow.

"We could skirt this," Sorin said, looking uneasily at the seam of light on the other side. "And not risk it."

Nissa had already consulted the map. "It is a low mountain, but very long," she said as she looked over her shoulder. "Going around would mean two extra days of travel at least. And *they* would surely fall on us in the meantime."

"Why are you whispering?" Sorin said.

Nissa did not know she had been whispering. But all day as they walked she'd been thinking of the huge knuckle prints in the mud in the foothills. *Where would such a large creature hide?* she thought. No rocks were large enough to hide behind.

Whatever had separated the top from the base of the mountain had not done it cleanly. Both the top and bottom lips of rock had long jags hanging down. The effect was that the gap appeared to have fangs and a dark maw. She peered deeper.

"I see metal hooks and swords smashed flat," she said, her voice echoing in the darkness.

They all knew what that meant, and nobody said anything until Sorin spoke. "Well, if we leave our steel out here it will not be crushed flat," he said.

Nissa turned and looked blankly at him. "We wait until it falls again and rises, and then we run through."

The goblins looked at each other.

Nissa waited, but not even Sorin had anything to say. So they waited all the rest of the day. Night fell, and they kept waiting. They spent the night huddled against rocks waiting for the mountaintop to fall. As the sun rose, Nissa was already at the cut, peering in.

The dry tack was gone, and all the goblins were accounted for. She suddenly threw down the dry twig she was chewing and stood.

"Where are you going?" Anowon said.

Nissa had been watching a small flock of birds bob from rock to rock. She ignored Anowon's question and approached the rock the birds had massed on. At her approach the flock flew off and to another rock, where they complained noisily. Nissa peered carefully at the base of the large boulder. Then she dropped down onto her knees and put her face within a foot of the seam where the sandy soil met the boulder.

Sorin looked over casually and raised one eyebrow as Nissa sniffed tentatively at the dry soil. Unsatisfied, she moved an arm's length to the right and sniffed the ground again. She moved six more times before she found what she was looking for: a small hole in the dirt. A small patch of bright green lichen grew in a spiral pattern above the tiny hole, Sorin noticed. Even Smara watched Nissa quietly.

Then the elf began digging. She dug with her hand, carefully piling the sandy dust next to the rock as she worked. After a good time at it, Nissa began to hum. The hole deepened. It was not morning anymore when Nissa began to heave. She pulled three times before looking over at Sorin and Anowon. They approached the hole.

"It's soft, so you have to grip hard," Nissa said.

"What little gift have you found here in the loam?" Sorin said, glancing over at Smara as he bent and took a handful of what felt like a wine skin filled with jelly. It had not rained in weeks, yet the soil was damp at the bottom of the hole.

Smara cocked her head at Sorin. She gave no indication she had understood his taunt.

"Now pull," Nissa said.

It took six heaves before it came free. A large, bright red blob of material popped out of the hole.

Sorin jumped back despite himself. Anowon bent for a closer look.

"A grit slug," Nissa said. She collected dead limbs from the low and gnarled evergreen shrubs clinging to the cracks between the rocks, and built a small fire.

"What will you do with *that*?" Sorin said of the fire.

"Cook the slug," Nissa said.

"With *that?*"

"Just so."

Nissa lit the fire with a flint and steel and constructed a small shelf of rocks around the fire.

"That fire will never heat that . . . thing," Sorin said.

"I only have to boil one area, and the slug will cook in its own skin," Nissa said.

It took hours to cook the thing, nonetheless. And the whole time the mountain did not fall.

When Nissa poked the slug and pronounced it cooked, Smara and the goblins flocked around. Even Anowon seemed interested and drew near.

"I thought you only ate blood," Nissa said to the vampire.

Anowon shrugged. "I prefer blood," he said.

Nissa used the eating knife stowed up her right sleeve to cut jiggling wedges out of the slug. The color was a dull red. The goblins threw their pieces down their gullets and put rough hands out for more.

"It tastes like . . . raw human fat," Anowon said.

Sorin scoffed from where he stood at the periphery.

Nissa made a sour face hearing Anowon's words. She cut the goblins more slug, and then ate three wedges of her own as fast as she could, with the viscous juices running down her knuckles and dripping off her forearms.

Smara held her piece up to the sun to watch the light diffuse through it before eating.

"How did you know the slug was there?" Anowon asked, licking the juice off his thin fingers.

"The birds were waiting for its eye to poke through that hole—they told me," Nissa said.

"I did not see anything like an eye pop out of that hole," Sorin said.

"It would not have," Nissa said.

"Why?"

"Because the slug was dead," Nissa said. "Had been for days."

Sorin shook his head and swallowed hard. Anowon looked away from the half-eaten slug.

Nobody except the goblins ate any more of the slug. Then they sat against the rocks and watched the flies ply the gelatinous corpse, waiting for the mountain to hurtle down.

"I think we should run through now," Nissa said.

Anowon stirred in his torn cloak.

"If we wait here any longer . . ." Nissa said. She did not need to finish. Even in her cold sleep she could feel the brood closing in on them from behind, and the others felt it too, she knew.

Sorin groaned and sat up. He blinked at the gap. Then he patted the pommel of his great sword. "But I love the shape it is in right now," he said. "It would not have the same charm if flattened."

"Walk around if you have fear in your heart," Nissa said.

"Fear in my heart," Sorin repeated. "I like that." He stood and yawned. Then he walked over to the gap, ducked calmly, and disappeared. Anowon hopped up and followed, and so did Nissa.

Nobody said a word while they walked under the mountain. Even Smara, who was last through, was absolutely quiet. Nissa put her palms on the damp rock above her head as she walked. Rough hewn, but split with the grain. No tool had done the work on the mountain. *But what had, then?*

Their foot falls echoed on the wet stone. The echoes that returned to their ears were affected by a strange chirping, so for a moment Nissa thought the brood must have entered the cleft from another part of the mountain. The more she listened, the more she detected the scurry of mice in the odd echo. But it was hard to tell.

Soon the line of sunlight opposite became wider, and Nissa could see rock through the gap . . . and something else. She stopped and squinted. Sorin had seen it too. He was in the process of very slowly drawing his great sword from its sheath.

They could only see the bottom half of it, but what they saw was large—easily as large as a forest troll, but not quite as tall as the trench giants. It had thick arms, hands, and torso, but its legs were stunted and tiny. Its tail was long and thick like that of a rat. It was sitting with its body against the rock and its tiny legs sticking straight out. Its overall appearance was almost comical. But judging by the keen way Sorin had his sword at the ready, Nissa guessed he was not in the joking mood.

They neared the gap and could see the whole creature—its massive shoulders and large-jawed, reptilian head . . . and its closed eyes. Nissa watched as its chest rose and fell rhythmically.

"Asleep," Nissa whispered. She stepped out of the gap on tiptoe. The sun had grown bright and seemed to be shining directly into her eyes. Still, she could see clearly enough the rusted, flattened remnants of armor and splintered bone strewn around the creature, and she could guess why the thing waited at the edge of the cleft. "The meat must already be well tenderized by the time he pulls it out."

Nissa motioned to the others and crept around the creature and through a cut in the rock. The huge thing smelled like rotting death lying in the sun the way it was, snoring softly. Soon Nissa saw why it stunk so badly—she passed the pile of cast off parts. Bright red flies buzzed off the rotting pile as the intruders passed.

But then one of the creature's eyes popped open.

Anowon noticed the open eye too late. The thing was up on its knuckles in a moment. The speed and quickness with which it swept its stunted legs forward and landed a kick on Anowon's chest shocked Nissa, and then he was tumbling through the dust.

Sorin drew his great sword with its blade as black as night.

Anowon was up on his feet the moment after he stopped rolling. His teeth were bared, and his long-nailed hands were up and ready for attack. Small trails of blood were falling from around Anowon's red eyes. A deep growl that Nissa did not like at all came from the vampire's throat. Then he charged at the creature.

Nissa drew her stem sword and swung, hoping to catch the creature before it reached Anowon, but it caterwauled forward and swung in on its knuckles for another kick. Just then Sorin's blade slashed through the creature's back.

As soon as the blade bit into its flesh, the creature's body began to shrivel. In two breaths it was no more than a dry shell. In three breaths it fell to a large pile of gray dust. Soon the wind was blowing it away.

Nissa exhaled and leaned against a rock.

"I thank you," Anowon said.

"Yes, you do," Sorin said, sheathing his blade. "And the Parasite Blade."

Anowon felt for his metal cylinders before smoothing his hair.

"It is called that?" Nissa asked, making a face as though she'd bitten into an unripe nectarpith fruit.

“Quite,” Sorin said, patting the weapon’s pommel. “It draws the mana from whatever it cuts. It can drain creatures to their doom, as you saw.”

“Where was such a thing created?”

“You would like to know.”

Nissa looked away. “No, I really would not like to know,” she said. “It smacks of vampires.”

“Rather,” Sorin said. Then he said no more.

They left the pile of dust and continued walking. Nissa thought they were still on the trail, but it was impossible to tell for sure. There were no tracks to follow, and the rocky gravel they walked on looked pristine and untouched.

Nissa took out the map and sat down on a rock. Even with the map, she could not be absolutely sure they were in the right place. Clearly the trail was descending, as the map said it would.

“What *was* that thing?” Sorin said.

Anowon said nothing, but stared at Smara and the goblins. The kor was in an advanced state of excitement, blathering more than usual so that two of her goblins were stroking her hair and singing to her. Nissa could tell Anowon was listening to the kor.

“I think it was a hurda,” Nissa said, without looking up from the map. “They’re not evil creatures, but they do throw tantrums that can be dangerous. I would have expected him on the plains more than here. They are shameless scavengers, so I guess it makes sense, really.”

“What does?”

“To see a hurda scavenging a meal where best it can,” Nissa said, rolling the map up and sliding it carefully back into the leather tube. “It is the natural way of things.”

Sorin shook his head. “Elves.”

Nissa stood. "We should be coming out of the mountains soon enough. If we push we might be able to make the Fields of Agadeem by nightfall."

Smara talked, and Anowon took out a piece of parchment and jotted something down with a bit of charcoal.

They descended into the foothills by late afternoon. The sun was bright, and the air was cool. The wind that had plagued them on the ascent was blocked by the mountain itself, and the path was clear and easy going. Yet Nissa worried. Catastrophe was surely waiting in the Fields of Agadeem. There was no reason to think such a thing; she just felt it to be true.

Anowon stopped and put his arm up in a fist. Nissa halted. The vampire had been walking ahead and to the left. He brought his finger to his nose, tapped it, and made an exaggerated motion of sniffing. Nissa understood and took a deep breath herself. There was a sweet smoke in the air. She sniffed again and pointed left. They followed the scent down a side canyon until they spied a small force of kor with a fire burning on the ground next to them.

As they watched, a kor dressed in a robe of beads threw a bough on the fire. It burst into flames, sending thick blue smoke into the air. His barbells were so long that he had tucked them into his belt. The other kor stood, gaunt, off to the side as the kor in robes went to a bundle wrapped in leathers and hanging from a rope anchored in the canyon wall. He began to spin the bundle, wafting handfuls of the smoke against the spinning bundle.

Anowon leaned into Nissa and whispered. "There is a body inside. Next they will cut it."

The vampire's mouth was too close to her skin for Nissa's comfort, and she took a step back.

"They hack it up," Anowon said. "For the eeka birds to eat. The spirit flies away with the birds."

Nissa looked at the bundle spinning in the smoke, then at Smara. The kor had become very quiet. As she watched the ceremony she pushed her crystal against her lips. In that instant Nissa knew she could not stay and watch the kor funeral. She turned and walked back up the canyon. Sorin was smiling when Nissa passed him. Anowon followed Nissa. She stopped and turned.

"That is horrible," she said. "To dismember the dead."

"Is it?" the vampire said."

"Is there anything else I should know about the kor?

"Nothing you do not already. They give away one of their children to the wilderness, as you know."

"They what?" Sorin said. He bent close to hear what they were saying.

"The elf knows what I saw is true," Anowon said.

Nissa said nothing.

"Truly?" Sorin said.

"It's called a *world gift,*" Anowon said. "Most die. Some wander out of the wilderness and are assimilated among other races. But many of those who were assimilated go back to the wilderness."

Nissa found herself staring at Smara squatting in the dusty rock dust watching the burial. She spoke without taking her eyes off Smara. "Are the world gift kor that survive accepted back into the group?"

Anowon looked back at the ceremony. "You know they are not."

Nissa felt her breath catch in her throat. The kor priest kept the bundle spinning near the smoking fire. A tear edged down Smara's filthy face.

"Do they want to come back more than anything?" Nissa asked. She stared off at nothing as she spoke.

"Do they ever try and see if their elders will allow them to return home and be part of the tribe again. Do they apologize?"

Anowon frowned at her tone of voice. "Are you ill?" Anowon said. To Nissa, his tone conveyed anything but concern.

"I am not ill," Nissa said, searching his smooth face for any expression that might explain the comment. Finding none, she straightened and put her chin up. "I just happen to know something about exile."

"I am sure you do," replied Anowon.

"Let us be away. Ghet . . ." Sorin said. His voice carried through the canyon, echoing off the walls so the kor priest looked up from his spinning. Sorin stood and began walking.

Anowon turned and followed.

Nissa caught his arm. "Why do you follow him thus?" she asked. "What power does he have over you?"

Anowon opened his mouth, then closed it. He was clearly about to tell her something. Finally, he shook his head and turned away to follow Sorin.

Nissa followed them both, and the sounds of the funeral and Smara's muttering trailed her as they all walked away. Soon she felt hot tears on her face and wiped them away hard with the back of her glove. She had been a young warrior. What did a young elf know about right and wrong? About proper and taboo? How was she to have known that the ability she possessed was something to be hidden away? But the truth was she knew, even then. She knew that she was different and she flaunted it. And when her mother and father exposed her to the Deep Council for displaying non-Joraga tendencies, it was exactly what she deserved. And she was better for it.

"Are you done with your little weeping?" Sorin said. "If it pleases you, we will leave now."

"I am coming," she said.

They walked into the foothills with no sign of pursuit. And by sundown the red foothills flattened to rolling grassland. Where the sward on the other side of the Piston Mountains had been bare, the plains were absolutely covered with huge diamond shaped stones—hedron stones. Most of the stones were the size of a houses, but many were smaller, and some were buried in the ground at various positions and depths. As Nissa watched, six stones pulled together so their tips touched and formed a huge star floating above the grass. She continued to watch as it broke apart and the pieces drifted away.

Most of the hedrons were floating above the ground with tips pointing at the sky and the green grass. On the horizon Nissa could see the dark shadow of the ocean topped by banks of purple clouds.

"Zulaport lies on that shore," Nissa said as she pointed. She could smell the salt air on the breeze. She glanced down at the rocky debris she was standing on and guessed that the trail had not been used for many weeks, and that it had last been used by goblins. She could see where the faint digs from their toenails had degraded with the rains and wind.

A hedron stone bobbed slightly as they walked past. Each of the stones was grooved with the strange designs found on all the crumbling edifices on Zendikar, but Nissa had never seen so many in one place.

"The Fields of Agadeem," Anowon said. "I have never actually seen them."

"The brood did not drag you this way?" asked Sorin.

He did not even turn at her taunt. "No, they did not," he said. He looked out over the fields as they walked. A bird of prey was perched on the tip of the nearest hedron. It watched them with shining eyes as they passed.

A bit further they found the blue striped, dead body of a juvenile sphinx. It floated in a knotted eddy of humid wind formed around a pack of stones. The mana in the gravity well refracted light like it was underwater.

Later, Sorin stopped and put his hand over his eyes to shield them from the low sun. "What would that be?" Sorin said.

Nissa followed his eyes to a bit of movement on the plains below. She looked closer and saw a half-built structure cut into the turf. The structure was simple, no more than four walls built as high as Nissa's chin. Something was moving around the structure's shell.

"What are they doing?" Nissa said.

Anowon squinted. "They are brood," he said. "And they are building."

They walked closer, being careful to creep from hedron to hedron. But Sorin ignored Nissa's and Anowon's attempts at stealth and walked straight for the strange building site. The wind was blowing into their faces, which was a stroke of good luck—perhaps the only one they would get.

Soon they were as close as they dared go without risking detection, and Sorin stopped for a moment, then walked even closer. Nissa would have liked to have remained concealed, but they had no choice but to follow Sorin as he bulled ahead. Smara followed some distance behind.

Nissa felt like cuffing Sorin when she caught up, but one look at his eyes and she lost that feeling. He had drawn his great sword and was looking at the brood in a certain intent, unblinking way that spoke of violence.

The brood were dragging stones, or rather their vampire workers were dragging stones using harnesses bound to their shoulder and elbow horns. Nissa looked at Anowon's elbow horns. The vampire caught her staring and turned away.

There were perhaps thirty brood, including something she had not seen before: juvenile brood. At least that was what she thought they were. They were half the size of the other brood.

"We will take them unawares," Sorin said. "Elf"—he pointed off to the right—"you start there and sweep in. Ghet, you go there and run straight in."

"Straight in," Anowon said, without the slightest inflection.

"Yes, that's what I said."

"And what will we—" Nissa started.

"We will destroy them all," Sorin said.

"We will destroy them all?" Nissa repeated. But then she thought of Speaker Sutina, the leader of the Tajuru whom the brood had slain. "Yes, we will," she said.

"I have no weapon," Anowon said.

Sorin looked at him, measuring him up. "Use your teeth, *Vampire,*" he said. Then one of Sorin's smug smiles spread across his face. "Are you not angry at that lot? Look at your brethren toiling there." Sorin's eyes stayed on Anowon. "See here, they are vulnerable to biting and tearing attacks. Most of them are unarmored, and their flesh is soft. They bleed easily. They will not expect us. They are building whatever they are building. We can take them in the flank."

Anowon's mouth twisted into a growl. Nissa thought it was more for Sorin than the brood.

But Sorin misinterpreted the look. "That is more of what I had in mind," he said.

Nissa moved off to the north to squat behind a hedron stone, awaiting Sorin's nod.

As they watched, a brood with tentacles for legs moved to the rock Nissa was hiding behind, and leaned its bony head against the hedron stone. It stayed that way, making sucking sounds. The sweat cooled on Nissa's forehead. *What was it sucking off the rock?*

Nissa was ready when Sorin nodded. She twisted her staff and slid the stem blade out. With a flick it went limp, and she used it as a whip, snapping it around the rock and neatly severing the brood's head from its shoulders.

Sorin began to run toward the half-built structure. After a moment, Nissa followed, and so did Anowon. The first brood had their backs turned, helping the vampires push a huge block along runners of logs. Sorin and Nissa cut the brood down, and they slumped over the block they had been moving.

The rest of the brood fled to the structure they were building. As they charged, Sorin spoke in his rhyming voice. Nissa listened as it rose and fell to its own rhythm. She could see the cone of sound ripple in the air as the energy tunneled into the brood. Within seconds, their flesh began to tumble off the bone. Before her eyes the creatures fell to pieces, their bones freed from the sinews that held them taught.

Nissa could see the toll such an expenditure of power made on Sorin. When he closed his mouth he had to reach out and steady himself on a hedron stone. His white hair was matted with sweat to his forehead, and his skin was so pale she could have seen veins.

But Nissa did not have time to look for veins in Sorin's skin. A group of brood peered out from behind the corner of the half-built structure, and as she watched they spread out in a line and started running at her.

CHAPTER 10

Many of the brood were of the tentacle-and-bone variety, Nissa noticed, but at least one of them was the large kind with the many blue eyes. Its tentacles were as thick as a man's chest as they churned up the dirt while running at her. The creature's squat front tentacles dug for purchase as lines of muscle rippled. Behind, four more brood with bone heads ran, followed by three of the kind that flew.

Nissa had a matter of moments before the flying ones were on her. She fell and put her forehead and palms on the ground and took a deep breath. In a moment, the vigor of life pulsed up through the dirt and shot up her veins and arteries and into her head.

And she was not the only one. Anowon charged forward and slashed savagely at one of the flying brood with his long-nailed hands. He bit and tore a head-sized chunk out of its tentacle.

Nissa formed an image in her mind. A moment later a shrill cry split the air and a huge, six-legged basilisk was blinking its oily black eyes in the sun. It swung its head and caught one of the flying brood by a tentacle and flipped it into a nearby hedron. The other brood fell on the lizard like a stone. The lizard hit the brood hard on the top of the head and

threw it off into the weeds. From the way it hit the ground, Nissa could tell the brood was dead. The basilisk shook its head, tripped, and almost fell. But it did not, and a second later the brood on foot reached it.

One of the winged ones had snuck past her basilisk. Nissa looked up just as the brood threw one of its long tentacle-arms out to catch her around the neck. Nissa caught the tentacle in her hand and gave it a tug, and the brood had to pull wildly to stay aloft. But stay aloft it did. It snapped its other tentacle out, and with a deft movement Nissa sheared it off with her stem. Still the brood did not cry out. Nissa marveled at that. Perhaps it did not have a mouth.

Another of the creature's tentacles came out and struck her on the forehead. Nissa fell back and pulled her feet up over her head and flipped as best she could. She landed face down, and the brood was on her. She rolled to the right, but the brood grasped her neck and pulled her up and threw her. Nissa flew through the air and was able to easily flip and land lightly on her feet.

To her left the basilisk she had summoned was making wide sweeps with its head. The two horns protruding from its forehead were already blood-spattered, and as she watched, the huge brood rammed into the basilisk's haunch. The lizard screamed and turned for a bite, but its fangs snapped on air—the brood-bull had backed away.

Nissa eyed her stem where it lay in the grass between her and the flying brood. The stump of the brood's tentacle was dripping blood, she saw, but the creature regarded her as mildly as if she had waved hello to it. She gauged the distance and guessed she could reach the weapon before the brood reached her.

Nissa had always been a fast runner, even for an elf. Joraga prided themselves on sprinting, and she had won most of her tree's weekly races while still only a juvenile. But she had never seen speed like the brood produced. It was past her stem and coming directly for her before she was halfway.

Nissa used her last step to jump up and over the brood. She put her hands before her and snatched her stem before tucking her head, rolling along the turf, and popping up on her feet. The brood was too far away, otherwise she would have snapped it while its back was still turned. Why should she, a Joraga, be concerned with the formality of honor when these plagues were running roughshod over Zendikar?

She started running at the brood again. The creature turned and, seeing her running, attempted to fly, but Nissa snapped its right, split arm off with her stem.

Nissa firmed the stem into a spike, tucked its handle under her armpit, and ran its tip into the middle of the brood. She drove it all the way in until it rested against its chest.

The brood stopped moving as Nissa drew the stem back out. Its tentacles and arm went limp, and its body pitched foreword.

The basilisk had destroyed almost all of the brood. The large brood lay on the ground gasping for air with a horn-puncture through its chest and brown foam at its mouth. She walked past the fray, toward the building where Sorin was wiping the blade of his great sword on a clump of grass. A juvenile broodling lay hacked in two pieces not far away.

Sorin looked up at Nissa's frowning face. Sorin glanced at the dead brood juvenile and smiled.

"Would you have rather taken him home?" Sorin asked.

She was about to respond. But when she opened her mouth, nothing came out. Perhaps he was right. What was wrong with killing the young of such creatures? Were they not brutes? They wanted Zendikar. They wanted to clear the trees and dig holes and suck on rocks.

"Look at this." It was Anowon's voice, and it came from near the structure. Nissa and Sorin followed his voice around a corner. A brood with a crushed skull lay slumped against the half-built wall. Nissa looked at Anowon and then up to see the vampire slaves fleeing through the hedrons to the mountains, with their harness ropes untied and trailing behind them. There was no sign of Smara and her goblins.

Anowon, however, was peering at the rocks used in a finished part of the structure. He had a small sliver of glass which he held before one of his eyes as he looked closely at some carvings.

A thought immediately occurred to her: how had the brood carved that? She looked around. There was no sign of any tools. How had they cut the blocks? Where had they quarried them?

Anowon waved them closer. "Look at this," he repeated. The stones he gestured at had strange glyphlike patterns chiseled into them like many of the other structures and hedrons that floated in crumbled glory across Zendikar.

Nissa looked up at Anowon.

"Do you see anything different?" he asked. He pointed at one of the hedrons floating nearby. "Look at that first."

Nissa looked at the floating stele, which was bobbing an arm's width away. Anowon was right. The design on the new structure was similar to what was on the hedron, but not the same. The structure's design was . . .

rougher somehow. The lines were neither as symmetrical, nor as clearly graven.

"Why would that be?" Nissa said.

The vampire gave a knowing curl to his lip. "Well, the designs are similar at first, but very different on closer inspection."

Sorin rolled his eyes.

"They are very different," Anowon continued. He pointed to the nearby hedron. "The big brood pushed that stone this close. It was what it was doing when we attacked."

"Why would it push it that close?" Nissa asked.

"To copy the design," replied Anowon.

Nissa was silent for a moment. "I would have thought those designs are a language, or some known part of the brood's life. A story perhaps?"

"They are language," Anowon said. "Power glyphs in ancient Eldrazi. This one says, 'There is no power but our power.' " The vampire pointed at a panel of glyphic lettering on the stele, then pointed to a similar marking on the building. "But this means nothing. This is not even close in shape."

Sorin sniffed.

Nissa bent for another look at the hedron glyph and then the glyph on the structure. They looked the same to her.

"Do you not see?" Anowon said, pointing to the hedron. "The words on this are copied imperfectly on this," he pointed to the structure. "Copied to meaningless gibberish."

"Why would they have to copy?" Nissa said.

"A good question," Sorin said. "Sharp as jurworrel thorns you are."

Nissa ignored him and turned to Anowon, who regarded her as he stroked his chin.

"They must be unable to write ancient Eldrazi," he said. "They are copying something that they have forgotten how to produce. They either have forgotten or they never knew."

"But who wrote them, then?" Nissa said. "And why are the brood copying them?"

"The brood idolize the authors, obviously," Anowon said.

"Gods?" Nissa said.

"Perhaps."

Sorin smiled. "As interesting as this little lesson of archaeosophy is, do you not think we should arrive at Zulaport? I am not feeling my best."

Nissa could hear the distaste in Sorin's voice, and she suddenly realized that she hated him for it. But it was true that Sorin did not look like he had when had they set out from Graypelt. He was noticeably thinner, and papery somehow. After rot-talking during the attack on the brood, he looked positively stricken, like he was possessed by a horrible disease that made his eye sockets deepen and his skin look like dead leaves.

Anowon paid no attention. He was staring at the building. A moment later a strange look crossed over his face. He muttered something to himself and began fumbling in the leather pouch on his belt. Soon he drew out his scraps of parchment and scraped something on one with a piece of charcoal. He stopped and felt for one of the metal cylinders hanging from his belt. He pulled the cylinder up and read the letters on it, holding it very close to his face, turning it slowly as he read.

Sorin watched with a bemused look on his face. "I suddenly feel like I am intruding," he said. "Do you want to be alone, Ghet?"

Anowon looked up and blinked. "What do you want?" he asked.

"Are you ready to visit beautiful Zulaport?"

"Zulaport?"

"You know?" Sorin pointed down to the sea. "The town that lies there . . . where we will hire a craft to take us over the water to Akoum? That Zulaport."

"Yes, of course. I am ready, master."

The smile dropped off Sorin's face. He glanced at Nissa before smiling again. *"Master* you say? What foolishness you speak? Let us walk."

And Sorin began walking.

Master, Nissa thought. *Interesting. That would explain many things. But why?*

The grassland swept several leagues until it ended abruptly at the blue ocean. The trail was clearly marked, and they followed it until the sun buried itself in the jagged pink and yellow surf. Soon the lights of Zulaport showed bright in the dusk.

They entered the town at total dark, greeted by the barking of feral Onduan hounds that howled around them on their three legs. Sorin fetched one a kick in the ribs and sent it yelping away, and the rest melted into the darkness.

Nissa frowned. She could hear Anowon sniffing the air next to her, smelling the many beings in the small settlement. At one point he closed his eyes, and his head bobbed to a rhythm only he could hear. Vampires could hear and feel the blood of prey. If a vampire let it, the pulse, as it was called, could be strong enough to whip one into a frenzy. But as Nissa watched, Anowon opened his eyes and took a deep breath.

Yet Sorin took Anowon by the scruff of the neck, and when the vampire turned, shoved him forward so he almost went sprawling on the ground. "Keep your fangs in your mouth," Sorin said. "Shed blood here, and I'll exact a toll on your flesh tonight."

Nissa stepped back from Sorin. Any vampire she'd ever encountered in Bala Ged would have attacked at such a provocation. But Anowon skulked ahead and did not even turn.

Sorin leaned in. "Anowon has wanted to feed on you, but I have kept him at bay."

Nissa did not know what to say to that. "Let him come," she said finally.

"Indeed," Sorin said, and moved away into the darkness.

The town itself seemed composed of small shacks of thatch and sod as was typical in a Zendikar settlement. The rush of the ocean surf punctuated the darkness as Nissa walked. The wind off the ocean was humid and cold, and the acrid smoke from the animal dung fires stung Nissa's eyes. Ahead a large fire burned, and they walked toward that light like moths.

A group of larger shacks were grouped around the large fire. It blazed huge and sideways with each gust of wind. One shack was larger than the rest. In the wild flicker of the bonfire a sign made from a piece of driftwood swung in the wind above its door.

Anowon drew the hood of his cloak up over his head. Nissa watched the reflection of the flames dance on his eyes for a second, and then Sorin spoke.

"What is that supposed to be?" Sorin said. He reached up and took hold of the swinging sign, stilling it.

"A kraken," Nissa said. "But what is it doing to that cuttlefish?"

Sorin, tilting his head sideways, looked at the

sign. "I do not . . . uh"—he righted his head—"I see now."

"*The Way of Things,*" said a voice from within the door. Eyes were looking out from the peat hole. The door opened to reveal a short human, hunkered as though by deformity. Or perhaps it was the man's heavy armaments—he was wearing a contraption strapped over his left arm. To Nissa it looked to be a mechanism that fed one of the many knives lined up along his arm into his hand. Humans loved such devices. And he was wearing armor—plenty of armor—another human weakness. Only his bald head and huge red beard were free from rusted plates fit together with only a small seam. Even though elves loathed armor, she could tell the suit he was wearing had once been quite expensive.

"Welcome to Zulaport. You will be wanting to speak to Indorel at your earliest possible convenience. He runs this place."

"And you are the welcoming committee?" Sorin said.

"In a manner of speaking, yes," the man said. "I keep this small inn here." He jerked a thumb over his shoulder at the large shack, an action that caused a multitude of squeaks and creaks to issue from his armor. "I watch. For Indorel."

When the man turned, Nissa noticed a great sword covered with runic etchings at his side. His armor was accented with various hooks, and riveted with small loops for affixing ropes and rope systems. And his hands were covered with what looked like tattoos of fire. Flames over every bit of exposed skin on his hands.

"Do you have coin?" the man said.

Nobody said anything.

"There are two places to sleep in Zulaport: Here or there." He pointed into the dark where the ocean crashed, and Nissa could just make out the outline of a small lighthouse on a hill. "And you are not getting in there without fins on your ankles." He held out his hand. "I take coin or trade." He looked them over carefully. "In your case I can see it will be coin."

That seemed to offend Anowon in some way. He straightened up and lifted his chin. Smara stumbled out of the darkness with her goblins behind her. Nissa waited for more, but none appeared. *Were they really down to only three?* she wondered. Had there not been nine when they had climbed out of the Makindi Trench?

"So, do you have coin?" the man said, in a tone more like a demand than a question.

"Oh, we have everything you would want," Sorin said.

The man smiled, showing teeth as brown as his armor, and lines at the corners of his eyes. But his smile fell away when he saw Smara and her goblins. "Superlative, but the goblins have to sleep in the stables due to the smell."

"I'm sure your little inn cannot smell *that* bad," Sorin said. "The goblins can endure.

The man did not smile at Sorin's joke. "I meant due to *the goblins'* smell. It is too much. And the kor too, cannot enter for obvious reasons."

"How do you feel about vampires," Sorin said, with his smug smile on his lips.

"Vampires pay double," the man said. "And if he slips his chain in the night we are not responsible for skewering him, be warned. And you still pay double."

The inside was worse than the outside. It smelled like seaweed and was as damp as a grave. Nissa could feel the shafts of wind through the cracks in the daubed timber-and-peat walls. But the man who said his name was Aleen showed them a room with slips filled with dry grass that lay on low wooden frames lined up against the wall. The beds were only a bit stained, but the grass was sweet smelling. Nissa fell asleep almost as soon as she layed her head down.

She was shaken violently awake. "Get up," a voice shouted in the dark. "Up."

A hand grabbed her by the hair and dragged her painfully to her feet. By the raw strength of the man she knew she could not attack directly, and her staff was unreachable next to her bed. Wincing in pain as he pulled her through the dark, Nissa planted one foot, squatted, and braced for the pain. The man stopped and began to pull, but Nissa shot her other foot out and planted it in the small of the back of his knee, forcing the knee to bend and the man to lose his balance and fall into her. He was a large specimen, she thought as she easily caught him, pivoted on her hip, and threw him head first into the wall.

She could see quite well once her eyes had become accustomed to the dark. She was on top of the man quickly. She had his belt off and around his neck in a split second, and she put her knee in the space between his shoulders and pulled until his throat made a certain gagging noise. Then she pulled more until he stopped making any noise at all. She walked back to their room and picked up her staff. The other beds were empty, but there was a small window cut into the wall.

Outside the wind was gusting as hard as it had been before. Nissa left the room and walked down to the water and the dock that the inhabitants of Zulaport had built in the crescent shaped Bay of Bayeen. Nissa had been on the ocean only once in her life, when she had left Bala Ged to sail to Ondu four months ago. In the bay. she saw tethered ships bobbing in the pitch of the surf. Some had sails and some did not. One had what must have been a sail bound in a tight bundle and lashed to the bottom of the beam that went perpendicular to the mast.

Nissa walked back to the inn. The bonfire had burned down, but a group of people stood around it. The body of the man Nissa had strangled lay on the sand before the fire. Smara and her three goblins were standing with men behind them holding their arms. Sorin was smiling in the firelight, looking like he was enjoying himself immensely.

"Where is the other one?" The being was tall, wearing black leather armor made in such a way as to be formed entirely of swirls. His hair hung in his face in stringy, black wads. Nissa realized it was a vampire, and a start of revulsion went through her.

She knew Anowon was there behind her before she felt him touch her shoulder.

"That is Indorel." Anowon hissed. "A credit to my race. He controls this shore-rat's nest. He makes his coin extorting the peril seekers, and sucking the weak among them dry."

"How do you know?"

Anowon did not say anything.

"Why is he so angry?"

"He found two of his henchmen," Anowon said. "Bled dry." She could hear the wet way he was forming his words, and the sound made the gorge rise in the back of her throat.

Nissa shook her head. "The goblins were not enough for you?"

"It was not I," Anowon said. She could hear the mocking tone in his voice. Why did he even joke about not killing the henchmen, Nissa thought. Who else would it have been?

They watched the vampire question Sorin and Smara. The kor babbled and Sorin smiled, responding with single syllables. With each of Sorin's responses Indorel became angrier and angrier until he was stomping around in the sand throwing his arms up in annoyance.

"I feel like that, talking to Sorin most times," Nissa said.

Anowon pushed his jaw out and said nothing.

The men around Smara and Sorin were heavily armed, and further out in the shadows, Nissa could sense something else. Something larger was waiting.

"Why does Sorin not give them coin and be done with it?"

"I do not know that he has coin."

"But he said . . ."

Anowon raised his eyebrows in a way that said, *I pity you for your foolishness.*

Nissa looked back at the fire.

"Maybe we should leave?" Anowon said. "Sorin will be fine without us."

"No," Nissa said. "Only he knows how to stop the Eldrazi and send them back into their slumber."

"I know where the Eye of Ugin is, do you not remember?" Anowon asked.

"Yes, but how do we work it?" Nissa asked.

The surf crashed behind them.

"Do you even know why we travel to the Eye?" Anowon said.

"No. But it must have something to do with imprisoning the brood."

"Right, of course," Anowon said. But the vampire did not sound convinced. "An outlander thinking about the good of Zendikar?"

Indorel suddenly shoved Sorin, who fell back in the sand. Indorel raised his arms and rivulets of black and purple power crackled and bled down his arms.

Sorin reached out and took hold of the ankle of the dead henchman. His body convulsed at Sorin's touch. But when it lifted its head an instant later, long drips of bloody fluid were coming from its eyes and from its mouth as it struggled off the sand and reached for Indorel.

The vampire stepped back and spit into the sand to his right. He extended one finger and touched the flesh between his eyes. He whispered some words, and his finger glowed. At the same time the zombie swung a clawed hand at Indorel, which caught the vampire in the ear and caused him to stagger sideways a step. But then Indorel took a step forward, reached out, and touched the zombie. It locked and fell dead.

Anowon began chanting softly.

Indorel seized the air, and Sorin fell onto the sand, writhing with convulsions. He arched his back and grunted.

Then Anowon snapped his fingers, and Indorel suddenly stumbled . . . releasing Sorin.

Anowon kept chanting.

Sorin hopped to his feet and began to run. Smara and the goblins followed, shaking off the henchmen's grasping fingers.

Nissa twisted her staff and released the stem sword. She rushed forward and caught one of the henchman in the chin as he struggled to grab the fleeing Sorin. The henchman's head slid easily off his shoulders and fell with a thunk in the sand, his mouth gasping.

The henchmen were all around her then, with more coming out of the inn. But she reached her target. Indorel stepped back as she neared him, and two henchmen stepped between them. Nissa joined her stem sword to the staff and dived between one of their legs. She twisted and hopped to her feet and in an instant poked the vampire with the bottom end of her staff. Then two henchmen were swinging, and she bent her knees and hopped back. Indorel looked down at the place where Nissa had jabbed him.

The henchmen pushed their advantage. They rushed forward into the darkness at the edge of the fire and brought their swords down where Nissa should have fallen, but struck only sand. Nissa snapped out the stem sword and one of the men fell with a grunt, clutching the stump of his right arm, severed above the elbow.

Nissa knew the seed she had planted in Indorel's chest would have rooted throughout the vampire's body. And as she watched from the darkness, with his body silhouetted by the raging fire, she saw a small bud poke out of his sternum and through his leather armor and burst into bloom. Nissa took a running start and flipped into the air over the henchmen squinting into the dark looking for her. She cleared their heads easily and landed with a thump in the sand in front of the vampire. Nissa stopped only a split second, just long enough to seize the flower stem and yank it out of the stunned vampire's chest. The fire-light flickered and, *pop*, there was the vampire's heart, still beating in the stem's roots. She dropped the flower and heart and ran.

Smara and Anowon were standing in the sand, as was Sorin. When Nissa reached the dock, she ran directly to the boat with the sail lashed to the mast. In a moment Anowon stomped onto the dock's lashed logs.

"How do you make this sail?" Nissa said.

The vampire's eyes glowed slightly in the dark. The sun was lighting the eastern sky, but even so it was too dark to see if they were being pursued. The fire in front of the inn blazed, but nobody was standing around it that she could see.

"I do not know how to sail this," Nissa said as she looked over her shoulder at the dark.

"Can we create wind?" Anowon said.

"But how do we get the sail up?"

Nissa heard running from behind. Sorin and Smara appeared on the dock. The goblins arrived seconds later.

"What is this?" Sorin said.

"A boat," Nissa said. "And we do not know how it works."

"We have little time," Sorin said. "Can we push it or pull it?" He looked genuinely harried.

Then Nissa had an idea.

"Find rope," she said.

Nissa sat down on the deck and took a deep breath. The plains that stretched around were foreign to her and held little power she could use. But Nissa recounted the route they'd taken to get here. In her mind's eye she followed their trail backward, over the grassland, down the trench and up onto the mesa to Turntimber Forest.

Soon the power from the turntimber trees was flowing into her. She collected it in herself until she felt so full of the energy that she could burst. Then she imagined the largest creature in the forest. A creature of the deep forest . . . a ziru behemoth. Ten humans standing head on foot would just reach its burly shoulder, and the Behemoth had plates of horn extending from the tip of its nose all the way over its shoulder in a loose row. The underside of its jaw had plates as well. Its legs were long and muscular, and its feet were splayed and slightly webbed, which was why she summoned it.

Nissa began drawing the image into herself, and when she opened her eyes the huge creature was standing on the beach, its feet sunk into the wet sand. It snorted its pug nose into the gusting wind and stamped a foot.

"Now *that* is exactly the creature I would have expected you to summon," Sorin said. He threw up his arms. "One with neither fin nor wing. Why not something with wings?"

Nissa and Anowon used every coil of rope they found on the dock to fashion a harness of sorts. While Sorin kept lookout, they looped the rope into a huge circle and put it around the behemoth's neck. To that circle of rope they tied other long pieces of rope. Nissa asked the creature to enter the water, and when it had, they tied the loose ends of the rope to the masthead of the small ship. The rope was not long enough at first, so they tied more on, and soon it was long enough.

CHAPTER 11

The ship responded surprisingly well to being dragged behind the behemoth. The creature swam with its head low in the water, so only its eyes, nose, and the top of the head jutted above the low waves.

By sunrise, the continent of Ondu was only a line of land topped with a fringe of round mountains behind them.

By midday there was no land to be seen in any direction. Nissa used Kahlled's pathway stone to point the way, and they followed it. If the behemoth veered, Nissa crawled over the rope and whispered in its ear.

Soon the azure water changed to dark blue, and its surface became choppy. All the rest of the day Nissa watched a line of clouds at the horizon grow larger, until finally they were overhead.

The map showed the blue ocean gap between the continents of Ondu and Akoum to be only the length from the tip of her middle finger to its first digit—not a long trip. But Nissa had no way to tell how fast they were traveling. So, by measuring with her finger how long it took them to travel from the Turntimber Forest in the center of Ondu to the coast, she guessed they would be traveling on the boat for two days.

Still, the behemoth never seemed to tire so it would perhaps be faster. The creature paddled its feet in the manner of an Onduan hound and moved along fast enough to create a small wake. Before night fell Nissa thought she'd seen a landmass on the horizon.

The behemoth would not sleep. Nissa shimmied across the wrist-sized rope to tell it to stop, and either the creature did not hear her or it did not understand. If the behemoth did not sleep, neither could Nissa. She leaned against the mast with her cloak pulled tightly around her, holding up the pathway stone as often as she could to check their direction.

Their dry tack was long gone. For water they had the little still residing in their canteens that they had filled before going to bed at the inn. If the trip lasted no longer than another day, they would survive. Nissa knew the Joraga fasting mantras, and she could last without food for another week.

There was no sign of any landmass when the sun rose the next morning. Had they missed it in the darkness? *Doubtful,* Nissa thought. More likely she had mistaken a cloudbank on the horizon for a landmass. The light *had* been fading after all.

They sailed the rest of the day with no sight of land. When the sun was five hands high above the ocean, a flock of something appeared at the horizon. Nissa had a bad feeling about the creatures immediately. Her apprehension rose as they beat closer showing no visible wings, and for the first time she wished she could jump away, as she had when she'd first learned to planeswalk. But Nissa knew that she had to see the trip to the Eye through. Where had running away ever got her? No, she would continue on her path.

Soon the creatures were close enough that Nissa could see tentacles. She narrowed in on the creatures. "Flying brood," she announced.

The brood flapped closer. When they were close enough that Nissa could hear the wind rushing through their tentacles, the brood lineage turned and circled over the boat. She watched their tentacles squirm as they circled. Nissa looked to Sorin. There were large dark circles under his eyes. He appeared as though he had not slept in days. Did he have the stamina to fight off the brood circling the ship? His was the only ranged weapon they possessed.

The behemoth's eyes showed their whites as it struggled to raise its head enough to watch the brood.

If they glided down slowly in just the right formation she could perhaps use the stem in its whip form and dispose of two in quick order. Conceivably, Anowon could use one of his teeth.

Nissa was just preparing to pull her stem from its staff when the brood lineage moved out of their circling motion and moved away, flying west. Soon they were specks on the horizon again. The wind gusted, and the behemoth's breath puffed. Sorin's left hand was on top of his head holding his hair out of his eyes as he watched the brood disappear. *Why had they gone?*

The others slept that night on the deck of the ship. Nissa was not looking forward to another night of managing the behemoth, but she sat at the front of the ship trying not to fall asleep, holding the pathway stone Khalled had given her, and watching the immense creature she'd summoned churn the brine water to foam.

The stars were bright enough to cast pale shadow on the deck. Anowon was at the other side of the ship with a nub of a candle burning as he read one of his cylinders. Nissa could hear Smara muttering somewhere below decks where the jars of turntimber bark were lashed . . . packed in Zulaport for the markets of Guul Draz.

Nissa checked the pathway stone again. Sorin was standing across from her when she looked up.

"Why did the brood leave us alone?" Nissa said.

Sorin's face showed the annoyance the question caused him. "How do you suppose I would know that?"

Nissa looked back at the stone hanging from the cord in her hand. A gust of wind blew it sideways, and she put it in the pocket of her cloak.

"I know what you are," Sorin said, suddenly.

"What did you say?" A knot immediately formed in Nissa's throat. *He knows.*

"I know what you are able to do," Sorin continued. "That you posses the ability to walk to other planes."

Nissa set her eyes on Sorin, and gave him what she hoped came off as a steady, level stare. "I am not oddity. Why would you suppose I was?"

"We are not 'oddities.' "

Nissa felt as though she might swallow her tongue. Her heart hopped. She found herself making a conscious effort to control her breathing. She took a deep breath and released it. When she opened her eyes she had her center once again.

"Why do you tell me that you know this about me? Who are you?"

"I am like you," Sorin replied.

"You are not like me. I do not slay juveniles. Not even brood lineage juveniles."

"You would if you had seen their parents."

Nissa let that statement hang in the windy air. She hoped he'd say more, and when he did she could barely contain her smile.

"The brood are only the minions," he said. "That is why we must put them all back in their prison, and hold their parents in check with them."

"Why must we?"

"Because if we fail to do so they will eat this and many other planes," Sorin said. "Planes that you perhaps have visited?"

Nissa had, in fact, visited only a handful. One had been a staggering metropolis of beings standing virtually cheek to cheek amid towering buildings. She had walked the street for about an hour and in that time it had seemed that the amount of people grew and the height of the buildings lengthened. There was nothing green that she could see. She had left soon after.

Another plane was stranger than the first. There had been natural features like mountains and forests, but on closer examination they turned out to have straight angles that showed they had been created. She had watched in amazement as a range of mountains were moved with the wave of a hand by a being with metal arms and an elongated head. She'd been taken prisoner fairly quickly by one of those beings and barely escaped with her life. She would not be traveling to anywhere like those places again, if she could help it. Still, she said nothing in hopes that Sorin would keep talking. And he did.

"If we do not contain the brood, they will free their titans, and Zendikar will cease to be what it is now."

"What are these *titans?*"

"They are terrible creatures that eat energy, as the brood do," Sorin said. As he spoke he stared out over the starlit ocean. Small white crests appeared on the low choppy waves. "They suck the very energy out of a plane and move on to the next one. Destroyers of planes. They are dreadful foes to anyone who stands against them."

"And they are imprisoned now?"

"Yes, in the Eye of Ugin."

"On Akoum?" Nissa said.

Sorin nodded.

Nissa looked out at the water. "How will we put the brood back in the prison the vampire saw them escape from?"

Sorin did not say anything for a moment. "We cannot," he said finally.

"Did you say 'we cannot'?"

"Yes."

"Why is that?"

"They are too dispersed at this point. But they are not the true danger. If the titans escape"—he raised his eyebrows in the starlight—"there will be utter catastrophe. And the brood lineage are trying to accomplish this, they just do not know how yet."

"So this brood will have to be hunted down, and their parents imprisoned?"

Sorin nodded.

"And what would happen if we allowed these titans their freedom?"

"They would wreck Zendikar," Sorin said, without hesitation.

But Nissa sensed something—a certain tightness around his mouth and eyes that she had not seen before. She looked again, and it was gone. *Could he be lying?* she thought. *And for what reason?*

"Why do you tell me all of this now?" Nissa said. "I am already helping you on this quest. You saved my life in the Turntimber, and I am repaying you."

"We are near Akoum. Somebody has to understand what we will shortly face."

"Why?"

Sorin exhaled. "I will need your skills later."

Nissa did not like how that sounded. "And if I refuse?" she said. "Later?"

"You cannot refuse. Zendikar depends on it."

Nissa sat looking out at the water. Why would the brood or the titans be on Zendikar in the first place? Were they native to that place? Clearly the Eldrazi had been on Zendikar a long time. Eldrazi ruins could be found in almost every corner of the plane.

And who *was* Sorin, really? Who had sent him to make sure the Eldrazi stayed contained, and why? Why would beings from other planes be so concerned with keeping the Eldrazi on Zendikar? How did he know the truth of the Eldrazi when she, a native of the plane, had never heard even a whisper of what he'd said? She only remembered the Eldrazi as a childhood nighttime story. And in those stories, the Eldrazi were the sort of beings that built castles that reached to the sun and ate golden fruit from trees that floated in the air. And Sorin was telling her they lived on energy, on mana from the land?

She turned to ask Sorin how he knew so much about this situation, but he was gone. She was left with the sound of the waves chopping against the hull of the ship and the behemoth's massive legs chugging in the water.

Nissa sat with her back against the mast and let her mind wander. Above her head the stars moved along their paths. Soon her mind was reworking what Sorin had said, and before she knew it, the eastern horizon went as red as blood.

Nissa could see a line of land ahead. Above the land towered high, strangely pointed spires of sharp tipped mountains. As she watched, the morning sun reflected red off the crystal-studded peaks.

Nissa felt a presence and turned. Anowon was standing on the other side of the mast, staring at her.

"Truly you are lucky to be a Joraga," the vampire said. "And to have taken the Joraga tincture of cut fungus and asta weed."

"Good morning to you," Nissa said, turning back to the blood-red shore of Akoum. "I wonder why Sorin has not fallen to your fangs?"

"Perhaps he is not to my liking."

"And I am?"

Anowon looked away from her and at the land on the horizon.

"Akoum," Anowon said. "The kor called it 'the place where things were lost.' Low level Roils are nearly constant. The very land is as sharp as a knife's edge. The sun refracts through those pointed crystals creating areas of extreme heat that could cook an unsuspecting elf traveler in a manner of moments. And the denizens," Anowon said as he grimaced malevolently, "taste horrible."

As if in response to Anowon's monologue, the ocean suddenly pitched to the right. There was a sudden, deafening rush, and the water immediately next to the ship began to impossibly lift up. Soon a huge globule of swirling water was floating above the tip of the mast. Nissa could see the dark shapes of ocean creatures—six times larger than the behemoth—caught in the huge bubble. And when she looked over the side of the ship, she could see the plant life of the ocean floor flopped to the side in the early morning sun. A loose fish flopped on a bare patch of sand.

"It's the Roil," Anowon said.

Nissa watched as the ball of ocean floated gracefully up into the sky, with its fish swimming within.

Sorin walked to the front of the ship, brushing his long hair with a silver comb. He glanced up at the piece of disembodied ocean. "Look! Even parts of Zendikar are trying to get away from Zendikar," he said.

They were still a league from the shore. Nissa unrolled Khalled's map to look for a possible port in which to land the ship. Akoum appeared like a large circular landmass. She wiped the map off with the palm of her calloused hand and peered closer.

"What troubles you?" Anowon said.

"Our map is wrong. The ports are not marked on here."

"The map is not at fault. There are no ports on Akoum."

"Oh, this *is* excellent," Sorin said.

"The shore is too perilous for ports," Anowon said. "However, the probability is high that a group of humans is forming a rescue party on shore even as we speak."

"To rescue us?" Nissa asked. "Boats!" *Why did I ever get on a boat?*

"It is possible to land a ship," Anowon said. "But the water is filled with crystalline points invisible to even the most trained lookout."

"And we do not even have that." Nissa said.

"Precisely."

"Why did you not say something about this sooner?"

Anowon shrugged. "One point more: There is a good chance that those human rescuers could also be bandits."

"But how did the brood that took you prisoner get you to Ondu?"

"By wing."

"Oh, lets do that," Sorin said.

Nissa ignored him. When she looked up, it seemed like the shore of Akoum had raised three hands higher, like a great maw opening to receive them.

"This must be the welcoming party," Sorin said, pointing off the starboard side. A great field of bubbles erupted on the surface of the water. Soon the water churned with movement, and huge tentacles began to break the surface. A fleshy dome the color of a bled corpse broke the surface. Even Sorin drew his breath in sharply when two great, malevolent eyes opened in the dome and focused their long irises on the ship. Soon the full head appeared, with the tentacles where the mouth should be.

Nissa held her staff up. *A kraken,* she thought. *What could happen next?* She glanced at Sorin. Had he recouped his power enough to strike down such a large creature? Even though Sorin was smiling, she could see the lines of exhaustion on his face.

The kraken rose immensely next to the ship. Its right tentacle held a huge, spiked shell, and on its back was another even larger shell. The creature's other limb was huge, an armored claw easily as long as the ship they were standing on. The six gills running up its chest opened and closed in the early morning sun.

"Why do you disturb the slumber of the sleeper in the deep?"

"Who is he?" Sorin said innocently.

The eyebrow shells above the kraken's eyes dropped. "He is Brinelin, the Moon Kraken. He is I," the creature said.

For some moments, Nissa could only stare at the tremendous creature, dripping and glistening in the light.

"Brinelin," Nissa said, raising her voice above the churning made by the kraken's tentacles. "We did not mean to break your slumber."

The Moon Kraken harrumphed. "An apology will not save you."

"What will save us, great Brinelin?" Nissa said.

"Nothing will save you."

Nissa remembered the rumor she'd heard about Speaker Sutina and the Moon Kraken. The rumor of a secret friendship.

Anowon stepped up beside Nissa. "Do you have a riddle for us, great Brinelin?"

The kraken regarded Anowon through round unblinking eyes. "Riddle?" it said. "Riddles are a sphinx's folly." It raised one tentacle to its mouth. "Brinelin demands red sacrifice!" The kraken swam to a small rock sticking out of the ocean, and hoisted itself up into a sitting position.

"Will you take this offering?" Sorin said. He casually took one of the goblins by the scruff of the neck and tossed it screeching into the water, where it thrashed wildly.

The Moon Kraken regarded the panicking goblin for a moment before sighing and falling off the rock. It hit the water with a large splash and slipped under the surface. The goblin, showing the whites of its eyes, scratched desperately at the side of the ship, looking for a handhold. It did not cry out, but whimpered in a way that made Nissa's stomach turn. The other two goblins stared down at their feet while Smara sang what sounded like a song under her breath, oblivious to the goblins' whimpers. Sorin chuckled. Anowon watched Brinelin's air bubbles approaching the goblin with a blank expression.

And then the goblin was simply gone, pulled under with a sudden jerk. The Moon Kraken surfaced a moment later.

Brinelin brought its huge shell out of the water and slammed it down on the water. The wave from the impact of the shell hit the hull and washed over the deck, drenching everyone on it.

"You will do me further tribute," the Moon Kraken said. One of the goblin's arms was sticking sideways out of the kraken's beaked maw, and as they watched, a tentacle swept it away and into the water.

The two remaining goblins looked at each other out of the corner of their eyes.

The shore was not far away. Nissa could see the long crystals jutting out of the water. They would never make it through them without being guided. A narrow beach of white sand started behind the crystals, and a high cliff of black basalt extended almost vertically from the white sand. Nissa thought she saw movement among the crystals at the water's edge.

"If you have nothing better to offer me," the kraken mused aloud. "I will crush your skulls and suck out your brains and make tributes of you all."

"You will not be eating anyone's brains today," Sorin said. "Surely you know that?"

The kraken regarded Sorin. "I am Brinelin, the Moon Kraken," he said. "I know nothing of the sort."

"And I am Sorin Markov. If you do not stand aside this very instant you will be destroyed, and we will leave your body for your subjects the fish to devour at their leisure."

Sorin's voice had taken on a different tone as he spoke. It was both deeper and sharper. It hurt Nissa's head to hear it.

But the kraken did not move. Instead it stood up to its full height and pushed out its white breast. "Your magician's tricks will not work on the Moon Kraken, little wizard," it said. "I have battled other, greater magic users than you."

Sorin uttered no words. He spoke no incantations. His eyes simply went black, and his hands began to glow with a smoky light. The kraken noticed it, too.

It dropped down into the ocean so that only its top gills showed above the surf.

"Do you not remember me, fishmaster?" Sorin boomed.

Nissa had to crouch down on the deck of the ship. Something about Sorin's voice made the parts inside her stomach and chest vibrate, and she suddenly felt nauseous.

The kraken looked closer at Sorin. "You?" it said after its examination. "You have returned?"

"Stand aside, or you will be disposed of," Sorin boomed. "Stand aside, now!"

The timbre and volume of his voice was so great that Nissa had to clap her hands over her ears.

The kraken moved out of the way of the ship, and the behemoth started paddling again.

"Why have you returned?" the kraken said.

Sorin frowned, and his voice returned to normal, as did his eyes. "Be a good little fishy and guide us through the crystal fields," he said.

The kraken's tentacles casually slipped out of the water and wrapped loops around the small ship; Nissa had to jump back to avoid being caught up in the sudden lassoing. Soon the ship was entirely covered with tentacles. Nissa pinched her nose. *How had Speaker Sutina endured this smell?*

"I will squeeze your ship to splinters before you end my days. Then you can make your sad way to shore with your tiny feet and hands," The kraken said. "And there are things in these depths that do not slumber."

Nissa looked again at the shore. She did not see the movement she'd seen before. The glitter of white sand looked terribly far away.

Sorin must have noticed it, too. That, or he realized that his power was at such ebb that he dared not call the kraken's bluff. The smoke wafting off his fingertips blew away.

Brinelin chuckled, and bubbles broke the sea's surface. The Moon Kraken began to squeeze and Nissa felt the ship buckle and crack.

Nissa stepped forward.

"Moon Kraken," she said, fingering something in her pocket. "I have an offering greater than blood sacrifice."

The Moon Kraken twisted its beaked mouth into a terrible smirk. It squeezed harder. Now Nissa was sure she could hear water shooting into the hull.

"It concerns Speaker Sutina," Nissa said. "Important news of her welfare."

The kraken's smirk fell away.

"What of the Speaker?" the Moon Kraken blurted.

Nissa could feel his tentacles loosen.

"Release the ship," Nissa said.

It did. The kraken pulled its tentacles back under the surface of the water.

"I will tell you what I know," Nissa said. "But you must promise to guide us to shore."

"If it pleases Brinelin," the kraken said.

Nissa thought about this. He might not be in the best mood after he hears that Speaker Sutina is dead.

"Take us to shore first," Nissa said.

The kraken thrust its fleshy chin out. "Tell me now."

"Do you promise to take us to shore after I tell you?"

"The Moon Kraken makes no promises."

"Then it saddens me to tell you that Speaker Sutina is no more."

The expression on the kraken's face fell. Nissa felt a twinge of pity for it. The creature sank deeper into the water, before floating higher again.

"You lie!" the kraken spouted water from its gills. All of its tentacles shot straight out of the water and into the air. "You are lying to save your barnacles. Your falseness will not save you."

"I am not lying. She died in an attack made by the new scourge that plagues Zendikar, the very scourge we are on a journey to stop." Nissa said. From her pocket she drew the pearl Speaker Sutina had dropped the day she died. Nissa held the pearl up. "Behold the pearl you gave her." The assumption was a gamble, but it was all she had. The kraken's eyes squeezed together when it saw the gift. A small tentacle lifted out of the water and came close to the pearl. With a gentleness that surprised Nissa, the tentacle caressed the pearl before taking it carefully. The kraken brought the pearl to the front of its face, and examined it through sad eyes.

"Tell me everything," the Moon Kraken said softly, without looking away from the pearl.

Nissa told the creature the story of Speaker Sutina's death and of their quest to imprison the brood lineage. When she had finished the only sound she heard was the not-so-distant sound of waves breaking on the white shore.

"What did she say before she fell away?" the kraken said.

Nissa cast her mind for a good lie. "She spoke of the ocean," Nissa said.

"That is not true. Sutina hated the water," the kraken said, softly. "But I will let you pass."

The kraken moved out of the way of the ship, and the behemoth started paddling again.

The kraken's white face crumpled as it slipped under the water. Soon it broke the surface of the ocean and waved them forward. The creature guided them through the deadheads lurking just below the surface of the water, and crystals as long as three of their ships, one of which had at its tip a human skull pierced through the brain pan and clacking in the wind.

Soon they were near the shore. The Moon Kraken moved to the side and let the behemoth clamber onto the shore, dragging the ship through the sand. The ship tilted right off its keel and onto its hull, and Nissa had to grab a railing to keep from sliding off into the sand. She dismissed the behemouth and immediately felt stronger.

"Go forth from here," the kraken said, glumly. "Brinelin will do his part to rid Zendikar of this scourge." With that, he slipped below the surface and was not seen again.

CHAPTER 12

A shaft of sunlight broke through the clouds overhead and sparkled on the white sand made of crystals ground to grains. The beach extended to a sheer cliff. Nissa's heart sank as her eyes followed the cliff up. It was a league high if it was an arm's length, rising in one uninterrupted sweep so high that Nissa could see clouds moving at the top. Crystals protruded at irregular intervals from the cliff's sheer face.

Anowon brushed past her to evaluate the cliff, suddenly the guide on the continent she had never visited. "The creatures that have adapted to live here are as hard and as spiny as this land," the vampire said. "And tougher by far."

"We cannot scale this cliff," Nissa said, suddenly understanding the kraken's malicious smile before it submerged.

Anowon looked up from the cliff's base.

"For one," Nissa continued. "We lack rope enough for even one ascent. Second, none of my pegs will penetrate that crystal."

Anowon turned as though he had not heard Nissa. He walked back to the shore, pushing through the goblins that drew back from him as he passed. Even

Smara stopped mumbling to watch what he was doing. When Anowon reached the shoreline he began to dig. He soon unearthed the badly rotted wooden mast of a ship.

"I saw another ship broken and scattered in the shallows there," Anowon said, pointing just off shore to a massive crystal as thick as their whole ship. "And now this one."

The vampire looked up from the hole he'd dug and peered at the top of the cliff, where clouds skittered by. "I wonder . . ."

Nissa waited for Anowon to explain what he was thinking. He walked a bit up the shore and began to dig again. Sure enough, he uncovered a broken piece of hull.

"This place is a graveyard for water vessels," Anowon said.

Nissa waited, but the vampire said nothing more. A moment later he knelt and closed his eyes. He stayed in the position for long enough that Nissa thought he might have fallen asleep, but then she saw his fingers moving like spiders over one of the metal cylinders dangling from his belt.

"Ghet," Sorin said. "Oh, Ghet."

Anowon opened one of his eyes and curled his lip at Sorin.

Sorin chuckled. "You were only just about to explain your hypothesis to us."

"We cannot scale that cliff," Anowon said.

"The elf said that already."

Anowon opened both of his eyes with a sigh. "If ships ruin here commonly, then there must be something taking advantage of it. On Akoum nothing is wasted."

The waves broke on the beach. The wind blew hard

across Nissa's ear. "So we wait?" Nissa said.

"Yes," Sorin said. "For imminent attack."

They waited the rest of the day and into the night. Brightness, Nissa learned, was never much of an issue on Akoum, where the ever-present crystals magnified even the dimmest light.

So it was easy for Nissa to see almost as clearly as day when figures slowly rappelled down the side of the cliff later that night. They rappelled in a way she had never seen before—face forward with their harness at their belly, belaying the rope that way. The figures were short and lightly armed. When ten were on the sand, they branched out and drew small knives.

Nissa waited to give the signal until the men were almost on top of them. Then she whistled, and they jumped up, Nissa with her stem sword drawn and limp next to her. Anowon's eyes glowed pale in the starlight and Sorin's silhouette, as black and as deep as velvet, drew in the surrounding light.

The beach combers looked from Nissa to Sorin to Anowon to Smara and to the two goblins, then to Sorin's parasite sword, which seemed to pulse darker than the night around it. They were clearly weighing their chances. The combers had obviously been counting on surprising them, and with that gone, they wondered if they had the numbers to carry the fight. The decision was made when the lead scavenger dropped his dagger. The others soon followed.

"Stop," one said, stepping forward and holding his hand with the palm facing out. "We are not your enemy. We have come to help."

"That *is* a relief," Sorin said. "Because I thought you wanted to cut our throats in our sleep and then plunder whatever goods we might have."

"We saw your ship from above," the head man said. He was a human, without a doubt.

Anowon threw down a tooth, which began to glow. The combers were a mixed group—some goblins, some humans, two world-gift kor . . . even an elf—a Tajuru-splinter by how he wore his quiver—with a dire look in his eye. Nissa put her stem sword back into the staff and stepped forward. "Come," she said to the combers, gesturing next to the tooth. "Sit here."

When they were seated under the eyes of Anowon and Sorin, Nissa went around and collected the knives. Each knife was different, clearly salvaged. One of them was even made of flint. She took the knives to the water and threw them in.

"Those took a long time to collect," the head man said.

"They will still be there when you return for them later," Nissa said.

"Are we your prisoners now?" the human asked.

"No," Sorin said. "You are now our guides. At least until we get to the top of that cliff. At that point we will decide if you have been helpful. If you have not, we will let our vampire drain your veins. I must say, you do look tasty."

The human looked at the sand between his feet and did not speak again.

As soon as the sun broke on the eastern horizon, they rose, stiff with cold, and proceeded to the cliff.

"How long will this take?" Sorin said.

"All day," the human replied. In the sunlight Nissa could see that he was a short man with every inch of exposed skin covered with puckered white scars. A scraggly beard clung to his chin, as did remnants of armor to his wiry body.

He began strapping his harness to one of the ropes

they had descended the night before. Nissa took the rope in her hand, feeling its odd, firm texture.

"What is this made of?" she asked.

"Dulam beast hide," the man replied, taking out a coil of thick rope and deftly looping it to his harness and then to the rope. "The crystal has trouble cutting it," he said before pulling himself up, catching each foot in one of the loops he had tied to the harness. He pulled so the loop cinched around each foot, raised one of them, and stepped up. The rope caught and raised him up one step. He repeated the action with his other foot, and soon he was ascending the rope as though it was a ladder.

"Stop," Sorin said. "Wait there. We would not want you getting up to the top and alerting whatever associates you have up there to our presence."

Three of the combers stayed on the beach while Nissa, Sorin, Anowon, and Smara ascended. The combers strapped them in and tied their foot loop tethers. Smara's goblins, both of them, looked at one another and simply climbed Smara's rope without harness or tether.

Nissa looked down at the beach after she had been climbing for a couple of hours. The three remaining combers were sanding at the base of the cliff, eyeing the ship tipped on its side.

Soon Nissa was too high to look down; the clouds obscured her view, and the wind blew so hard that it caused the rope to bow and snap against the crystals. But the rope did not break, unlike the sleeve of her jerkin, which sliced easily when she grazed a crystal halfway up the cliff.

The crystals were everywhere as they climbed. Sorin managed to cut his hand, and the blood fell in rivulets, only to be blown away in the wind. When the comber climbing near her saw Sorin's blood blowing away he made a certain whistle and pointed to Sorin. The head man stopped and looked down.

"You must bind your gash," the man said. "Certain animals can smell blood on the wind." He closed his mouth and turned back to climbing. Nissa noticed that all of the combers doubled their pace. Nissa doubled hers also, and soon they were above the misty fog and in the bright sun. The ocean below was a blurry outline.

And still they climbed, Nissa becoming more confident with the ingenious rope system. At midday the combers stopped on a small ledge, the flat side of a crystal that had had its sides chipped and dulled enough that it did not cut them. They sat on the shelf with their feet dangling over the edge and drank water sloshing in canteens made from the exoskeletons of large beetles. There was no food—there had not been any for more than three days, and Nissa's stomach had stopped hurting. She did not even miss it.

They attained the top of the cliff by late afternoon. Sorin poked the top of his head over the edge and seeing no sign of movement, scrambled up. The dulam hide ropes were tied to huge crystals that had first been wrapped with more layers of hide as thick as Nissa's finger.

When they were all up and resting in the strange, wavy shadows created behind the crystals, Sorin looked over at Anowon. The vampire had closed his eyes again and was kneeling on the hard rock, moving his fingers soundlessly over the writing on one of his metal cylinders. The combers sat opposite Anowon, pretending not to notice him.

"So," Sorin said to the combers. "You were not totally unhelpful."

"We traveled down to help you," the head man said. "We never meant you any harm."

"Um," Sorin said, and then turned. "Ghet?"

Anowon opened one eye.

"Ghet, do you know the way from here to the Teeth of Akoum?"

The vampire's eye moved to the head man and stayed there. "Not precisely," Anowon said.

Sorin addressed the head comber. "You will come with us and act as a guide. You will bring another . . ." Sorin turned to Anowon and asked, "Two?"

Anowon nodded.

Sorin turned back to the comber. "Bring two of your associates," he continued. "One of them might be eaten by the end. I feel I must tell you."

"And if we refuse?" the comber said. He spoke very calmly, without fear or uncertainty. Nissa found she liked him for that.

"If you refuse, then we will destroy all of you," Sorin said, jerking his thumb over his shoulder at Anowon. "And he will turn you into nulls."

They spent that night at the top of the cliff, protected from the nearly continuous wind by a huge crystal lying on its side. In the morning two of the beach combers had gone, and the others got together to decide which of them would accompany the party.

The head man volunteered, as did a merfolk who Nissa had not seen at first. The rest of the combers said hasty goodbyes and left, disappearing into the rocks. Sorin and Nissa noticed how brief their parting words had been.

"If I were you," Sorin said, turning to the two remaining combers, "I would have told my associates to meet us somewhere up the trail. Maybe a loose boulder could be pushed. Maybe there is a certain ledge or hole only you people know about. No?"

The two combers stood looking down at their shabby sandals made of what Nissa took to be dulam hide stitched to other, older pieces of the same hide. Their shins and knees were wrapped with the same material.

"Is that what you were talking about before they left?" Sorin asked.

"No," the headman said. He stood up tall. Nissa thought he really was a fine specimen of a human, despite his thick, black beard. Growing a beard was an ability human males seemed to relish, for most of the human males she had seen displayed some type of one. The head man's beard was long enough that it touched his chest. "You have my word," he said. "We spoke of no such thing."

Smara muttered to herself off behind a crystal. One of the goblins cooed at her. Sorin narrowed his eyes at the head man.

"You are an interesting human," Sorin said. "I feel there is more to you than meets the eye."

The head man said nothing.

"Perhaps it is the first blood," Sorin said as he squatted before the head man, as one might with a child. "Your people were some of the first in this place. You and the kor. Now the vampires," Sorin said, brushing his hand in the direction of Anowon. "They are relative newcomers. The merfolk too."

He was speaking in the same tone he had used to tell Nissa of the Eldrazi titans, still buried in the rock. What Sorin had not told her was why he knew all of this about old Zendikar. Could he have been on Zendikar in the first place, to see the old races and know about the vampires of old? And how old would that make him? she wondered.

Without bothering to reply, the head man turned and slowly began to walk, with the merfolk who had also volunteered following close behind. They stopped and shouldered the supplies that the other combers had left.

Nissa pulled on the pack that Khalled had prepared for her in Graypelt. Sorin brushed off his hands and walked behind Nissa. Smara tripped after them, with a goblin fore and aft as she walked. Anowon followed last, turning a metal cylinder and running his fingers over it as he walked.

They walked up a series of small rises until they stopped at the top of the last one. Stretched out before them was Akoum. Below lay a rick of hedrons of all sizes jumbled together, with most being many times larger than any Nissa had ever seen. A mist sat low on the land, obscuring the ground, but in many of the cracks of the hedrons, Nissa could see the faint pink glow of molten rock. Scattered among the fields were crystals, some of them as large as the hedrons. They fit so close together, there was hardly a space between them. Broken bits of hedron stones floated above the larger hedrons.

"How do we move through *that*?" said Nissa.

"There is a way," the head man said. He looked until he saw what he wanted. The group made their way over to where the constitutent parts of a shattered large hedron were floating just above the ground. The head man took a bit of dulam rope and fashioned it into a lasso. He waved them to a larger chunk of the hedron, and carefully they climbed onto it and clung as it bobbed.

Then the head man scaled the chunk of hedron. He stood atop it and swung the lasso until its loop went around a nearby tip of a hedron. Then the head man pulled. At first nothing happened. Then slowly the rock began to move. When it moved past the hedron he'd lassoed, the head man yanked the loop off and swung the lasso onto another hedron and pulled again. Their hedron moved a bit faster. Soon they were floating at a walking pace over the hedrons in the fields.

"We dare go no faster," the man said. "Some of these stones are higher than others, and we may need to slow to dodge one of them."

"How long does this rock field continue?" Nissa asked.

The man turned to her and blinked.

They traveled in such a way for three days. Another of the goblins disappeared in that time, as did the merfolk who had come with the head man. Anowon made no pretense. He shrugged when Nissa found the goblin's left sandal hanging near the edge of the hedron.

The head man had already shared the meager tack he had. He looked at Nissa and pointed ahead.

"The land changes ahead and there should be game," he said.

Nissa looked. There seemed to be no end to the hedron and crystal fields. The horizon was dotted with more floating hedrons. She knew she could rig a snare or some form of trap if they could only find a place where living things could be found. She glanced at the head man again. "He said the terrain is about to change," she said to the others.

Anowon, who was nearby, looked past her at the head man pulling on the rope looped around his chest and arms.

"The man is Eldrazi feed," Anowon said.

Nissa did not know what to say.

Anowon continued. "His people were the feed of the Eldrazi."

"I thought they did not eat like we eat?"

"True," Anowon said. "They live on pure mana. But they had my people collect energy by feeding, and then tapped us."

"Why?"

"Our blood condenses mana," Anowon said. Nissa edged closer a bit, as much as she dared. "Our blood is a sort of distillate of the mana from every victim. The Eldrazi beasts kept us for that sole purpose."

"And the hooks?" Nissa said, pushing her luck, she knew.

But the vampire smiled faintly, something Nissa had almost never seen him do. He looked down at the hooks that extended from his elbow.

"For labor. They could strap us into their harnesses all day, let us feed, and then tap us all night," Anowon said. "The arrangement was wonderful . . . for them."

"You said *was*," Nissa said. "But the brood do the same thing. That is how we found you in the Turntimber."

"But they were copying their masters. They did not know how to strap us in. I virtually had to show them."

"How did you know?"

The vampire looked out over the hedrons. "Some memories are kept alive, by the Bloodchiefs."

Bloodchiefs were the very old vampires. "You were created by a Bloodchief?" Nissa said. Anowon was of that lineage, of course—not your normal shadow creeper.

"Yes," Anowon said. "My Bloodchief was an original slave. She told me about the hooks. She told me about The Mortifier, the first vampire who sold his own kind to the Eldrazi as slaves." Anowon looked out at the hedrons. Nissa looked down.

The sun crossed the sky, and by late afternoon the hedrons had started to become less frequent as the land split into deep canyons. The trenches radiated away on all sides and echoed with strange calls.

CHAPTER 13

Each canyon was almost a league wide and many more deep, and composed of dark gray rocks covered with crags. The canyons were not empty, however. The tops of vast pillars formed a patchwork level with the top of the canyon. Branches from vines and trees climbing up and around the pillars filled the spaces between them with dense growth. The top of each pillar was covered with grass or rock, and raw crystals protruded through some.

Standing some leagues away was a pillar larger than the rest. It did not originate in a canyon, but stood on flat ground atop a raised hill. Even from a distance, the strange, geometric designs that covered the tower drew their eyes. As they watched, a loud grinding sound filled the air and the tower began to move. Like an immense puzzle, shapes poked out of the tower as its sides shifted. When its angles had rearranged themselves into an altogether different configuration, the protruding shapes snapped back into place, and the tower was still.

The crumbled hedron that they had been riding slowly came to a stop. They stood and stared at the huge tower.

"Tal Terig," Sorin said. "Where the Eldrazi buried

their dead. We will skirt well around that place, I think."

The head man stopped coiling his rope. "The path into the mountains lies behind the puzzle tower. We have to pass near it to enter."

The mountains extended away to the right and left. Nissa had a moment to look at the tower. Something about it seemed impossibly wrong: its angles appeared off somehow, as though it was suddenly top heavy and might fall at any moment. As she watched, the tower started to grind and squeak and rearrange itself.

"That sound has brought woe to many an archeaomancer's ears," Anowon said. "The tower is full of unimaginable treasures . . . ancient weapons too deadly for the Eldrazi beasts, it is said. But the halls are riddled with magical traps of every clever devising, and every time the sun changes its angle, the tower rearranges itself, guaranteeing that the halls you have just memorized and the traps you have just uncovered are forever changed so you do not know them anymore. Beings that know their way through those towers are uncommon in the extreme."

"Something is there," Nissa said. She squinted, and noticed many tiny figures milling around the base of the tower.

"Brood, yes?" Sorin said, looking back at the ocean, not at the tower. He slowly turned around.

"Yes, brood," Nissa said. "A very great host of them."

Everybody stared at the tower and the huge dark splotch, clearly visible, of brood milling at its base.

"What are they doing?" Nissa said.

"Seeking egress, I should think," Sorin said. "They know it is the burial place of their masters, and they want to enter."

Nissa made note of how Anowon's pale eyes trained on Sorin as he spoke. His face clearly betrayed his disbelief.

"Can they enter?" Nissa said.

"Doubtful," Anowon said, pulling his eyes away form Sorin. "Very doubtful. The entrance shifts. The door is obscured and locked with powerful magic. There are some that have found the door and ventured within. From them we know that the tower you see extending above the ground is but a fraction of the its true length. Most of it is underground."

Nissa could hardly imagine. "It must be a league deep!" she said.

"Yes," the head man interjected. "And the mountains lie on the other side of it. I have only traveled as far as the tower. Past that I do not know the way. Perhaps you do not need me anymore?"

"You do not have leave," Sorin said.

Suddenly Nissa heard a whoosh. She turned and had a brief look at the floating creatures that swept down on them: large brood with masses of tentacles extending from funguslike bodies composed of pocketed lattices. One brood's long, split arms reached out.

Nissa had only a moment. She sucked mana from the æther and concentrated on making her self appear as a patch of dirt to the flying brood. Her camouflage spell had been effective before, but this time the brood made a guess as to where she was squatting, and snatched her off the hedron despite her spell.

Nissa was flying through the air with thick tentacles wrapped around her. She had to struggle to move her head enough to get a good breath, and even after she did, she could not see or speak. She felt the air rushing on the backs of her calves.

The tentacle wrapped around her face smelled like dirt and rock dust, and she could feel the blood pulsing through it. Nissa thrashed against the tentacle, but it seemed only to tighten, so that by the end she was barely able to pull in a breath at all.

She flew like that for a time, and then the brood holding her suddenly jerked. It spasmed three more times, and as the tentacle around her face went limp, Nissa began to freefall through the air.

It should have been a common enough feeling for Nissa, but she could only think of childhood nightmares as she spiraled toward the sharp surface of Akoum.

Her impact was sudden and punctuated with the sickening crack of bone. She found herself rolling with the sun filling her eyes and the colors blurring.

Nissa rolled over and cast a wary eye around. She stood. The bodies of five other floating brood were strewn over the top surface of one of the columns in the canyon. Arrows with fletches made from the stiff leaves of some unfamiliar green plant stuck out of them. Nissa fell into a crouch and ducked behind the body of the brood that had been carrying her. She looked around.

She had crashed quite near the tower. She could see the different sizes of the brood milling around the base of Tal Terig, and see the holes they had dug. Some brood were bent over the holes or moving their tentacles in the air above the holes. *Doing what, exactly?* Nissa wondered. She looked around hoping to catch a glimpse of the bows that had struck down the brood.

But instead she saw Sorin and Smara tossed in the grass near the brood that had been carrying them. As she watched, Sorin rolled over. She waved to him, and he began crawling toward her. She heard a groan and saw Anowon stumbling in her direction. When he was near, she grabbed his cloak and yanked him down. She brought her finger up to her lips and listened.

The breeze stirred the clump of grass next to her. The dead brood's tentacle twitched once. Anowon leaned against the flank of the creature, and when Sorin finally crawled the distance to them, he also leaned back.

Nissa could neither see nor hear anything moving. But whatever had shot the brood was waiting somewhere nearby. The gap between pillars was the height of a man. Nothing moved except the grass caught in the wind.

One of Smara's goblins stumbled over to Smara's insensate form, the other perhaps lost to the gaps. The goblin took her gently under the armpits and swore under its breath as it pulled the mad kor to where Nissa and the others were squatting behind the dead brood.

"Where is the human guide?" Anowon asked the goblin.

Sorin rolled over and looked at Anowon, who was watching Smara. "You only want to know where the human is because you want to feed on him," Sorin said.

The goblin did not reply. Instead it propped Smara against the cooling beast and began fanning her face. The kor stirred, and her eyes popped wide.

"The titans stir," she said quite clearly.

Anowon said nothing. Sorin stood.

A movement caught Nissa's eye. "Look there," she said. Nissa saw the tip of what looked like a bow disappear behind the edge of a pillar. They all turned to look. When the bow did not reappear they waited. But there was no bow, no movement of any sort.

"Do not move rapidly," said a voice from behind. Nissa turned. A small force of elves was arrayed behind them, with bows drawn and nocked arrows trained. Nissa immediately recognized the arrow fletches of their shafts as the same ones sticking out of the dead brood.

"Throw down your weapons," said a female elf with a strange accent. Nissa could not place it. She could not tell what kind of elves they were—their skin was darker then hers, and they were shorter and stockier. Their bows glittered in the sun, and Nissa realized with a start that they were constructed of some wood she had never seen before.

"Who are you?" Nissa said.

"Close your mouth, foreigner," said the female elf. "Throw down your staff."

Nissa let her staff fall with a thump. Sorin slowly took his great sword out and laid it carefully on the grass. Anowon kept staring down.

The elf commander turned her head. "Collect the weapons and bind the vampire's hands," she said. "Drag the human out from under the tentacled menace."

An elf collected Nissa's staff. Nissa watched him move. He was muscled like a human and harnessed as heavily as a kor. There were scars all over the exposed skin of his hands and face, and the tip of his right ear was missing, replaced by a thick edge of scar tissue.

The elves all crouched as they worked. The commander kept her eyes on the sky, holding a nocked arrow in her bow. She was as scarred as the other elves, and her eyes glowed.

Nissa's eyes lingered on the mass of brood moving around the base of the tower. They looked as though they were building something. A square wooden form was clearly visible in their midst.

"What are they doing there?" Nissa asked.

The commander turned and took a quick look at Nissa before looking away again. "They are preparing an attack," she said, simply.

The elf pressed Sorin and Nissa's weapons into the commander's hand. *Was that really everything we have? No wonder we captured by the elves*, she thought.

The elf commander turned Nissa's staff in her hands. Her fingers detected the seam and pulled, then twisted.

"Be careful with that," Nissa warned.

A drum started beating at Tal Tarig, and once it started, others pulsed behind it. The elf commander twisted the staff back together and turned. "We go," she said.

They were crowded together into a tight group by the elves. The human was there too. The commander broke into a run and launched herself into the air at the end of the pillar, landing on the other pillar top. One by one, each of them jumped the pillar gap. Nissa looked down when she jumped and saw the deep undergrowth of the trees and shrubs that grew between the pillars, and below them a long, long fall into darkness.

When it was Anowon's turn to jump, the elves jabbed his ribs with the tips of their bows. "Run, blood slurper," they hissed. "Run, run." Anowon took a running start and easily jumped the gap, but an elf shoved him as he landed. Trying to regain his balance, Anowon spun, tripped, and went sprawling in the grass of the pillar. The elves broke into peals of laughter at this humiliation.

Nissa closed her eyes so as not to watch Anowon, hands bound, struggle to his feet. *Did he not deserve the ridicule?* she thought. He was a vampire after all—a merciless vampire. He could not be trusted. On the other hand, he had conducted himself fairly, and who could blame him for feeding on the goblins, who were, after all, barely lifeforms. They were not children of the forest, but rather opportunists of the stone and dell.

In fact, Nissa reflected, most times Anowon was a scolar. He had not chosen this affliction of vampirism.

The elves lined them up, and they all jumped the next gap between the pillars. They jumped again and again, until everyone was at the other side of the canyon. With Tal Terig grinding itself into different positions behind them, they made their way through the rocky outcroppings that puckered at the edge of the canyon. Without the elves, the maze of rocky hills and crystals would have been impassable. But throughout the remaining daylight, the elves walked ahead and behind.

The sun was halfway below the skyline when the commander elf raised her hand and all the elves stopped. The commander looked behind and in all directions. Using her foot she brushed a patch of ground bare. Then she bent over and with her hands cleared away the branches and brush that had been pushed into the dusty soil. She revealed a hole, and without a word lowered herself into it, disappearing.

One by one the others followed. When it was Nissa's turn, she lowered herself down and felt ladder rungs. She descended the ladder in the dark, with the blotch of daylight above her head filled with the dark shadows of elves climbing down after her.

They climbed through the ground for so long that the hole that they had climbed through became a tiny dot and then disappeared completely. The elf above Nissa kept stepping on her fingers or putting his foot on the top of her head. The wooden ladder creaked in the small tunnel, swaying slightly.

A patch of light appeared below. It grew larger, and the elves below her were exiting though it. Nissa put her foot through the hole and crawled out onto sand. The light was too bright at first, and Nissa closed her eyes. When she was able to open them, she saw that they were in the bottom of a dry basin. Crystals poked out of the ground with their tips touching.

The elf commander started walking, and the others followed. They walked along the dusty basin until it was deep dark and the various night birds had arrived and were swooping around above their heads, snatching the singing gnats and piercer midges out of the air.

Anowon tripped, and one of the elves delivered a kick to the vampire's forehead that knocked him sprawling. The vampire rose and began walking again. The elf next to Nissa chuckled.

Then Nissa noticed something strange. The elf that had kicked Anowon was glowing. She looked closer. His veins were glowing. She looked at the other elves. Not all of them had veins that glowed, but many of them did. Some of their eyeballs also glowed.

Nissa turned to the elf that had kicked Anowon. His face was a spider web of glowing veins. "Why do you glow?" Nissa asked.

The elf put his hand over his mouth. A moment later the ground began to shake.

The shaking became violent. The vial of water around Nissa's neck began to boil telling her that the Roil was occurring. She threw herself on the ground, wishing more than ever for her staff.

A moment later the ground split open like ripe fruit. Amid the dramatic shaking, Nissa could see the orange glow of magma in the crack. She attempted to roll away from the fissure but only succeeded in bouncing back and hitting her head hard on the ground. For a moment Nissa lost consciousness, and when she woke a column of writhing magma was streaming upward out of the crack in the ground. It cooled to black rock almost immediately. In the next moment Nissa saw shoots peeking out of the basalt. Soon the spar was covered with the dense green fuzz of growing plants as the ground continued to shake. The plants grew until they covered the column.

The elf that had refused to speak to her before leaned close to her ear. "A life bloom," he said. "Truly we are blessed."

Nissa looked again at the strange living pillar. The ground stopped trembling, and the plants started moving in the wind. Well, maybe not blessed, she thought, but it was an interesting occurrence.

"How long will it last?" Nissa asked.

"Not more than a day," the commander elf said. "But you shall soon see one that has lasted over a hundred years." And with that, he turned and began walking.

Soon a different tower than Tal Terig appeared on the dark horizon. When they were nearer, Nissa saw that this one did not have the same smooth sides of the Puzzle Tower. Its irregular form stood out like a natural monument in the dry basin.

"Ora Ondar," the elf commander said. "The Impossible Garden."

Nissa knew the stories, as did every elf and most humans. Examples of every plant that grew on Akoum grew on a basalt tower that shot up out of the wastes. The tower was shaped similarly to the pillar that had formed after the lava Roil she'd seen, except Ora Ondar was larger.

As they neared, Nissa could see the fabled plants growing off the pillar in a lush cascade.

"Formed by the Roil more than a hundred years ago," the commander said. "And tended continuously by the Nourishers. Come."

She led them to a hole at the base of the tower. Stairs chiseled out of the black rock spiraled upward. Again, the commander led the way. Nissa noticed with a pang of alarm that the elves waited to go last, and that they did so with arrows nocked on their bowstrings. As the group walked up the staircase they passed doorways that led out into the rooms where the plants grew. Each level of the tower seemed to grow another kind of plant. One level had only a plant that smelled like water and produced flowers as large as an elf. Another was all tall ferns. Yet another had plants with flowered mouth parts that lunged at the elf keepers who protected themselves with huge shields of skins stretched across frames.

"Where are we going?" Nissa asked.

The elf commander said nothing.

They climbed the spiral staircase until Nissa's thighs burned and she was huffing with exertion. On the top level, the sky was dark and huge. A group of elves with crystal lanterns was busy picking something off the small trees that grew there—a white fruit that glowed slightly as it hung off the boughs.

The elves that had come behind up the spiral staircase pushed the group forward with their short bows. Soon a figure stepped out from behind a tree. He was an older elf with fruits in each of his hands. As they watched he took a large bite out of one of the fruits. Juice ran down the corners of his mouth as he gave a wide grin. His teeth glowed. His eyeballs glowed. His unkempt hair looked like a snipe falcon's nest on his head. He smiled again.

"I had a dream last night," the figure said. "In this dream a voice said, 'Ser Amaran?' and I said 'yes?' " Ser Amaran took another bite out of the fruit in his right hand. He chuckled as though he had just remembered a good joke, and more juice ran from the corners of his mouth. The he frowned, and his whole face seemed to fall. "This voice told me that Ora Ondar would fall. The voice told me that our sacred kolya fruit would be scattered across the barren waste that the Eldrazi will make of our world . . . those parasites in the deep." His glowing eyes flashed from Nissa, to Sorin, to Smara, to Smara's goblin, and finally rested on Anowon.

"You have all been captured for being too close to the forbidden tower," the elf chief said. "What were you doing there?"

Nobody said anything.

"Speak. Or are you minions of the tentacled creatures with the beautiful hearts?"

Nissa looked out the corner of her eye at Anowon, but the vampire's face had the same perplexed look she imagined she had. *Beautiful hearts?*

"Very well, do not tell me," he said, taking another bite of the fruit in his hand. "But I will know this vital piece of information. An odd party such as yours clearly does not travel for pleasure. You are spies, of course. Vampire spies for the tentacled invasion.

The elf commander hurried forward and whispered in the chief's ear. Ser Amaran turned his head as the commander spoke, but he did not take his eyes off Anowon.

"Lock them away, all of them. At dawn throw the bloodied one from the grove, and feed his crushed body to the slaughter shrubs. Throw the guide to the salt flats."

CHAPTER 14

Nissa, Sorin, Smara, and her goblin were thrown into cells carved out of the basalt. They tried to sleep, but the spiny floor would not allow them.

Anowon was in another cell, and all that night the stone door of the cell opened and closed, opened and closed. Once Nissa heard Anowon moan. But aside from that, there was no sound from inside the cell.

"We have to free him," Nissa said.

Sorin shrugged. "Vampires do not fear pain or death," he replied.

"He is not that way," Nissa said.

Sorin turned to her and raised his eyebrows. "He is not what exactly? A vampire?"

"He is not that *kind* of vampire."

Sorin smiled. "He's the kind that wanted to drain you before I dissuaded him."

The door of Anowon's cell slammed shut.

"But he is our only guide," Nissa said. "The human is gone."

Sorin said nothing.

The goblin coughed and glanced at Smara. "I know the way," the goblin said. "To Teeth of Akoum."

They both turned to the goblin, who had not spoken

since Smara had bumbled into their camp in the Makindi Trench.

Smara also stared at the goblin, who clapped its claw over its mouth.

Sorin turned back to Nissa. "You see, there is our new guide."

"But Anowon saw how the brood was released. Perhaps he knows how to put them back?"

Sorin's smile dropped a jot. "The vampire does not know how to put the brood back," he said. "You can trust me."

The door to Anowon's cell opened. Someone laughed as they exited his cell. Then the cell door slammed again. She could understand some of what the strange elves were saying. Two were talking about "the fruit eater" whoever that was.

"Who is this Ser Amaran from the grove of fruit trees?" Nissa said.

Sorin waved his hand. "Some minor figure."

"Anowon would know who Ser Amaran is," Nissa said.

Sorin snorted. "We should be more concerned with how we are going to get out of this cell."

"When they open the door, you can use your rot talk to destroy them."

"I cannot risk that . . . not with this many crystals and lava rock around. The sound could echo. And nobody wants that."

"Then I will have to end whoever opens the door," Nissa said.

"Perhaps if there is one guard or two," Sorin said. "But six? I think not."

Nissa pushed her chin out. "I am Joraga," she said.

"You are unarmed," Sorin said. "Anyway, I don't think they plan to let us out."

"They have to some day."

"Do they?" Sorin said. "Did you happen to notice what the kolya trees were growing in? Or were you too busy watching the minor elf stuffing his mouth with his sacred fruit?"

"I did not notice anything unusual about the bed the trees were growing in. This pillar is the remains of a life bloom Roil. Did you not hear the elf?"

Nissa waited for Sorin's response.

"Yes," Sorin replied. "But I also heard her say that most life blooms last a day or two at the most."

Nissa's trap had worked: Sorin had been listening. He had good ears for a human, as she had been at the end of the line and he'd been the first. She would have to watch him closer. Humans did not have ears capable of hearing a whispered conversation from half a mile away. That was an elf's ability . . . or a vampire's.

"I saw bones protruding from the soil under the trees," Sorin said.

"Bones?" Nissa said. Could elves do something like that—kill and bury beings to ensure their plants lived? *Sure,* she thought. Her own people often killed any sentient beings they found in their forest, regardless of species. If these Nourisher elves tied their way of being, their tribal identity, with those trees, then they would do any sort of thing to ensure that they thrived and prospered.

"Yes, bones," Sorin said. "If they are to use us for fertilizer, why not kill us here in this cell with poison?"

Nissa looked down at the empty bowl of gruel her jailer had shoved at her. She'd eaten it all without a word, gagging slightly at the grubs which she had seen the elves picking off the kolya leaves earlier that day. But at least she had known they were fresh.

"Then we need to free ourselves quickly and rescue Anowon," she said.

"Are we not back to the discussion we were having before?" Sorin said.

From far away Nissa heard the low drone of a horn. It was a tremendous dusty sound, the loudness of which increased then dropped off then built again to a crescendo. She heard the sound of thick-soled sandals shuffling in the hallway.

"What was that?" Sorin said.

"Death," Smara said, suddenly. "Death, death, death, death."

"Hush," Nissa said. She listened to the horn for a while longer. "A signal horn. They use a similar code to the Tajuru—a force approaching."

"Well, we must get out now," Sorin said. He cast his eyes around the cell. They had been over the cell in the daylight and found nothing. The simple bench was carved out of the wall, and there was no window. The solid door was the very piece the builders had cut to make the doorway, presumably. It fit into the doorway so snugly that Nissa could not see light at the seams.

Sorin got to his knees before the door to look at the lock. After a moment of inspection he inserted his long first finger into the keyhole and drew it out again.

"If the door were wood," he said, "if it had ever been alive, I might have had some enchantments that could putrefy it or make it an entity for us to command." Sorin pushed on the door, and when it did not move he strode over to the bench and sat down.

Nissa bent down for a look in the keyhole. She'd heard the elf unlock and lock the door three times—when he and the others put them in the cell at Ser Amaran's order, and the two times they had been brought food. She had never heard the jingle of keys, or the scrape of metal on metal, or metal on rock. They were elves after all. If she were to design a lock, it would not feature metal . . . a useful but untrustworthy creation. She would use something natural. Nissa looked into the lock hole again.

The hole was dark, or course. But Nissa could see clearly enough the hallway on the other side of the door. There was no keyhole shape to the hole, just a circle. *What kind of key would fit a circle?* she wondered.

One thing was certain: the cell had not been built to hold elves. Either the occupants of the Impossible Garden never thought they would imprison an elf, or there were other cells for elves elsewhere in the tower. The door was very small, and Nissa concluded that the cell had been built in all likelihood for goblins. Even the cruellest elf would leave a window if he knew elves were being held. Not being able to see and smell the outside world was paramount to the most inhumane torture for an elf. No, their cell had not been built for elves.

Nissa looked into the hole again. Silent figures passed in the hallway. Inside the lock's hole the opening from keyhole to keyhole was absolutely smooth. She pushed her finger into the hold and felt a sensation. The feeling was neither hot nor cold, but buzzed slightly.

"There is a field of power here," Nissa said.

Sorin rolled his eyes. "You are coming to that realization only now?" he said.

Nissa ignored him. "Goblin," she said. "Have you looked? You are of the Lava Steppe Tribe, are you not?"

The lead goblin stood and walked to the lock. He did not glance at Nissa. With a grunt he bent and peered in the rock. He looked up at Nissa, then back at the lock, and then back at Nissa, before shrugging.

They heard footsteps approaching in the hall. Soon something was inserted into the keyhole from the other side, and the door swung out into the hallway. A force of six armed elves strode in. They had bright bladed scimitars and armor composed of pieces of chipped slate wired together.

Nissa could smell the fear on them, and it smelled like warm copper coins. She peered closely at them. *They are not afraid of us,* she realized as their eyes jumped toward the hallway. The lead elf tucked something into a pocket in his robe. A key, Nissa supposed. He closed the door and frowned at Nissa.

Sorin took a deep breath. Nissa saw what was to happen, and she just had time to clap her hands over her ears. A moment later a string of rasping, somehow vile sounding words emanated from Sorin's open mouth. Many of the words came with a guttural boom from the back of his throat. Sorin snapped them off in such a way that his tongue clicked wetly in his mouth.

The effect was instantaneous. The elves fell dead and rotting a moment later. Nissa found herself on the basalt floor as well. The very room vibrated when she stood, as did the contents of her skull.

Sorin stood in the middle of the floor, cleaning his fingernails with his small eating knife, which he pointed at the mess on the floor. "Now," Sorin said. "Who will find the key in all that muck?"

The smell in the small cell was overwhelming. The sloughed bodies of the elves were already in an advanced state of decay, and just looking at them caused Nissa a bit of unease.

"I thought it was to risky too use your rot talk among the crystals?" Nissa asked.

"I decided it was a risk worth taking. Now, goblin . . . Fetch." Sorin pointed at where the head elf's slate-plate armor lay crumpled and wet.

The goblin looked at Sorin for a long moment as though he had not fully understood the language he was speaking. For a moment Nissa thought he would say something, but instead he blinked once and then stood and proceeded to the bodies.

It took some mucking about in the bodies, but finally the goblin produced the key and held it out to Sorin. The human eyed the dripping key warily.

"Well," Sorin gestured at the door. "Use it."

The goblin walked to the door, inserted the key in the hole, turned it, and . . . nothing. The key did not click in the lock, and the door did not open to either pushes or pulls.

Sorin threw up his arms. "Wonderful," he said.

The horns had grown louder. And Nissa thought she could hear something else: a deep growling, maybe. Like boulders dragged across a flat place.

Sorin took the key between two pinched fingers and tried it in the lock. It turned but would not open.

When it was Nissa's turn, she stood before the door and looked closely. The basalt was worn smooth around the keyhole, and a similarly smooth area was visible where the elves put their hands to push the door closed. There were also two patches on the floor where the elves' feet had worn it smooth. Nissa placed her sandaled feet in the smooth areas. She inserted the key and turned, and the door snapped open.

Sorin stood and moved to the door. He took a wary look out to make sure some of the scuffling feet they had been hearing in the hall were not passing. Smara was muttering under her breath behind Nissa as she slipped out of the cell. Sorin was standing in the middle of the hall. The doors of four similar-sized cells were visible in the light of the torches that sputtered in the hall. Nissa opened them all and found them to be empty until the last. Anowon was waiting, and he brushed by Nissa when the door opened. Without stopping, he walked down the hall, sweeping past Sorin.

"You could at least thank the elf, Ghet," Sorin said. "I would have left you."

Nissa followed Anowon, and the others followed her. They passed empty rooms, some with plates of warm-looking food still in them.

"Wait," Nissa said. She ducked into a room. Sorin's great sword and Nissa's staff were propped in a corner. She seized them and left.

The first attack involved something large hitting the tower. The tremor seemed at first like the Roil, until Nissa checked the vial of enchanted water hanging from her neck and saw it was not boiling. But the tower shook all the same. Anowon was some distance ahead, and they all ran to catch up. A brace of elves charged out of a room to Nissa's right, and Sorin drew his sword and cut them down where they stood. Their bodies were withered husks when Nissa stepped over them, and Sorin's sword pulsed deep and black. He sheathed its hungry blade, and they ran after Anowon.

Once free from the cells, they descended the stairs. On every level elves were among the plants shooting arrows out. Nissa saw forms flying through the night. On the level where the plants with mouths lived, Nissa watched as a plant snatched a flying brood lineage out of the air and chewed it down. She also saw eight elves pulled out of the bushes and dropped by flying brood.

Nissa stopped. "How are we going to get out of this tower?" she asked nobody in particular. But Anowon did not stop. He charged down the spiraling stairway. Soon they were at the second to last level—Nissa recognized the giant ferns—and she could see the assembled host. Their dark shapes extended far into the darkness. There were no torches and no battle cries—only the screams of elves pulled from their positions and the harmonic music of bowstrings released in *staccato*.

Nissa stopped again, taking Sorin's shoulder. "We cannot win if we step out through those doors," she said. Sorin nodded. Anowon was ahead, but Sorin ran after him and caught the vampire before he turned the spiral corner. Sorin spun Anowon around, and the look on Anowon's face made Nissa start. His lips were stretched back and showed his fangs. His eyes were red and narrowed, and blood was coming out of the corners of his eyes. He was crying blood.

None of that seemed to bother Sorin, who dragged Anowon back up the stairs as though he were a toy. Nissa threw down any elves they met with her staff. There was a tremendous collision, and the tower shuddered. Elf screams erupted from below.

"They've broken through," Nissa yelled.

The stairs ended, and Nissa and the others found themselves on a wide platform. Kolya trees grew in raised beds. Three brood were standing next to the stairway entrance, and Nissa charged through, tripping on the body of an elf and falling. She twisted her stem sword free and connected with the verdant energy of the Turntimber.

Mana moved through her and she camouflaged herself to a patch of basalt. The brood that had been descending on her pulled up and hovered above the entrance. The brood's head moved back and forth, searching for Nissa's form.

But the creature did not have long to look, for Anowon came through the doorway behind her and grabbed one of the brood's hanging tentacles. The creature tried to pull away, but the vampire punched the tentacle with his fist, and the creature fell dead. A glyph glowed red on the tentacle where Anowon had struck.

Sorin was next. The two remaining brood took a look at Sorin, tall and pale with his great sword unsheathed and glowing like the starry night sky, and they turned to fly. But a keening song came to Sorin's lips, and the brood froze midair and fell as lumps of flesh into the darkness below.

They turned to Anowon. In a moment the dead brood stirred and moved slowly back into the air. The Glyph glowed softly on the tentacle as it moved.

"Come," Anowon said. "This will fly us down."

Nissa's skin itched seeing the effects of Anowon's vampire-rapture.

Another tremendous impact shook the tower. That was enough to dispel any unease Nissa had about the zombie brood. At Anowon's command, the creature wrapped one tentacle around her waist and stepped off the edge of the tower. The flying brood lineage could not fly normally while holding all five of them in its tentacles, but it controlled itself enough and glided fast toward the ground in a sort of controlled freefall. As they passed, Nissa could see that each of the tower's ledges held hundreds of roosting brood. In the starlight Nissa could see the land around the base of the tower. Six massive brood had planted their shoulders against the tower and were pushing it back and forth.

The zombie brood held them tightly as it glided far out into the night on wings of flesh. It finally skidded to a landing in the dusty flats half a league from the tower.

Anowon took a deep breath, and his jaw tightened as he gnashed his teeth. The veins in his neck stood out, and the muscles in his cheeks and arms clenched. A series of grunts emanated from deep in the vampire's throat, and when he opened his eyes they were red and without pupils. He looked at the null brood, and the creature dropped dead.

In a normal situation, Nissa would have felt a bit of pity for the dead brood. Nothing deserved what a vampire gave. But there was no time for pity. The night spread on all sides. Nissa turned and realized her pathwaystone was back in the tower, as was the pack that Khalled had given her.

"I do not know what direction we should travel," Nissa said.

Anowon was in a similar quandary, Nissa could tell. The vampire was looking at the stars, trying to gain his direction. His blood tears had dried on his cheeks and flecked off. But the curl to his lip had not disappeared. He jerked his hand up and pointed. "That way is west," he said. "It is somewhere there."

"Ghet?" Sorin said. "You told me you were at the Eye of Ugin. How can you be unsure how to travel to the Teeth of Akoum, Ghet?"

Anowon looked hard at the smiling Sorin. Both sides of his mouth curled back, and he spoke in a voice as menacing as any Nissa had ever heard. "Having visited a location is different than knowing the way there," the vampire said.

"Ghet," Sorin said, his face clearly showing his mock disapproval. "You have lied to us, and we demand an apology."

Smara's goblin looked from one to the other of them, then at Smara. "I know the way," he said.

Nobody said anything. Smara cocked her head and stared at the goblin as though she'd only just noticed him for the first time.

"You?" Sorin said. "Again?"

All eyes were on the goblin, and he swallowed hard before speaking. "I was in the Teeth for my mistress," the goblin said, motioning at Smara. She had suddenly become quiet, listening to the goblin speak. "My mistress sent me through the Cypher of Flames to find the Eye of Ugin and return with a path to it. We were traveling to the eye when the fates of the ancient ones put us in your path."

"The ancient ones?" Sorin said. "Do you mean to think that the Eldrazi sent us to you?"

The goblin clapped its clawed hands over its ears. It peered at the dark sky from under a furrowed brow. "You must not speak the ancients' name," it said.

"The gift is in the loam," Smara said, her pupilless eyes staring up at the sky.

"Yes, the gift in the wherever," Sorin said. He turned to the goblin. "Well, lead on then," he said.

"Wait," Anowon said. The vampire had advanced on the goblin and was not less than an arm's length away. "I did not see you. I did not smell you," he said.

"But I saw you, vampire," the goblin said. "I saw you held outside the doors as the magic wielders fought. And the dragon. And I saw you . . ."

"That is enough," Anowon said, holding up his hand.

A sly smile spread across the goblin's dry, cracked lips. "The vampire does not want me to speak of what I saw?"

"You will remain quiet, or you will sleep with your friends."

The goblin bowed, turned on the ball of its right foot, and pointed into the darkness. "The Teeth of Akoum lie there."

They walked all that night. The wind that blew across the flats was cold, and soon Nissa's teeth were chattering. But when the sun rose, the flats heated quickly. By the time the sun fell shining in their eyes, the ground was so hot that none dared stop, for fear that their sandals might start ablaze. The goblin was the exception—its feet were the color of rock and seemed as thick and as hoary as dulam hide.

For three days they walked. At the goblin's request they traveled at night until the land split into shallow canyons with long-dried stream beds at their bottom.

Anowon remained in a dark mood. He traveled far behind the others and began to lose weight. There was nothing for him to eat, as Sorin slept next to Smara and the goblin, knowing that if they lost the goblin they would all be lost and at the mercy of the crystal flats.

To make matters worse, there had been no water since they had found a hedron plant, a low gray plant covered with thorns and roughly shaped like a hedron. They'd found it in a low draw, and without a moment's hesitation, Nissa had cut the top off. They had scooped out the pith and sucked the water from it. That had been the day before. At that moment, Nissa's tongue felt so large from lack of water that she could barely close her mouth.

Nissa and the goblin topped the bank of an arroyo and saw shapes moving on the flat before them. Nissa squinted at the moving shapes, but the sun was in her eyes, and she could not see well.

"Brood?" Nissa said. "Goblin, is it them?"

The goblin looked at the movement. "Mudheel," it said. "I have told you. My name is Mudheel. Or will you not like to speak the name of a goblin? I am not some Saltskull. I have a brain and a tongue, and I know how to use them."

"You are certainly the most unusual goblin I have ever met," Nissa said.

"Mudheel, my name is Mudheel," the goblin said, bowing mockingly. "If it pleases my lady."

"Mudheel," Nissa said. "What I said before."

Mudheel looked to the flats. "It is the City that Walks. The Goma Fada Caravan."

"Does it have water?"

"I do think," Mudheel said. "If not they would die in this waste. A body needs water."

"Thank you, Mudheel. I'll keep that in mind," Nissa said, struggling forward. Speaking hurt as much as walking, and her throat burned from talking to the goblin . . . to Mudheel. Still there was one question that was burning her as much as it had before, as much as the scorching air around them. Nissa turned to Mudheel.

"Why do you stay with this party as the other goblins have slowly disappeared?" Nissa asked. "Are you not afraid that you are next? Why have you not fled in the night?"

Mudheel turned to Smara. "She needs me."

Nissa waited for more.

"She is like a wife to me," Mudheel said.

A wife? Nissa thought. Of all the responses the goblin could have given, that was the one that Nissa had least expected.

"A wife?" Nissa said.

The goblin nodded and turned to look at Goma Fada. Nissa also turned toward the mobile city, her mind reeling from what Mudheel had said. *A kor and a goblin?* she thought. Nissa understood then why they traveled. Either of their people would strike them down for being together. Suddenly Nissa felt pity for Mudheel, but also shuddered at the though of their unnatural coupling. *Goblins!* she thought.

In the bright glare she could barely make out hundreds of small buildings, some with pointed roofs and others with flat. Large dulam beasts were pulling the buildings.

The Goma Fada Caravan was slow moving and they made their hobbling way to it just as the sun was fading. It was a huge caravan, composed of hundreds and hundreds of enormous wagons. Each cart held a small building of wood or mud. One that Nissa saw was a small stone holdfast with turrets and a portcullis. Some of the carts were long and flat and pulled by braces of dulam beasts. Those were filled with dirt and plants. One such cart had a small grove of fig trees growing in it.

A flock of birds flying above the caravan cried out as the party approached. Soon a merfolk riding a slim beast rode out to meet them. He pulled up on the reins, and the animal snorted and stopped. Nissa noticed that the bit and bridle were studded. She had never liked bits and bridles. She was not sure she liked the merfolk rider, either.

He was dressed in long flowing white robes. A hood was pulled up over his head to keep the sun out. His lips, painted to accentuate their natural blue, pulled tight into a mirthless smile. His green eyes glinted beneath the shadow of his hood. "Yes?" he said.

"We mean no harm," Nissa said. Suddenly the sun felt very heavy on her shoulders. She took a step, and the world moved its alignment. She touched the vial around her neck, but it was not boiling. "We are in need of water," she said.

The rider looked from her to Sorin, to Smara, to Mudheel, and finally to Anowon, where his eyes stayed. "The vampire is not welcome," he said. "But I will be the benefactor for the rest of you. Do you have coin? Strangers must have a benefactor to enter the caravan. There are no exceptions. Hurry, the Caravan Sheriff will arrive shortly."

Nissa waited for Sorin to speak. When he did not, she opened her mouth. "We have no coins," she said. "But we have items of power."

The merfolk rider waited. "If you say hedron chips I will call the Sheriff myself right now," he said.

Nissa thought desperately for something they could barter with. "We have teeth," she said.

"Teeth?"

"Magic teeth."

"Let me see," the merfolk said.

Nissa turned to Anowon, who was scowling. "The teeth are owned by the vampire," she said.

"Perhaps he can enter if properly bound. Let me see these teeth," the merfolk repeated. He held out his hand, palm up. "What kind are they?" he asked. When Anowon did not move, the caravaner snapped his webbed fingers.

"They are merfolk teeth," Anowon said, and seized the emissary.

CHAPTER 15

The hardest part was hiding the body. Anowon had the sense to grab the merfolk and drag him between two carts to do what he did there, while the rest of them kept a look out. Nissa felt the bitter gorge rise in her throat as the merfolk thrashed. Amazingly, nobody in the caravan had seemed to notice. At least nobody had said anything. An if someone *had* seen Anowon drain the merfolk, they had not raised an alarm. It was the time of the day when people eat before the night comes, Nissa guessed, and the occupants of the caravans were inside.

Anowon disposed of the body by hoisting it and propping it against the side of a smooth adobe house built atop a wagon. The merfolk's legs hung over the side of the platform.

They walked into the midst caravan, where it was shady and strangely cool. A wagon with an immense tower built on a steel bed lumbered by. Two carts on a dray rocked and bobbed, each carrying a small crop of grain planted in straight rows. They wandered deeper into the caravan, hopping over the steaming dung piles left by the dulam beasts.

It appeared that the caravan never stopped moving. Beings tossed their privy pots from high windows.

Even a huge wagon, three of its steel-shod wheels turning and squeaking, was being repaired on the move—a wheeled jack held the corner up as a human hammered a new wheel onto its axle.

Soon they were in in the middle of what was a small village. Many small carts, each pulled by a male and a female human, traveled together, virtually touching edges as they rocked. On each cart was a small wattle hut, each identical to the one next to it. There were even guards. At four corners sentries stood, naked except for turntimber-bark armor. Each grasped the shellacked stalk of a vorpal weed.

Past the moving village, a strange beast with long white fur and twirled horns plodded with a group of humans and mermen surrounding it. There were two immense copper tanks strapped to its back. Two of the men wore various sized metal disks that clinked against each other as they walked. Each of the men had a cup on a lanyard around his neck.

"Water," one cried. "We have water."

Nissa looked down at her feet. Her boots were not worth much anymore, and she would need them. Still, if she did not have water soon . . . She turned to Anowon, who drew back the white hood of the cloak he'd taken from the merfolk. He held up his hand. Pinched between his fingers was a glowing tooth.

"Is it fresh?" Sorin croaked, through cracked lips.

Anowon smiled. "The teeth in that merfolk's mouth were not fit for magic. This is one of the original teeth."

"Whose are they?" Sorin said. "I've been curious all this time."

Anowon did not look at Sorin. "You will never know, Mortifier."

Sorin had been grinning, but when Anowon called him *Mortifier,* his smile disappeared.

In exchange for the tooth, the water vendors let them drink all the water they could from their cups. Then they turned a spigot on one of the tanks and shot a glistening stream of cool water into three new skins and gave them those. The water was piney tasting, flavored with Jaddi sap. It tasted like the finest thing Nissa had ever had in her life. Even better than a roasted thrak toad.

Nissa looked ahead, but could not see the end of the caravan. Buildings lumbered, and whips snapped. The smell was that of sweat and dung. The spicy dust blowing in between the wagons off the barren land mingled with the smoke from fires. Overhead a small creature, perhaps a young kor, was flying, being towed on a rope, with a pair of hide-and-wood wings strapped to its back. In the hard desert wind the winged creature dipped and soared, and the sun flashed off the reflective objects it wore.

Nissa took another deep drink and wiped her lips with the back of her hand.

"What did you mean by *Mortifier?"* Nissa said to Anowon. Anowon was watching Sorin walk some paces ahead.

"He knows what I mean," replied the vampire. "He knows. Did you see the expression on his face?"

"Knows what?"

"That I know he speaks the ancient dialect of the vampires."

"Oh," Nissa said.

"Yes," Anowon said. "His rot talk. It sounded strange at first, and then I consulted the cylinders. He rot talks in a language that appeared suddenly during the reign of the third Eldrazi titan. It did not evolve as most languages do. It had no precedent in other, earlier languages. It simply *appeared* in texts at exactly one time."

"So, where did it come from?" Nissa said.

Anowon smiled and shrugged. "Ask the Eldrazi," he said.

Nissa took another gulp of her excellent water. With each drink she felt more like herself. *"You* ask the Eldrazi," she said, smiling.

"I leave that to you, Nissa the elf," the vampire replied.

"I will tell them if you will answer this one question, Anowon of Ghet?"

Anowon held up his water skin and squeezed it, sending a concentrated stream of water into his open mouth.

"Why do the Eldrazi Titans have to be kept in the Eye of Ugin?" Nissa asked. "Perhaps they would flee if released, and this place would stop being so dangerous. Perhaps they would flee to another plane."

Nissa closed her mouth. She's said too much. She'd *assumed* that because of his knowledge he'd figured that bit of fact out, but apparently not.

But Anowon just continued walking, seeming to consider her words.

"I just meant Sejiri, in the north," Nissa said. "They could go there and leave the rest of Zendikar."

But Anowon was looking at the dry ground as he walked, keeping up with the rest of the caravan. His fingers moved down to one of the metal cylinders hanging from his belt.

"I just meant Sejiri," Nissa repeated. "You know. The region in the north?"

Still Anowon did not speak, but walked with his eyes on the ground and his fingers reading the ancient scripts copied on the cylinders that hung from his belt.

"I am aware that there are other planes of existence," he said, turning to her as he walked. "That certain creatures can travel between here and there."

Nissa felt the blood rush to her face. But Anowon was not done talking, and he began again before she could speak.

"The Eldrazi are clearly these types of beings. All the texts claim they came from nowhere. That they simply snapped into existence. Obviously they came from another plane."

"Obviously," Nissa repeated.

Over the next days, Anowon walked with the hood of his white robe pulled down low and his fingers moving slowly over a different cylinder. The caravan moved like a lumbering city over the dry pan. Nissa could see the fringe of a mountain range rising out of the haze at the horizon. As they had no coin, and Anowon simply did not answer questions leveled at him, they had no choice but to sleep where they could. One night Nissa slept in the window of a building pulled by dulam beasts. The next night she curled up in the fig grove as it shook and swayed in the starlight. On the fourth day they saw a dulam beast die. The large wheeled tent it had been pulling slowed a bit until another younger beast was led from the trailing herd trail and harnessed in. The other wagons simply turned to avoid the beast's carcass as a human bent and butchered it, slopping the meat and vital organs into a wheeled barrel.

One night Nissa was able to steal some grilled dulam sausage from a seller—the next day she found two loaves of bread rolling in the dust near the communal oven. The goblin took whatever she offered it, breaking the food in half and feeding part to Smara, who stared into the goblin's eyes as he fed her.

"What does she see in your eyes?" Nissa finally asked.

"The oracle sees the ghost she channels in my face," Mudheel said. "And she is content."

"Teeth of the dragon!" Smara blurted out.

Mudheel stroked the kor's hand. "Yes, we are going there. We are going."

But the caravan stopped later that day. Every cart, wagon, and dray slowed and then stopped. Nissa and Sorin walked past the wagons until they found the front of the caravan. The front wagon was stopped just behind an area of what looked like plants made of rock. The rock garden had maybe sixty plants, and some trees and each one was black and stone.

A human stood near them, leaning on a staff as he looked at the fossilized plants. Nissa watched is disbelief as a tear rolled down his cheek, leaving a trail in the grit and dust. "Beautiful is it not?" the man said. "Truly luck is with us. We will make the mountains by the day after the day after next, surely."

Nissa turned back to the formation, for that was surely what it was. "What is it?" she said.

"An igneous Glen, of course," the man said. When he saw she did not know the name he continued. "Caused when a lava Roil burns the site of a Roil bloom. This reminds me that plants grow here on this rock. The kor say they are sacred. It is truly a great omen. We need such omens now that the tentacled menace has sacked Ora Ondar."

"They have?" Nissa said. "Does it still stand?"

The man shrugged.

More humans and some mermen had gathered at the edge of the stone glen. Nissa even recognized a couple of elves with glowing eyes, and the white kolya fruit emblazoned on their flowing robes. The elves did not appear to be searching for anyone—their eyes

stayed on the bloom. *Refugees, possibly,* Nissa thought. Still, she would have to keep an eye out.

Each of the onlookers, Nissa noticed, acted as if they were in the presence of a miracle. One merfolk with his ankle fins unbound and his beard a scraggly mess fell to his knees and planted his face in the dust.

Nissa turned back to the strange forest—a monument to something that had once been alive and teeming, but was dead, cold, and no more than a sad memory. It was certainly nothing compared with the beauty of a true green growing place. The Roil had created it. And if she was to trust both Sorin's and Anowon's hints, Roils had more to do with a perversion of Zendikar's nature and more to do with Zendikar's desperate attempt to contain the Eldrazi in their restless slumber.

How could humans and merfolk find the garden beautiful? she asked herself. *Beautiful?* It was an abomination.

If the Eldrazi kept spreading like an alien plant, like the choking linnestrop Khalled had mentioned, they might devastate the wilderness to such a degree that such a garden would be the only nature many ever saw. The thought made Nissa's stomach twist and her nostrils flair.

She walked forward into the glen and started swinging her staff, hitting the fossilized remains of the plants and shattering them. They were more brittle than she could have hoped. In a matter of minutes the whole grove was reduced to shreds. A mermen rushed forward and seized her.

CHAPTER 16

The crowd yelled and cursed at Nissa as she was dragged out past the wagons and thrown down on the flatness. One of the mermen spit at her before he turned.

"I will never understand elves," Sorin said, evaluating his fingernails. "Such a confabulation of dirt worshipping notions.

The caravan began moving again and slowly went past. Nissa, Anowon, Sorin, Smara, and Mudheel squatted in the dust, with the hot wind snapping at their clothes. They had three skins half full of water, no food, and the red mountains on the horizon.

"How far might those be?" Sorin said. Like the others, he'd taken to wearing his hood up as protection from the sun and lashing a headband around it to keep the wind from gusting it off.

"Two days?" Nissa said.

Mudheel coughed and said, "Those are the Teeth of Akoum, and they are three days journey, I should say." The goblin put its hand above its eyes and peered at the mountains, which appeared to float above the ground on a pillow of air. "Or four. Yes, four days," it added.

"And we possess how much water?" Sorin asked.

"Three skins," Anowon said. "Half empty."

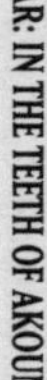

Every member of the expedition figured how much water they would need for a four day walk in the wastes. Each put that number against how much water they actually had. The silence that followed left nobody in doubt about the findings of their grim calculus.

"We should all perish," Sorin said.

Nissa started walking. "Then let us fall dead as we walk."

After the first day they moved only at night. During the day they slept face down with their cloaks and hoods wrapped around their bodies, so that anybody who saw them lined up on the wastes would think they were a line of corpses shrouded for the grave.

By the end of the second day their water skins were empty, and they threw them away. They rose at dusk on the third day and stumbled toward the high mountains. Suddenly to their right, a huge dark form moved. In her weakness Nissa tried to pivot and raise her staff, but instead she lost her balance and fell. Sorin managed to pull his sword, but dropped it when it proved too heated by a week of desert air to hold.

The form floated in the sky. At first Nissa's thirst-addled mind saw a huge baloth with claws forward in mid pounce. But she shook her head and looked again. A tremendous congregation of boulders floated above the flatness, banging together. She watched the rocks float until she saw one rock with lines cut in it. Upon closer inspection she recognized stairs and a turret thrown together and chipped to almost nothing. The ruins had once been a palace.

They stood and watched as the rocks passed over their heads and moved out to the wastes from which they had come.

Nissa would have liked to ask Anowon about the

huge palace, but she was too weak. There had been no water for a day, and her tongue filled her mouth completely again. Her lips were cracked to scabs. She could barely see, and her whole body hurt. Stepping was agony where the hard pack had burned the bottoms of her feet right through her worn boots.

Nissa started to fall the next morning. They had decided to not sleep during the day, knowing that if they did not attain the mountains soon, they would all die. So they continued. By midday the sun was so intense that Nissa felt as if she were made of fire.

And she fell. The first time she felt her legs weakening, and she pitched forward onto her knees. Mudheel helped her up, and she started walking again. The second time she did not remember falling. She simply blinked, and she was sprawled out in the dust. She struggled to her feet and walked a couple of steps and fell again. Nissa looked for the others, but she could not see anything but the sun glaring in her face.

Through the brilliance a figure appeared. At first she thought it was Anowon with everything that was hanging from his belt, but then Nissa saw the two dulam beasts yoked together following behind the figure. He was wearing a huge cloak with a hood and a piece of wood strapped over his eyes in which there was carved a thin slot. He reached down and took Nissa under the armpits and lifted her onto her feet. He took a cup from the folds of his cloak and poured it full from a small earthen jar. The water he offered her smelled of sulfur, but she drank it and the next cup he offered.

Sorin had made it a bit farther before collapsing. Nissa helped the man in the huge cloak hoist Sorin to his feet and give him water. Anowon was still stumbling after the goblin who was carrying Smara on his back.

The man collected each of them and gave them water. Soon they were staggering along behind a brace of snorting and bellowing dulam that pulled a huge wagon with an even larger tank strapped to it, water sloshing back and forth in the tank as the beasts lumbered on. The man was tiny, Nissa noted, if indeed he was a human at all. His clothes were too billowing for her to see his body. He held a crop as long as himself which Nissa never saw him use on the dulam beasts, to her great relief.

With the water, Nissa's tongue returned to a manageable size and stopped throbbing. After a time spent sitting on the back of the wagon she walked to where the tiny man moved ahead of his beasts.

"We cannot repay you," Nissa said. Even those few words sent stabs of pain down her tongue and throat.

The little man nodded and kept walking.

"Where are you traveling?" Nissa asked.

The man pointed at the mountains, red and looming high ahead.

"Do you live there?"

The man nodded and made a guttural choke in response, a sound that brought the hairs up on the back of Nissa's neck. *No tongue*, Nissa thought. *His tongue has been cut out.*

Over the next day, as the man guided his wagon up and over the gentle hills, Nissa developed the strong feeling that something was watching them from the foothills they passed into. Suddenly the man jerked the rope that controlled the dulam beasts, and they bellowed and came to a stop. He ran back to the wagon and yanked out a leather bag.

He then ran back past the dulam beasts, and Nissa

saw what was causing him so much excitement. A small pond of crystal water was floating two of Nissa's foot's lengths high in the air. The man approached the shimmering glob and scooped a cup from it. He took some small bottles from his bag and began mixing powders into the water.

Sorin stepped up next to her. "Imagine what kind of magnet this water is to every creature for two leagues in any direction. It is too dangerous to stay here."

Nissa looked down at the ground, knowing he was right. There were the tracks of many creatures scratched into the dirt, only some of which she knew. She recognized the hydra's claw scrapes, the drake's two footed hop, and the scute bug's scrabbling sign. But of the tracks she did not recognize were many humanoid ones. Nissa got down onto one knee and traced the outline of two particular tracks with the tip of her first finger. The first did not cause her as much concern as the second. The first was a made by a very heavy creature. Even in the hard land the splayed, three-toed footprint was stamped deeply. It was about double the size of a man's footprint, but not nearly the size of, say, a mountain troll's.

The second track was actually many tracks. Whatever had made them had come in a sizeable group. The tracks were thin and of average depth—not disconcerting in themselves. Nor were there claw digs at the tips of the toes. The problem came in how much she could see in the track—everything. She could see virtually every bone in the creature's foot. Whatever had made those tracks either had no skin or no fat under their skin.

"We need to leave this place," Nissa said, standing.

"Ghet!" Sorin yelled. His voice traveled over the low hills.

Nissa cringed at the loudness of his voice, and the thought of what could have heard it in the hills.

"Ghet," Sorin said when Anowon came limping over to them. "We are about to depart. Do whatever disgusting thing that you will."

Nissa looked from one to the other of them. Anowon turned and walked away. The little man had extended a long hose from the back of his wagon and affixed it to the tank. The other end he was about to stick into the globule of water.

"Nobody will miss one water scout," Sorin said.

"Wait," Nissa said. She took a step toward the wagon.

Anowon walked up behind the small human, and in one fluid motion he swept down, sweeping his hood back. But Nissa was ready. She lunged and jabbed quickly with her staff. The end of the staff caught Anowon in the middle of the chest and knocked him off balance, and he stumbled backward and onto one knee. When she charged, the vampire seized a handful of sand and hurled it in her eyes. Nissa stopped dead in her tracks and swung her staff where she thought Anowon was, but she swung through empty air.

A moment later Nissa heard a snap followed by a rhythmic slurping. She sat down hard and moistened a corner of her jerkin with saliva from her mouth, what little there was. As she cleaned the sand and dust from her eyes, Nissa had to listen to the cracking of the water scout's ribs as, presumably, Anowon squeezed the body to drain it fully of blood.

When her eyes were clear enough to see, she glared at Anowon. The vampire was standing above her smiling contentedly. The body of the water scout was off to the side. Two razor-thin lines ran vertically along each of the big veins in his neck. Nissa understood immediately why Anowon kept long fingernails.

"Next time it will not go so easily for you," Anowon said.

Nissa looked out at the flatness they had just crossed and swallowed hard. She was not sure what angered her more—that Anowon had killed the scout that had saved their lives, or that Anowon had out maneauvered her.

"Why not the witch vessel. Why not her?" she asked, pointing at Smara.

"The kor woman repulses me," he replied.

When she turned, Sorin was looking down at her with no recognizable expression on his long face. Nissa went over to where the goblin was sitting in the shade of the wagon trying to act as though it had not seen Anowon kill the water scout.

"We should go," Nissa said.

The goblin nodded and rose, then helped Smara to her feet.

"We'll take the wagon," Nissa said.

And they did. The terrain became more and more rugged as they traveled. Surprisingly there was a trail of sorts that led upward, and the dulam beasts pulled the water tank easily. They had not bothered to fill the tanks from the floating water, but even without filling they could hear that the tank was perhaps a quarter full.

By daybreak of the following day they passed the first plant Nissa had seen in weeks: a foul-smelling shrub that began to dot the draws between the foothills. The path turned to the east, and the shoulders of the mountains became noticeably steeper for the next two days.

The strange signs of the skeletal feet that Nissa had seen criss-crossed the trail, but never quite followed it. Whatever the creatures were, they seemed to move as a pack of maybe twenty and seemed to always be barefoot. Others traveled with them. But the beings that traveled with them wore boots and had tracks of average length, depth, and stride. Nissa suspected that whatever was making the tracks was probably aware of their presence, and was in all likelihood shadowing them. Who could know for what reason?

Anowon noted the signs with a grunt. When he did not think we was being watched, Anowon scanned the hilltops around. Once she found him taking big gulps of air and deep breaths through his nose, hoping to get a scent from the surrounding air. Whatever he detected in the air made him edgy and even worse tempered than before.

At one point the vampire stopped suddenly and closed his eyes for some moments. The rest of the group also halted. After a short time Anowon opened his eyes and kept walking as though he had not stopped.

"Ghet," Sorin said, after Anowon had stopped twice. "What foolery are you engaged in?"

But Anowon said nothing. That night he insisted on taking first watch, and he pushed Nissa away when she tried to relieve him later. In the middle of the night they were woken to the sound of a bellowing echo in the mountains and hills. It continued for some time then stopped abruptly.

The next day was no better. They walked higher, and the hills became taller and taller until the mountains seemed to loom no more than a day's travel away. Anowon became more agitated as the trail became steeper. At one point he stopped the party.

"We cannot go that way," he said, nodding to a rather level way that turned sharply behind a swelled outcropping.

"Why not, Ghet?" Sorin said.

Nissa looked at the turn he was talking about. "He's right," she said. "It's the perfect place for an ambush."

"We must leave the wagon here and travel rougher," Anowon said. "If we can."

"Are you going to tell us what you know?" Nissa said.

"No," Anowon said.

"Why?" Nissa asked.

"Because I might be wrong," the vampire replied.

"Vampires *are* wily trackers," Sorin said.

Nissa could not be sure if he was saying that Anowon was a good tracker, or that they were being tracked well by other vampires. She turned to check Sorin's expression, but it did not reveal his true meaning. The possibility that vampires were tracking them made her skin tingle with fear and excitement. Vampires were one of the two creatures she actually enjoyed killing.

"Are we being tracked by vampires, or is Anowon a good tracker?" Nissa said.

"Yes," Sorin said. "We will see just how good a tracker our pale friend is."

Nissa shook her head. *A straight answer would be nice just once. Just once.*

The group left the wagon and started on foot. They moved slowly over the boulders, staying away from possible ambush sites. They avoided blind angles, swinging wide around corners so as not to be surprised. Before they left the tank they drank as much water as they could, wishing very much that they had not thrown away their skins on the flat plain.

But by dusk they were thirsty. They had just moved up a steep alluvial fan of loose rock, a hard scramble but one with no blind spots, no possibility of ambush, when Anowon stopped suddenly.

"There is something ahead," he hissed.

"Where?" Nissa said.

"There," Sorin said, without pointing. "At the base of that rock formation that looks like a cascade of blood."

Nissa saw where he meant. In front of an undulated red stone formation was what looked like a statue of a very tall, stout human with no face. What struck Nissa was the fact that the statue was not constructed of red stone . . . It was light brown, almost a mud color.

"It is a statue," Nissa said.

"It moved," Anowon said.

Nissa looked back at the strange statue. It did have a face of sorts: its nose was a hole, as were its eyes and mouth. She noticed that rock cairns were piled up on either side of it. She watched the statue for long enough that her knees started to sting as she squatted in the loose rock. She was just about to stand when the statue moved.

"I saw it too," Sorin said.

The goblin was standing very still with one of its large ears cocked up and a worried expression on its face.

Nissa took a long, slow look around. The Teeth of Akoum were different from any other mountains she had ever seen. The steep sides of the high foothills were strangely bare and featured steep faces of rounded, almost bubble-shaped rock. There was no soil to speak of, only rock crushed to various degrees. Natural rock bridges formed by the wind joined canyon walls. Fingers of rock jutted high in the air, topped sometimes with boulders that floated and bobbed above their tips.

Clear crystals shot through everything, making walking difficult in the daytime, where rays of heat were concentrated through the crystals and had to be avoided if one wanted to keep from being badly singed.

Nissa's green lands were very far away indeed, she felt. But when she closed her eyes, she could sense the roots that extended out of the bottom of her feet and led all the way back to her forests.

They could not be taken by surprise on the wide fan, where a high canyon above deposited all the small debris carried by runoff from the high peaks. Nissa knew if the party left the scree fan they would leave the protection of the open and again enter into the maze of boulder ways, where every turn could be an ambush. They had to continue up the fan, and that meant passing the statue.

Sorin had been watching her. "You go first," he said. "I'll cover your flank. Ghet, go with her."

"You are too kind," Nissa said.

"Think nothing of it," Sorin replied, chuckling.

Nissa walked forward, her staff at her side. There was no point in sneaking. If something was following them, it had clearly watched their progress. It must have figured out that their way would bottleneck at the strange outcropping.

On closer inspection the statue appeared to be made of clay, which struck her as odd. Odder still was its position; it was standing with its arms out straight on each side. The cairns of stone that she had struggled to see clearly from farther down the fan now turned out to be the sides of a rock window. Like the rock bridges, the windows were formed by the wind blowing away a middle portion of the red stone. The statue stood arms wide in the middle of this.

They neared the statue and stopped. It was covered with symbols and decorative etchings.

"Third-reign Eldrazi," Anowon said, without hesitation. "See the tentacle flourishes at the corners of those boxes?"

"What is it?" Nissa asked.

Anowon shrugged. "That is script on its forehead. It says, 'mover.' "

"Mover?" Nissa said.

They stood staring at the statue. A rock tumbled ahead. "I have the strangest feeling," Anowon said, stepping away from the strange statue. "That something moves ever closer."

CHAPTER 17

What is this?" the goblin said, looking at the statue.

"We were hoping you knew," Nissa said.

The goblin stared at the statue. It brought the finger from its right hand up and inserted it into its own nostril and began digging. "Interesting," Mudheel said.

"It was a golem slave, I'd wager," Anowon said. He spoke with his eyes on the surrounding boulders.

"Ghet," Sorin said. "I'll hear none of your learned descent today. Let us remember that we have long way to go and still no water to wet that treasonous tongue. There are vampires, apparently, tracking us—though Ghet here has known that for days and not seen fit to tell the rest of us."

Anowon pulled his white hood off his head and scanned the boulders huddled at the edges of the scree fan. "Let us travel," he said.

They clattered upward through the loose scree. Behind them they could see the tumbled boulders and the far off flats at the feet of the mountains. Nissa kicked free a small boulder, and it rolled, bounced, and clattered away into the larger boulders, echoing off the hills around.

Reaching the top of the fan, they moved through

a slot in the rock and into a shallow cayon, dark and silent. Their footfalls echoed as they walked, and the valley began to shut them in. Soon the low sheer walls were close enough that they could not walk three abreast.

Anowon stopped them. To avoid waylay they climbed up and out.

As they pieced their way through the boulders, night was upon them. The moon rose and cast a pale light that turned every shadow deeply black. On a large outcropping of rock they came upon a guard tower of clear Eldrazi origin, tumbled and broken, with many of its blocks miraculously piled one upon the other in tall columns.

"We must stop," Nissa said, panting with the effort of the climb. "Let us take our rest in that guard tower."

Ahead, the goblin piloting their path stopped. It dropped into a squat, and its eyes darted from boulder to boulder.

"What is it, Mudheel?" Nissa asked.

"There is something there," it replied.

Nissa looked to where the goblin pointed. The pale light from the moon laid silver swaths of light between the boulders. Something glinted in the shadows. Many somethings.

"Fly," Nissa whispered, and she started running to the tower. She heard footfalls following behind, but her mind was not on the others. She twisted her staff and drew her stem sword as she ran. She heard the clatter as Sorin drew his sword. She was the first to the tower's crumbled stone ladder, which she scaled in three bounds.

The goblin was the next up, then Sorin and Anowon, and Smara running for the first time on her own.

Nissa's eyes were on the boulder field behind them. From the shadows many forms emerged and started to run. They were thin and dressed in all manner of rags and fragments of armor. Their skin was as white as the moon above their heads, and their long, emaciated shanks showed the fine outline of the bones under their withered skin.

But what made Nissa's breath catch in her throat were their faces. They ran out of the shadows and into the moonlight, and Nissa saw that they had neither eyes nor noses. Instead, a perfectly flat piece of skin covered the front of their face. Only a round, lipless mouth remained filled with sharp yellow teeth.

The creatures ran recklessly. The front-most creature tripped on a rock and fell into a sharp boulder, gashing its arm and head open so that a huge flap of skin flopped at the side of its head. Still, there was no blood that Nissa could see. The creature staggered to its feet and started running again, its mouth open in a dry scream.

"Not nulls," Anowon said. "Anything but nulls."

Nissa could hear the tension in his voice. She'd seen nulls before in the jungles of Bala Ged, but never so many. Nulls. They were what remained after a vampire drained a creature to an inch of its life but did not kill it. What remained was a mindless husk.

There were so many of them. Nissa lost count at thirty, before Sorin stepped forward with his sword drawn.

"My rot talk has no effect on the undead," he said.

Nissa settled the soles of her feet on the rock. She reawakened the roots of her body, and felt the energy of the forest slither across the wastes and mountains. Then the charge shot through the roots that extended from her brow and connected her with the green growing places she knew well: the Turntimber Forest of the Tajuru and the fetid jungles of Bala Ged.

She thought of trolls. Forest trolls with bug eyes and mossy hair and thick arms like tree trunks. She felt the energy dripping off her fingertips and pulling to a place in front of her where it distilled into two trolls holding long blood briar branches for weapons.

She did not need to point to the nulls who were almost at the base of the tower. The trolls hobbled on their knuckles down the side of the tower and into the frenzied host. Nissa heard fingernails scratching on rock behind her, and when she turned there were six nulls struggling over the back edge of the tower. Sorin swept past, bringing his great sword down and splitting one from the crown of its head to its chest. The creature fell bloodlessly to the side. Nissa whipped her stem sword out and snapped another's head off.

"Stop!" Anowon commanded in a booming voice.

The air seemed to drag as the remaining four nulls at the tower stopped in their tracks. One had a dented metal plate strapped over the top of its face where its nose and eyes should have been. They lowered their hands with their long, curling fingernails, closed their mouths, and waited.

Anowon pointed down at the other nulls, who were fighting the trolls. The trolls swung their arms out, sweeping up nulls in wide swathes. "Attack!" Anowon commanded.

Without a moment's hesitation the four nulls turned and threw themselves off the edge of the tower. The three that rose from the boulder below ran at their brethren and began tearing flesh and limbs.

"They are easily controlled by other vampires," Anowon said. "But only in small numbers. This force is no small number."

"Something must be controlling them," Nissa said.

Below, the forest trolls were swinging at nulls with all their might. The many gashes they had received from the vampire zombies had begun to regenerate closed. But Nissa did not worry about the cuts that covered her trolls. Hers was another fear, soon borne out. For every null that the trolls mowed down, four more seemed to clamber onto the dead one's back. Soon mounds of nulls surrounded each troll, and when the piles were high enough, the remaining creatures simply surged up and over the trolls. They clawed the trolls' eyes out and snaked their long arms down the trolls' throats to yank out handfuls of whatever they could clutch. The trolls regenerated, but not fast enough. Some of the nulls scrambled over the trolls' thrashing forms and charged at the tower.

Below, the last forest troll fell atop a pile of ruined null.

A primal yell came from Anowon's throat as he launched himself into the horde. Nissa was momentarily awed by the attack. As she watched, Anowon drove his long fingers into the nearest null, tearing out hunks of flesh. With his hands wrist-deep in one null he turned, and with a quick snap bit deep into another's neck and tore most of its throat out with the jerk of his chin. He freed his hands and mouth, sidestepped another null's clumsy swing, and countered by shoving his hands through the creature. His mouth began tearing chunks out. When that null fell, Anowon hopped up and spun to do it all again with a new null. A chill ran down Nissa's spine. It was one of the most savage attacks she had ever witnessed.

Nissa snapped her staff back together and raised it. Only about half of the nulls were incapacitated, and the rest would clearly not stop until they were playing in their blood. Nissa raised her staff above her head, feeling the power rise in her like the sap rising in a spring tree. She moved her mind to the one creature she knew could destroy all of the creatures. She only hoped it would take a mortal wound before it got to her and the rest. Soon the rough outline of an Onduan baloth appeared in her mind.

"Will they not . . ." Sorin began. She heard him grunt, and the next moment he was falling over the edge of the tower. Nissa received a blow from behind that knocked her forward and against a crumbled rampart. Darkness came abruptly, and she remembered no more.

She woke to a rhythmic jostling. Something was running as it carried her. Her eyes hurt, so she didn't open them. A sharp jab of pain spread through her head with every footfall, and she felt as though she were being torn apart. When she cried out, the running stopped, and she was thrown down on the hard ground. When Nissa regained consciousness, she opened her eyes and found that something was pulled over her face to keep her from seeing. A moment later the hood was yanked off, and the bright sunlight stabbed into her eyes, causing even more pain.

Nissa forced herself to make note of her surroundings. She was still in the high foothills, that much was obvious—there were some small plants eking from a fissure.

A blurry figure approached. Nissa shook her head so the figure came into view, and soon wished she had not. A female vampire bent so her head was almost touching noses with Nissa. Her breath, rank with the smell of blood, was all over Nissa's face. A lip curled back to show one stout incisor, pointed and white.

"It moves," the vampire announced. "What a shame. I was hoping for a broken spine." The female vampire pulled a pink tongue over her white teeth. "Easy meat."

Nissa looked past the female vampire. About eight nulls stood around them, their mouths gaping and drool running down their chins. Nissa noticed that many of the null had ruined limbs that dragged, or gashes and other signs that they had been in the brutal battle Nissa and the others had given.

"You will rue the day you survived that fray, meatling," the vampire said. "Rue the day."

"It is you who will regret," Nissa said under her breath.

"It speaks?" the vampire said. "Insolent animal?"

The vampire backed up and turned, snatching a long, obsidian-tipped bampha stick from the hands of a skeletal null. She was dressed in tight leather with her head shaved around the side, front and back so that only a swath of black hair grew in tangles. Her skin was as pale as a null's, and she was almost as thin.

But as she took the bampha stick and swung it, she appeared to be the lithest thing Nissa had ever seen. She executed a complex hand over hand spinning attack that took a split second to execute and concluded with the obsidian tip coming to an abrupt halt an inch from Nissa's right eyeball.

Nissa could no more have dodged the attack as she could have flown on golden wings. But when the female vampire looked down, Nissa had slipped the top of her foot around behind the heel of the vampire's foot. Nissa lifted her other foot and pushed on the knee. With the vampire's heel caught on the top of Nissa's foot, the force of Nissa's push transferred to the upper body, and the vampire pitched backwards. She fell on her back, dropping the bampha.

Nissa did not have her staff, but even without it she was able to call down the mana and channel it into her mind where the outline of a giant Onduan python had formed. The huge coiled serpent snapped into being next to the female vampire and opened its mouth.

A second vampire appeared by the serpent and touched its scaly side. Immediately the animal shook and dropped its head. A moment later its head raised, a pale glow emanating from its eyes, and its tongue lolling out the side of its mouth.

The second vampire turned to Nissa. "Thank you, elf," the vampire said. "We need more bodies in our troop after you and your associates had your ways with us."

He turned to the female vampire, who picked herself up and snatched her stick off the rocks.

"Biss," the male vampire said. "Would you scout ahead for us?"

Biss bowed and left, casting a hard look at Nissa before departing.

"We have been tracking your progress for days," the male vampire said, turning to Nissa. "And her hatred of the Mortifier is very great indeed. As is mine." The vampire raised one hand and snapped his fingers.

Behind the vampire, the zombie python began to writhe, knocking one of the nulls against a rock with its huge coils. Then it lay still. The male vampire looked at Nissa and shrugged.

"What can I say? I love to kill things," he said. "Plus, it would have been another mouth to feed."

"Why am I still alive, blood slave?" Nissa said. They had called vampires that when she'd been younger and in the jungles, mostly because vampires hated the name. But the vampire only smiled.

"A good question," the vampire said. "And you may call me Shir."

Shir must have sensed Nissa's disappointment that the name she called him had not angered him. His smile widened so that Nissa thought for a moment that he would lean over and bite her. Every yellowed tooth in his mouth showed as he spoke.

"I would expect names such as that from one who travels with the Mortifier."

"What is this *Mortifier* you speak of, blood slave?" Nissa said. "Or are you as dim as the rest of your kind?"

The vampire studied her face for a moment. "Could it be that this elf is not aware of whom she travels with?" he said. "Perhaps she does not know what the Mortifier is?"

CHAPTER 18

They stopped only briefly. At Shir's orders, the nulls seized Nissa and ran with her bound on its shoulders. The nulls ran like they were being chased with Biss and Shir at the front and back.

At several points Nissa had to pull into herself, into the forest within, to avoid the pain of the thrall's sharp shoulder blades impacting her ribs, and to avoid the mineral smell of its breath in her face.

They ran all day and most of the night for two days, and by the second day they had passed through the foothills and onto a wide plateau surrounded by the jagged aeries of the Teeth of Akoum.

If she had her staff she could slice them apart, but it had been left at the tower she guessed, most likely among the bodies of her dead comrades. At one of their short and infrequent rest stops, Nissa attempted to connect with her mana and summon a creature, but when she reached her mind out for the lines of power that connected her to her known places, she found herself too weak. Once she managed to summon a gravity spider, but Shir simply touched the animal, and it rotted before her eyes.

Nissa was neither fed nor given water and by the second day was passing in and out of visions of her

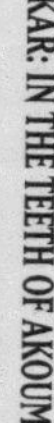

homeland of Bala Ged. She was near death when they stopped in the middle of the grasslands of the high plateau. The null threw her down in the sharp grass, and Biss stood taunting her. When Nissa did not reply to Biss's ridiculous questions she received a kick in her already excruciatingly painful ribs.

"Null," Biss would scream when Nissa rolled over to protect her face. "Roll her back over."

The nulls were the only creatures treated worse than she. Two of them fell and could not get up on the two-day run, but the others kept running. Biss even laughed at the struggling wretches.

But when they stopped on the high grasslands of the plateau, Nissa knew it was no rest stop. Shir had been stopping frequently to look at the dirt. At one point he even took a pinch of the dry earth and put it on his tongue and tasted it. Then he put his hand over his eyes to protect them from the sun as he scanned the distance.

"There," he said, pointing, and broke into a run.

One of the remaining nulls grabbed Nissa's feet and began dragging her. When they reached the place where Shir and Biss stood waiting, they released her feet. She was scraped and bruised but also interested in what Shir was doing.

The male vampire fell onto his hands and knees and began touching the ground, feeling for something.

"Why are we running?" Nissa asked, but nobody said anything.

Nissa noticed some oddness in the grasses of the area as the vampires searched. Some looked a bit trampled, as though others had already been to that particular spot. And she saw signs in the dusty soil—signs that Biss and Shir were not bothering to examine, which meant they knew who had made the tracks.

Or thought they knew who had made the tracks. As

Nissa looked at the tracks the pulse of blood through her body began to speed up. Soon it was hammering at her temples, and it was all she could do not to smile. She looked around the great expanse and saw no forms in the distance.

"Why are we here?" Nissa repeated. "Why were we running?"

Shir looked up from his searching. There was sweat on his forehead and a sour look on his face. Somehow Nissa knew that the vampire did not like to have sweat on his face.

"Null," he called. "Come here and look for a seam."

The nulls fell to the ground and began scrabbling their long claws about in the dust.

Biss said something to Shir in the vampire tongue. Even though Nissa did not understand the language, the female vampire's facial expression told Nissa that she was not convinced the null could find what they were looking for.

Nissa stood and began scanning the soil a body span away from the vampires and their nulls. Her elf eyes were good at finding patterns, and instead of looking at the soil, she looked at the patches of grass that blew sideways in the wind. Soon she was able to see a rough line where the grasses did not grow.

She saw the sign that had given her such hope again near the seam—footprints, and recently. Footprints she thought she recognized.

"The seam you seek is here, I believe," Nissa said.

Biss looked up and sneered. Shir walked over to where Nissa had slumped back onto the ground, then to where Nissa pointed.

"Yes," he said. "It is here. Nulls, to me."

The nulls scrambled over and began feeling for the seam.

"Thank you, elf," Shir said turning to Nissa. "For this your death will be quick. I will not leave you to Biss. I shall do it myself."

"Why not kill me back at the tower?" Nissa backed up as the null got their fingers in the seam.

"We would have liked to, but your party escaped. We plan to use you as bait."

"Who are you?" Nissa said.

"We are charged with fighting the Eldrazi brood lineage. When we came upon your band we saw an opportunity to kill or capture the Mortifier, who is perhaps the greatest Eldrazi sympathizer of all time."

"How do you know this Mortifier?"

"We know. Vampire legend talks about him frequently," Shir said. "He lives in infamy in our stories about slavery. He sold us into slavery to the Eldrazi, who utilized us as a food source, and when that was not diverting enough for them, as labor. They enjoyed greatly seeing how hard we could be worked until our bodies failed. The Eldrazi put us in chains all our lives. "

I would have put you in chains as well, Nissa thought. But instead of speaking Nissa backed up, as the nulls heaved, and the outline of a stone became apparent in the loose soil. Soon they had the stone high enough that they could slide the heels of their hands under and push. The grasses that grew on the stone were planted in such a way that they did not slide off.

Biss smiled as the stone was raised. But the smile faded on his lips when the stone flew back and Anowon and Sorin burst out of the hole. Sorin had his sword out, and he and the vampire charged the stunned nulls, cutting down the remaining creatures in a matter of moments. Anowon swung hands with their sharp, claw-like fingers in savage arcs, tearing chunks out of the nulls, his mouth set in an ugly sneer. He spun his body around pivoting first on one foot and then jumping onto another to generate the inertia for his sweeping attacks. He even used his slashing feet.

Finished with the nulls, Sorin and Anowon turned to the vampires. Anowon bent and yanked a bampha from one of the null's hands. Biss was searching the ground, looking desperately for her own bampha, as Anowon lunged, driving the obsidian blade of his weapon firmly into her chest. The impact of his thrust knocked Biss off balance, and she took a series of steps backwards before falling still into the dust.

Shir sneered and made a grab for Nissa. But she had been expecting such a move and spun easily away. Anowon stepped forward. Shir hissed.

"This is all your doing, Mortifier," Shir said to one of them, Nissa could not be sure which. "We were driven from our land because of you, and we have been fighting the Eldrazi fiends because of you. And you will die before this moon's cycle has moved beyond the mountains."

Shir took a deep breath and closed his eyes. In a moment the air around them turned cold, and with a shock of revulsion Nissa noticed the grass around Shir's feet wither and die. *Why do they have to be so creepy?* Nissa thought as the vampire raised his arms. His skin began to hang off his body in patches, then without warning, the vampire's body fell to pieces before Nissa's eyes. First the arms hung so low that the attaching skin tore, and the arms fell. Then the legs buckled, and the corpse of Shir fell. When it hit the ground, its head bounced off the pebbles and rolled a short distance before stopping.

Nissa watched as the headless corpse withered to a bloodless husk. Sorin was not smiling for once.

Anowon was already looking away to the west at the tallest mountains. Their peaks were so sharp that they truly looked like an upheaval of red fangs.

"Did you do that?" Nissa asked Sorin.

Sorin shook his head.

Nissa did not look at the loose pile of bones and skin. Instead she looked down at the square hole in the ground and the stone that had covered it for so long. "What was this place?" she asked.

"A hiding place," Anowon said. "I knew of this barrow. We have them in all areas of Zendikar. Many are joined with tunnels, as this one is. We entered at a location over there." He pointed.

Just then Mudheel came clambering out of the hole. He bent over and pulled Smara out. The kor did not notice Shir's body. In fact, she almost stepped on the vampire's now gelatinous thigh as she made her bumbling way to a small mostly buried hedron. Mudheel tilted his head as he stared at Shir's body, as though he was having trouble figuring out what exactly it was.

"It is called a body, you turnip." Sorin said to Mudheel.

"A turnip?" Mudheel said, looking from Sorin to the pile of body.

Nissa let her eyes linger on the goblin.

Sorin handed Nissa her staff. "Ghet was the one who insisted on tracking you," Sorin said. "I would have left you, you know. You must know that?"

"I know that," Nissa said. "You have a mission."

"Yes," Sorin said. "A mission." He took out a comb and began brushing his hair. *Has that comb been with Sorin the whole time*? Nissa wondered.

"I know those mountains," Anowon continued, still staring at the extremely jagged red peaks. "The Eye of Ugin lies there in that part of the Teeth."

"That is true," Mudheel said. The goblin had received a cut across his forehead in the battle, and the tip of his ear hung at an angle. Both wounds he had dressed with a mud poultice. "Affa lies at the base."

"Before he died, the vampire Shir—" Nissa began.

"—He is not dead," Anowon interrupted. He spoke with his back turned, as he looked out at the high mountains. "I know of this vampire Shir. He unincorporated. He dropped his body. He is from an old family. His line was made of a famous Bloodchief and has the funds to hire dementia summoners to dream him back into blood."

Nissa shook her head. She was rarely pleased to learn anything new about vampires. Such knowledge tended to keep her up at night.

"Before the autumn of his flesh, this creature Shir spoke of the Mortifier," Nissa said.

Anowon turned. Sorin raised an eyebrow.

"Mortifier?" Sorin said. "What did they want with this Mortifier?"

Nissa shrugged. "They did not say why they were looking for him. But I had the feeling that their main purpose was to find and destroy brood lineage, and finding this Mortifier was a coincidence."

"They were attacking brood?" Anowon said.

"That is what I think," Nissa said. "But neither vampire spoke much, except to taunt."

"So they were not specifically tracking the Mortifier?" asked Anowon.

"It seemed they stumbled upon us." Nissa said. She watched Anowon's face for a tell—something that would show her that he was the Mortifier, as she suspected him to be. The Mortifier was a vampire, after all. A vampire.

But Anowon's facial features did not vary or appear agitated. He simply nodded when Nissa told him about the vampires. Then he turned back to the mountains.

"The Mortifier," he said.

Anowon was far ahead when they began to walk through the clumps of grass toward the thin lines of smoke drifting sideways from Affa at the base to the aerie peaks. They kicked through the grass all the rest of that day. That night they slept where they fell on the hard ground, with no food and not even a fire.

They rose before dawn and stopped to lick the dew off the blades of grass and their weapons. The sky to the east was a dull gray when they started walking again. They moved across the high grasslands, and midday found them with their cloaks thrown over their heads to protect them from the high-altitude sun which Nissa could feel as a weight on her skin. Clouds passed close overhead, carried on the constant wind.

In the late afternoon, the ground began to jump and jitter. The air seemed to pull in on Nissa. The tiny flask of water she kept around her neck boiled, and tremendous crack appeared in the earth. Moments later, lava shot into the air and pulled into a massive ball that quickly cooled to black, at which point plants began to grow all over it. It happened in a matter of minutes. Soon the floating ball was engulfed with greenery.

Nissa had fallen next to Anowon. They stood when the Roil was over and the cooling ball of magma floated in the air blasting heat. Nissa looked sideways at Anowon.

"Thank you for getting me from the vampires," she said.

Anowon nodded. "You did the same for me in the tower of the elves. We vampires drink blood, but some of us have honor, if it suits us. I gain from your presence, which is why you are still here."

"How do you gain?"

"You are effective against the brood," Anowon said. "Perhaps you will be the same against the Eldrazi themselves."

Nissa changed her grip on her staff. "Eldrazi?" she said. "You mean the ones that are still imprisoned? How would we fight them?"

"If we woke them from their slumber?"

"But we are traveling to the Eye of Ugin for Sorin to strengthen the spell of containment on the Eldrazi tomb. If they escape, it will be red slaughter."

"That is what *he* told us."

"And you do not believe him?"

"There are other places out . . . there," Anowon said, waving a hand at the sky, referring to other planes. "Since we talked I have become suspicious. This Sorin is from another plane, and he wants to keep the brood and their masters here?" Anowon stamped his foot on the ground. "Why? Why does he not keep them somewhere else?"

Nissa opened her mouth and then closed it. The vampire had put voice to a question she had been wondering herself. "I do not know why he wants them kept here," she said.

"None of us do," Anowon said, casting a sidelong glance at Sorin.

"What do you propose we do?" Nissa said.

"Freeing the Eldrazi," Anowon said. "Let them go . . . back out there." Once again he waved his hand at the sky. "Have you noticed how the Roil has grown in severity lately, since the brood escaped?"

"I do not know when they escaped."

"I was there. It was three moons ago."

Nissa thought back. It did seem as though the Roil had increased. But that could just be her remembering incorrectly.

"And, according to what I've read, the Roil was not always on Zendikar. Ancient texts first speak of the Roil only *after* the Eldrazi disappeared," Anowon said, pointing at Sorin. "After that one imprisoned them. And I know from my research that the hedrons did not appear until after the Eldrazi disappeared off the face of Zendikar. There were no hedrons on Zendikar when the Eldrazi walked its surface."

"Well," Nissa said. "What are they?"

Anowon threw up his hands. "Whatever they are, they clearly have something to do with keeping the Eldrazi asleep . . . with channeling energy. Many of the strange phenomena of Zendikar occur around them, have you noticed?"

"That seems true," Nissa said.

"And did you notice the inscription on that building the brood were building? The one in the hedron field near the ocean?"

Nissa remembered that they had taken the brood by surprise and left none alive. But as for the building itself, she could not bring any of the inscriptions into her mind's eye. She shook her head.

"The inscriptions were made by the brood copying the ancient Eldrazi style of decoration," Anowon said. "Just as the markings on the hedrons are copies. The only original markings are on the palaces and crypts and various other buildings that once housed the ancients."

"The hedron were not made by the Eldrazi?" Nissa said.

Anowon pointed at her and nodded somberly.

When Nissa looked, Sorin was looking out over the distance singing a song under his breath.

Nissa took a deep breath. Hedrons or not, the Mortifier was a vampire, and there was only one vampire in their group. "Did *you* ever meet the Eldrazi?" she asked Anowon. "The titans I mean?"

Anowon looked at her. "How would I have? They died long before I was made." The vampire narrowed his eyes at Nissa. "Why do you ask me this?"

"I would not blame you," Nissa said. "Every vampire I have ever met is a beast, except you. I can see where you might have tired of your own. I am sure you had your reasons."

Anowon kept staring at her with a confused look on his white face. "What are you talking about?" Anowon said.

"The Mortifier," Nissa said. She squeezed the staff in her right hand, glad to have been given it by Sorin when they rescued her from the vampires and the nulls. With the tiniest twist, she could have the stem sword out.

"You must be he," she said. "The Mortifier."

It was many moments before Anowon spoke. He stood glaring at Nissa.

"Let me not mislead you. I would break my teeth off before I helped the Eldrazi in any way whatsoever," he said, a snarl in the back of his throat. "And I would never enslave my own people. Never. I am as much *a beast* as those weaklings with the null. More so." With that Anowon turned and stomped away. He stopped for a second to look up at the plants hanging off the cooling magma ball, then stooped under it and began walking to the smoke fires of Affa.

Anowon passed Mudheel, who was relieving himself as he gazed at Affa, moving his body to make glyphs in the powdery soil. Smara was sitting on the ground to the side of Mudheel, stroking her crystal in her lap.

"Why does he stomp away so?" Mudheel yelled over his shoulder.

Nissa watched Anowon go. If he was not the Mortifier, then that left . . . She turned to where Sorin was tending his hair with his comb, still intact after their many encounters. He carefully swept his long, white hair back and tied a piece of leather around it. He did not have the vestigial horns at his shoulders and elbows. *A vampire*? she thought. Sorin was too tall. He had no tattoos. *When does he feed?* His hair was not black, like the hair of every other vampire she had ever seen. *A vampire?* Nissa felt like drawing her stem sword and trying to strike Sorin down where he stood. *A vampire?* But instead she turned and walked toward Affa as she considered her best course of action.

CHAPTER 19

Affa lay in the distance. They walked without stopping until the tents of the herders and small-time relic seekers began to appear. The tents of the stonecutters—those that eked out a living selling shards and chips from hedron stones—were the shabbiest, amounting to little more than hides stretched over the ribs of undra stompers. The goblins among the stonecutters preferred to sleep in burrows with hides thrown over the entry hole.

Anowon disappeared shortly after encountering the outlying tents. Nissa knew what the vampire was looking for, but she tried not to think about it. Luckily it was past dark when they straggled past the first bonfire, so Nissa doubted Anowon would be detected as he hunted.

Nissa watched Sorin as they walked. At first he appeared to be unaffected by the presence of edible creatures. But soon they passed the tents of the cutters and relic seekers and entered Affa proper, and the amount of life increased. Soon there were humans, merfolk, goblins, elves, and even other vampires moving around the cookfires in the dark. Nissa thought she could hear Sorin's breathing quicken. If he was as hungry for blood as she was for a drink of water, then she had best take the others and leave him to his unutterable desires.

The center of Affa was more built up than Nissa would have guessed. More than just a tent city, it had permanent stone-and-mortar buildings with steep roofs of slate and weathervanes of wrought dragons. The streets were cobbled with intricate designs. The steep mountain peaks stood out in stark contrast against the light brown clay shingles. A small, turreted keep hunched in the middle of town, surrounded by semi-permanent stalls built of wood and manned by merchants selling all manner of wares. *Where did they get the wood?* Nissa wondered. She had not seen a forest in leagues.

Braziers burned on the street corners, and when Nissa exhaled she was surprised to see her breath outlined in the chilly mountain air.

Nissa turned to Sorin, only to find him gone. Only the shadows around the various braziers remained. Smara muttered behind her as they walked. Nissa turned and caught the goblin Mudheel looking at her in a curious way. *Even the goblin knew about Sorin*, she thought.

Had Sorin been sneaking off the whole time? she wondered. She had spent so much time watching Anowon for the slightest glimmer of aggression directed at her that Sorin could have supped on her blood twenty times over, if he had had the interest.

Smara's muttering behind became louder as they walked.

"May I ask how long we will be walking tonight?" Mudheel said with more than a bit of acid in his voice.

Nissa turned. The goblin was carrying Smara over his shoulders, and she struggled on the goblin's back. As Nissa watched, the kor kicked her legs out and generally writhed.

The goblin fought to gain control of the kor's flailing body. After struggling for some moments, a grumbling Mudheel switched his hold, moving Smara from his shoulder so he was cradling her forward across his arms. Nissa was never more impressed to see a goblin's strength as she was at that instant. Mudheel bent its snout close to Smara's ear and hummed the kor a low song. It was a moment so strangely touching that Nissa had to look away. When she turned back, Smara was singing to herself, stroking the smoky, dagger-length crystal she clutched at all times.

"I thought we should sleep at the side of the camp that faces the mountains," Nissa said. She lowered her voice a bit. "So we can leave undetected."

The goblin nodded. "I have not seen sign on the ground of brood lineage for many days," he said.

"Neither have I," Nissa said, looking out of the corners of her eyes at the outlines moving around the fires. "But it is not the brood I am worried about just now."

The goblin kept walking, holding Smara in his arms as one might a child. "Lady elf, we will need supplies if we are to ascend into the Teeth, you know?"

"I know." Nissa said. She was still getting used to the goblin speaking and thinking as well as he did. Mudheel could surely be the leader of a whole goblin nation if he wasn't bound to Smara as he was. As kor to goblin.

"Where will we find the coin for this?" Mudheel said, snapping her from her thoughts.

"We will steal it," Nissa said, looking straight ahead. After her talk with Anowon about Sorin and the Eldrazi, her opinion about the importance of the expedition had changed significantly. "We will steal and acquire what is needed to climb to the Eye of Ugin and save Zendikar."

The goblin looked at her a moment longer than normal, blinking.

Nissa continued. "How many days can we expect to climb to the Eye?"

"From Affa, two perhaps three days," the goblin said.

"And what will happen then?" Nissa said. "What are your and your mistress's reasons for traveling there in the first place? I suppose I never asked."

Mudheel looked down at the face of Smara, who looked up at the pocked, mole-covered face of the goblin. "She feels drawn by the spirit in her crystal."

"There is a spirit in that?"

"A most fabulous one," the goblin said. The words were barely out of his mouth when Smara began struggling again. She bucked her body up and snapped her legs out. Mudheel struggled to hold her. When Smara's struggling became more violent, Mudheel gently put her down on the ground.

"The gift is in the loam," Smara screamed, suddenly. She kept screaming it.

"Should we both carry her?" Nissa said.

The goblin nodded. Nissa took the kor's ankles and Mudheel her wrists, and they hoisted Smara and began walking with her, struggling, toward the edge of the settlement. She stopped screaming.

Nissa waited a couple of beats before speaking again. "What ails your mistress?" she asked.

Nissa could not see the goblin's face as it walked ahead, but she imagined a wince.

"It started after she heard you and the vampire speaking yesterday."

"You heard that?" Nissa asked.

"I did not," Mudheel said. "She did."

"But how do you know she heard it . . ."

"She speaks to me," the goblin said as he stopped walking for a moment. "In my head."

"What did she hear?" asked Nissa.

"She was bothered by the Sorin vampire's plan."

"Was she?"

"Her ghost tells her to release the Eldrazi," Mudheel said. "He tells her to kill you all. He tells her to burn things."

The hairs on the back of Nissa's neck stood. "Really?"

"Yes," the goblin said. "Kill you in the fire of the Eye of Ugin."

"I see."

"The gift in the loam must be released."

"You want to free *them?*"

"It is not I," the goblin said. "It is the desire of my mistress's ghost."

"And who is this ghost?"

"The knower of all things," the goblin said. "The predictor of everything."

"And it says free the Eldrazi?"

From the back, Nissa saw the goblin look left and right at the mention of the word *Eldrazi.* "It says: *free those who shall not be named.*"

Once again the hairs on the back of Nissa's neck went up. Smara began to thrash violently and to scream words Nissa did not know. Nissa watched the goblin wrestling with the kor. The kor had been cast out of her tribe and given to the wilderness and somehow lived. She had grown up apart from her people through no fault of her own, and after all that . . . a crystal that spoke to her, telling her to burn things and free the Eldrazi.

Smara kept screaming. She thrashed out of the goblin's arms and staggered around as Mudheel spoke in a low voice trying to calm her. The inhabitants of Affa turned and watched the kor. Soon a small crowd had formed outside of a small dry-stack stone building with a flagon of wine painted above the door. Mudheel began shoving Smara none too gently down the lane, and soon they were out of the center of the settlement and hurrying between the tents.

The tents and rough stone shacks started to thin as they reached the far side of the settlement and the boulders started. The huge rocks had been in the settlement, of course—people had leaned wood and bones against them as a roofs. One could not hope to move boulders of that size without true magical talent, and from what she saw in the camps as they walked, there was not a great deal of that to go around. The inhabitants were mostly petty peril seekers.

The real power seekers would be excavating other locations like Tal Terig, the tower they had passed that lay under brood siege, or the Hagra Cistern. A real adventurer would not be hovering around at the base of the Teeth of Akoum like an eeka bird. Affa was a place where goblins brought the small relics and Eldrazi charms they had found and could not make work.

As she walked, a form appeared out of the deep shadows that lay far from the fires. Smara kept screaming as hard as her lungs could.

"What is that lovely sound?" Sorin said. "Oh, it is the kor, of course."

Smara reacted to Sorin's sudden voice in the darkness. She struggled and pulled free from the goblin's hands, turned on Sorin, and let loose a string of words Nissa could not understand. Smara sputtered as she spoke. To Nissa they sounded more like complete sentences than the ravings of a mad person, and Sorin listened with a smirk forming at the corner of his lips.

And then Sorin did something that Nissa could never have predicted. He spoke back to Smara in the same tongue she had been speaking to him. They were talking back and forth, arguing really.

From behind, Nissa detected movement and smelled the dusty smell of Anowon. But the vampire stood still, listening.

The arguing continued, with Smara becoming more and more aggravated. At one point the kor stepped forward and swung at Sorin, who stepped back and let the blow pass harmlessly in front of his face.

Nissa remembered how long she had gone without food or drink. She suddenly felt too weak to go any further, and she sat down on the ground. The stars were bright, and the fires of Affa were behind them. They had no coin and no hope of finding any. They would need to steal, and after that they would need to flee. She was tired enough at the thought.

The screaming continued until Smara began spitting. Sorin laughed, and Smara turned and wandered away into the darkness with Mudheel trailing after her. They did not see her again.

Nissa forced herself to stand, and they kept walking. Ahead the dark shapes of the long mountains loomed. Nissa walked up behind Anowon.

"We need supplies," she said. "Rope and food and water. We will *all* die without water."

The vampire stopped. "Then you had best get some."

"We still have no coin," Nissa said. "Nothing has changed there."

Sorin stepped up behind her in the dark. "It looks like a bit of theft might be just the thing."

"I do not want to do that," Nissa said. "But I will."

"It just so happens I would like to make a stop," Sorin said. "I will see what is lying around unattended."

When Sorin had left, Nissa caught up to Anowon. "I should have known Sorin was one of you."

"He is not one of me," Anowon snapped. "He is an outlander—a barong, as you elves say. He is an enslaver, from out there. My people do not enslave their own."

Not so sure of that, Nissa thought, but she swallowed the words. Instead she said, "What was Sorin saying to Smara?"

"They were arguing over what to do at the Eye. Smara wants to free the vile ones and let them live among us, and share their wisdom with us."

That did not sound like a good idea to Nissa, if the Eldrazi titans were anything like their children, the brood lineage.

"Do they suck the mana from holes in the earth like the brood?" Nissa said.

"The ancient texts say different things. Some say they lived off the blood of their vampires. Others say that they 'drank the land.' "

Nissa sniffed in the cold breeze blowing down out of the mountains. "That does not sound very good," she said. "If they are large I would reason they could drink plenty of land."

Anowon kept walking with Nissa next to him. *How long had they been walking?* Nissa wondered. She had lost count. It felt like months. Every step was slow and heavy. She stopped and plopped down on the ground for a rest. The fires of Affa were well behind them now.

Anowon stopped and turned to look at Nissa sitting on the ground.

"Anyway," Anowon said. "The Eldrazi will not tarry here. The mad kor wishes in vain. They would flee into the sky."

"How do you know?"

"All the texts agree they came from there," Anowon said. "Why stay here?"

"You yourself said they eat mana. Why not stay here and enslave us all?"

"If what you said before is correct, then there are many other places," Anowon said as he raised his hand to the dark mountain. "Out there."

Nissa looked up at the star-strewn sky. She recognized the constellations she had seen her whole life: the scute bug and the vorpal weed, the dragon's claw and the hedron. And there were the other vast planes separated by gray areas in space. Would the Eldrazi prefer these places to Zendikar?

"Nissa," Anowon said. "We must rid Zendikar of this parasite."

Nissa turned and regarded Anowon. "What did you see at the Eye before the brood took you prisoner?"

The vampire's voice appeared very close suddenly in the dark. "I was there looking at the strange crystal formations and the even stranger writing on some of the crystals. Writing I could not read. Writing that is utterly unknown to Zendikar. I imagine it is writing from Sorin's place, but I was unaware that the Mortifier was more than myth."

Nissa nodded.

"I was studied these unusual writings before I found two strange beings, perhaps one like you and Sorin—not from Zendikar?"

"I am from Zendikar," Nissa said. "I have always been from Zendikar."

"Well, the female had fire for hair. I wanted to feed on them both, to be truthful. But before I could, I was waylaid. By whom, I do not know. She moved on without me, but I met a mind mage on the trail who was pursuing the fire mage. I led him to the Eye of Ugin.

I was locked out of the chamber, though. I don't know what happened, or how they released the scourge."

"What is Ugin?"

"Ugin was a dragon," Anowon said. "I do not know what Ugin is now."

Ugin is a bother and a pain, no doubt, Nissa thought. *Like everything on this expedition.*

"Why did they release the brood?" Nissa said.

Anowon had been looking down at Nissa as he spoke. Now he folded his legs and fell into a cross-legged position.

"I don't know that it was their intention," Anowon said. "But whatever they did, it weakened Ugin's ability to hold in the brood."

"You think they *accidentally* released the brood?"

Anowon bowed his head a bit. "As you say."

"How do you think they released them?" Nissa said. If she knew how the planeswalkers had released the brood, perhaps she could release the titans—if she could convince Sorin to allow it. *And if he does not consent?* Nissa thought.

"They found a way to open the lock of Ugin," Anowon said. "A lock that has defied the Eldrazi for thousands of years. I have no idea how it was done. Perhaps it was their very presence that triggered the lock."

Just then there was a scuff, and Sorin appeared out of the darkness. He pushed his hair out of his eyes and moved his great sword's scabbard so it was in the proper position. He smiled.

"I have found what we need, and it is close," he said.

"What?" Nissa asked.

"Supplies," Sorin said as he turned and began walking. "Come."

They walked through the darkness back in the

direction of Affa. Nissa could hear Sorin's scabbard thumping softly against his thigh as he walked. They neared a fire, next to which a figure was lying, apparently asleep.

Why does this settlement appear so calm and unprotected? Nissa thought. *The brood are running feral over the land, and I have not seen an armed guard yet in this settlement.*

As they neared the fire, Sorin put one finger up to his lips and pointed at a large tent. The two dulam beasts tethered next to it snorted as Sorin approached, but Nissa stroked their necks and they calmed.

Nissa was unsure how it was going to work. They would wake the man if they went through his tent. He would hear them, surely. Sorin carefully threw back the flap of the tent and entered.

The vampire started handing items out to Nissa and the others. Rope appeared, as did wedges and mallets for climbing, small bags of zim grain and dried meat. Sorin kept handing out goods, but when Nissa saw the jar filled with a glowing substance appear in his hand, she snatched it and tucked it into an inner pocket of her cloak. It was Berm-bee honey—a kind of honey made by a berm bee which only collected nectar from the mana imbued flowers blooming in the surging growths after the Roil. A drop filled one with euphoria and prophesies. Three drops caused brief flight. More than three drops caused death.

Soon each of them had more than they could carry. Sorin stepped out of the tent, and without even looking at the sleeping figure, began strapping all they had on one of the dulam beasts. He used a length of rope to strap on two large panniers and filled these large baskets with goods. The rest, long tent posts and odds and ends, he strapped lengthways along the beast's back.

Sorin took the beast's halter rope and led it away into the darkness. Nissa looked back at the sleeping figure before following. If stealing from that poor man would allow her to save Zendikar, then that was how it had to be. The man would probably be glad if she told him the full story. As she reasoned with herself, Nissa fumbled for an earthenware canteen of water Sorin had placed in the left pannier, and helped herself to a long draught of warm, sulfurous water.

They walked into the darkness for a time before Nissa felt comfortable speaking.

"We must have the stealth of a baloth." Nissa said.

Nobody said anything.

"Did you drug the man?" Nissa asked. "He could have woken at any moment."

"End this charade of innocence," Sorin said. "He will not ever wake. I slaked my thirst on him. I even supped on his heart."

She walked in silence holding the dead man's water jug. They had not slept in days, and suddenly Nissa felt very tired. *Yes, it was time to end the charade.*

They stopped to sleep at the base of the mountains. The Teeth of Akoum jutted straight off the plateau. It would be a hard climb, she knew. To compound the difficulties they would encounter, they had lost Mudheel when Smara left. Goblins could be unbearable, but they always knew a good path and how to proceed along it. And Mudheel had been easier to live around than any goblin Nissa had ever met.

Each of them stooped and kicked hip grooves in the dirt before falling on the ground and asleep.

"Do you know the way?" Nissa asked Anowon. She was beginning to wonder if Anowon had fallen asleep when the vampire spoke.

"More, or less," he said.

"That *is* reassuring," Sorin said.

"I know the general path," Anowon said. "My camp had been here in the Teeth, but it was raised in the wake of the brood. I can get us to the Eye."

"Perhaps," Nissa said. She fixed her eyes on the tall mountains above her.

Later, in the dark, things seemed unusually quiet. Nothing moved. A lizard croaked somewhere far off, and then another closer by, and suddenly Nissa was wide awake. She rolled onto her stomach and took hold of her staff, waiting for the next lizard call to signal an attack.

But none came. She heard no more lizard calls. The stars blinked above in the empty sky, and in a moment her eyes felt heavy again.

She woke in the dawn darkness as Sorin jostled her shoulder with his boot.

"Up now," the vampire said.

Nissa rubbed her eyes and looked around. *What had happened to the ambush?* She wondered. When the light was good enough she got on her hands and knees to look for signs among the scrubby grasses. But she found only that of a nurm rat.

There was not time to look further. Anowon began to walk.

The climb up the mountains started out hard and never stopped. After just three hours ,Nissa was breathing as hard as she ever had. The well worn trail was riven with runoff channels and switched back and forth on an ascent so steep that she felt like roping in. But that would have slowed her down. Nissa knew she could not afford to be slow—when the man was found dead beside his fire, there was a high likelihood that someone from Affa would send out a search party.

There was also the issue of last night. Nissa was sure someone had been in the darkness watching them. The lizard calls had been too uniform and their distance too staggered. But Anowon had been on watch, and he had not mentioned anything about the strange calls. Perhaps Affa had sent their party out sooner than she thought, and they were watching for a chance to attack?

Below them Affa was an unmemorable scrabble of huts and tents, and above them the peaks appeared to go on forever. The mountain was constructed of the same red, gritty sandstone as the other mountains in the area, with one large difference: the Teeth of Akoum were as smooth as incisors. Where the earlier mountains had been bulbous and rounded, the Teeth were buffed smooth by the winds which blew continuously and hard. It blew so hard that whoever had created the trail had been forced to cut it into the very rock to allow feet purchase. Without the trail's lip the group would have been blown off the side of the mountain and away within two hours of starting their ascent.

The wind howled so that Nissa finally had to tie a piece of her cloak around her head and ears to protect them and keep her brain from feeling like it would explode.

And exploding was a distinct possibility. The Roil occurred frequently. Nissa could feel them erupting, echoing off the mountains. As they staggered along the trail, the Roil rent the rock above them, and lava gurgled forth from the cracks. The very mountain seemed to rock on some axis before straightening and settling. Another Roil was so severe that Nissa had to fall to the ground and brace her arms and legs against the rock.

Sorin, on the other hand, had begun to float away, pulled by the Roil. But Nissa managed to whip out her stem sword and catch his ankle before the crackling mana drew him far out into the chasm.

After the last Roil they all agreed to use the rope they had stolen in Affa. Nissa was the only one with a harness. She rigged a harness for Sorin out of the rope, which Anowon sneered at as he tied his own.

"Vampire style," he said. The harness Anowon tied on himself looked strange to Nissa, constructed as it was with long pieces of rope that wrapped around the hip *and* shoulders, a style she had never seen. Elf harnesses, and human ones for that matter, looped around the legs, hips, and abdomen. The strangest harness she'd ever seen was surely the merfolk's—little more than two pieces of rope strung through the crotch and around the shoulders in a figure eight. Anowon's harness took more rope, but appeared, she had to admit, very stable.

The trail became steep enough that they had to use their hands to half-climb, half-walk along the rough scree.

Their end rope was belayed crossways around Anowon's shoulder, so the vampire could with his weight act as the anchor. Nissa had counseled Anowon against the idea. *What if he fell, or was carried away by the Roil?* But Anowon was leading the ascent, and that meant he chose the rope system. Their climb would be in the vampire style. Nissa sighed and started climbing again.

Nissa wondered how Smara and Mudheel would have made their way up the trail *Would the goblin have led? Was theirs even the trail the two would have taken?* There were other trails; Nissa had seen them branching off. They were mostly small trails, more than likely used by animals, but Mudheel had been the only one among them that actually knew the way to the Eye of Ugin. Anowon had, by his own admission, only the roughest idea of where the Eye lay. In fact, as Nissa watched the vampire take each of his toe-holds, she wondered more and more if he had *any* ideas at all where the Eye was.

Nissa wondered where the kor and her goblin minder were. Surely they did not give up their quest to get to the Eye just because Smara argued with Sorin? What if they reached the Eye first and managed to free the Eldrazi?

Nissa had never seen Sorin with so little to say and with such a serious look on his face. Every time the switchback turned back on itself, Sorin stopped and closed his eyes and did not move. Whatever magic the vampire was utilizing was not giving him the answers he desired, for he was frowning when he opened his eyes again and scrambled over the rock.

The way became steeper. and at the same time the switchbacks stopped and the trail steepened. It clung to the side of a cliff that fell away below and spanned above past all their abilities to see. The trail was just wide enough for the dulam to move through. Nissa led the beast as it inched along.

Twice Nissa heard a loud crack and looked up to see a boulder bouncing off the cliff with great bounds as it plummeted toward them. One crashed past, knocking a divot out of part of the trail, which Nissa guessed happened fairly often judging from the chewed-upon state of the trail.

The second rock that fell was larger than the first, and Nissa knew the moment she looked up that it was falling directly at her. She waited until the rock was almost upon her before jumping to the side. She slipped in her haste, and tumbled off the trail.

The wind blasted past her ears. The thought flashed through her head that her rope had not held, but it took up the slack, and her harness jerked her to a jarring stop. She hung leagues above the ground swinging in the gusts.

Nissa has fallen before, of course. Falling was nothing new. Even zeem monkeys fell from trees, after all. But hanging so far above the ground—where Nissa had to squint at the ground to make out even a boulder—was something new. With shaking hands she hoisted herself up and continued to climb.

By late afternoon the group was higher than the clouds, and the air had turned cold. The crystals that stuck out of the red sandstone were red themselves and as sharp as sword blades. Sorin cut his arm as he passed one, and when he turned to look at the cut he tripped and teetered. Nissa reached out and caught him just before he fell off the side and onto one of the many tipped crystals jutting out of the cliff.

The light of the setting sun shone directly in their eyes as they walked, making stepping even more dangerous. Nissa's breath was a cloud in the high air as she stopped. At that moment the dulam beast missed its footing and struggled desperately as it slipped off the edge and fell soundlessly into the void below with all their supplies. Nissa waited for a sickening thud.

There was no sound. Finally Nissa turned and began walking again.

The night was frigid. The wind had mostly disappeared, but still the air was icy and bit hard at their shoulders and faces. Twice Nissa thought she heard the lizard call that had woken her out of a dead sleep days before echoing through the peaks.

"Do you smell smoke?" Nissa whispered. Any sound

echoed off the crystals, sounding deceptively close or far away.

Anowon shook his head, but Nissa was sure she smelled smoke. And when she stood first watch, the smell drove her to stand and go for a look around. Nissa knew it was not a good idea to walk in the mountains in the dark, especially *those* mountains, but she could not stand smelling wood smoke without trying to find where it was coming from. It could be some travelers that knew where they were going, after all.

As good as her eyes were in the dark Nissa still tripped. The land around was red from the sandstone and stretched out and down in long jags. She stepped around an outcropping of crystals and stopped. She could tell something was standing against the rock. She wished she had thought to bring her staff and cursed herself for making such an unwise mistake.

"Come out," she said.

A figure emerged from against the rock. Mudheel pieced his way to her walking carefully in the dark.

"You?" Nissa said.

The goblin bowed slightly.

CHAPTER 20

Nissa watched as the goblin approached. She'd last seen him some days before, following Smara as she stormed away after hearing Sorin's plan to refortify the Eldrazi's prison.

"Are you following us?" Nissa asked.

"It is you who should be following us," Mudheel said.

"Why?"

"You are on the wrong path."

"How do I know you are not trying to mislead?"

"You do not know this," The goblin said. "Except why would I, young elf?"

He was right, Nissa thought. The goblin and Smara had left, not the other way around.

"Why are you telling me this?"

The goblin smiled, showing lines of teeth like stones in a graveyard. He hesitated a moment before speaking.

"I miss you," he said.

Wonderful, Nissa thought.

"And I did not want to push the rock."

"You pushed that boulder down on us?"

The goblin nodded slowly. "Twice."

"Both times?"

The goblin nodded again. "But I did not want to. She made me."

"Where is she now?"

"Sleeping." Mudheel said. "She has been sleeping more and more the closer we get to . . . *them.*"

"Why are you here?" Nissa said. "To finish the job?"

The goblin frowned. "It was not you I was trying to knock off the mountain. It was the vampire. The one who wants to put the ancient ones deeper into their mountain. My mistress decreed it."

"Then why are you here?"

"I want you to take the true path. Your days are few if you do not."

"Why?"

"These mountains contain a protector. You have not seen it yet, but it has detected you. It stalks you."

"And you have evaded detection?"

Once again the goblin bowed slightly. Nissa wished he would stop doing that.

"What is the nature of this enemy?"

"They are children of the ancient ones."

"Brood lineage?" Nissa said. "We have handled them before."

"Here in the Teeth they are"—the goblin wet his cracked and purple lips—"wilder."

"Why have they not attacked us then?"

"I have been watching them for many days. They do not act as I thought they would. They seem to consider things more than I had thought."

Nissa looked at the goblin queerly.

"So you want us to travel a different path to avoid the brood?"

"Yes, please."

"I will tell you what I think," Nissa said. "I think you are trying to direct us down an incorrect trail by telling me that the brood are tracking us. I have not smelled brood or seen any sign in the dust."

The goblin sighed. "On the morrow you will come to a split in the trail," he said. "See if you do not. Take the right trail. It is the smallest trail."

"And it ends at a sheer cliff?"

"No," the goblin said. "It ends at the Eye of Ugin."

"Assuming this trail does lead to the Eye," Nissa said. "You know that Sorin will fortify the prison of the Eldrazi, correct?"

The wind picked up suddenly and howled past Nissa's long ears at the mention of the ancient ones.

"I know the Mortifier intends to do that. But you and the reading vampire have decided to release the gift in the loam," Mudheel said. "My mistress will do the same thing. But . . ."

"But what? Why should we come along if that is what she is doing?"

"I am unsure she can control whatever comes out of that hole."

Nissa thought for a quick moment.

"And you want us there if the Eldrazi do not do what she says . . . if they decide that Zendikar is as good a place as any to dwell?"

The goblin nodded slowly before bowing and stepping back into the shadows.

Nissa slept that night on the hard rock. The next day she and the others ascended higher and higher into the mountains. The clouds flicked by so close overhead that Nissa felt she could reach out and touch them.

The trail entered into a series of switchbacks that took them until the sun was past its zenith in the sky to complete. Then the trail split. The main trail continued forward, but two small offshoots extended right and left and disappeared behind the rock. Of the two splits, the right one was the smallest path by far, composed of gravel and dust that had not been disturbed in days. *How had the trail not been disturbed?*

"Let us take this smaller trail," Nissa said.

"Why would we do that?" Sorin said. "It does not lead anywhere."

"And this large trail does?" Nissa said.

"It looks more like a trail that leads somewhere than the small one."

Nissa paused. What could she say to convince them? "I'm telling you we should take this one," Nissa said.

Anowon stopped and cocked his head at Nissa.

At that moment Sorin pointed, and two mass-of-tentacles brood floated into view ahead. Each of them was different and larger than any the group had seen before. They had very large and thick looking obsidian-like rock mantles that floated around their writhing bodies.

At the same time, three brood with large bone heads and no faces scrawled their ways onto the large trail, pulling themselves on thick tentacles.

Both groups advanced on the party.

Sorin immediately began to sing. His voice boomed forth, knocking both of the large brood on the ground into heaps of blood. The wind blew the smell of putrefaction toward them. Nissa fanned out to the right to get away from it. The flying brood drifted closer. They seemed ponderously large to Nissa, incapable of quickness. But her thoughts were shattered moments later when one of the flying brood shot out a tentacle and caught Sorin around the neck.

Nissa twisted her staff and snapped her stem sword out, severing the creature's tentacle and freeing Sorin. Sorin pulled off the severed tentacle and flung it aside. He spoke two words and raised his right hand to the creature. The air around them went icy cold, and motes of power bloomed around Sorin's hand. The brood missing one tentacle trembled. The next moment a piece popped free from the brood's body and fell beating to the ground. The creature had no face that Nissa could see, but she had the distinct feeling that the brood was looking down at the beating thing on the ground, which could only have been its heart. In the next moment it crumpled and fell to the ground and lay like an empty wineskin on the red rocks.

The last creature flew at her.

Nissa put her staff on the rock of the mountain. When she took a deep breath her deepest fears were confirmed: only trickles of power were reaching her from the various mana tributaries she depended on. Nissa closed her eyes and took another deep breath. She seemed to be unable to catch her mana bonds. It was Zendikar herself that was hindering her, almost as if she wanted Nissa to fall here on this rocky spot. It had happened to Nissa before, of course—it was part of the unpredictably of Zendikar—but never at such a vital time. There was mana here, gouts of it. But it seemed to flutter around her, like a mothling around a lantern.

To make matters worse, two more brood appeared at that instant. One was the bone-headed variety—the other, floating. As Nissa watched they both began moving toward her at an alarming speed. The floating brood tucked its tentacles close to its body, and charged.

Nissa had only a moment. She channeled what little mana she could and formed an image in her mind of an eeka bird—a large, pest bird with a long beak. Nissa brought the bird to her and sent it hurling, beak-first at the brood.

The eeka flew straight and buried its beak deep in the brood's mass of concentrated tentacles. The brood stopped its charge and used one tentacle to find the bird and throw it aside. By that time Nissa had drawn her stem sword as rigid as a spike and was charging forward. She pushed off from a boulder and jumped high into the air where she executed a flip and hurled downwards. She plunged the spike into the center of the mass of squirming tentacles, burying it all the way to her fists. Nissa knew that once inside a body, the stem would put out rhizomes and use the blood vessels and arteries to travel through the body. Eventually the roots would fill it.

But that did not happen to the brood beneath her. Instead it found her and began winding tentacles around her neck and body, squeezing until she could not breathe. Nissa clawed at the tentacles and pulled, but the brood's tentacles wrapped around her wrists and ankles and squeezed. She struggled, and the brood's grip tightened. Soon the red rocks and blue sky went black and white, and spots began to appear before her eyes. Nissa felt the strength pass from her.

Anowon ran to the brood and swiped a swath out of its tentacles. Another tentacle swept down at him, and he caught it and bit out a sizable chunk before flinging it aside. But before he could climb any closer to Nissa, another tentacle seized his ankle and threw him back and away.

The blackness was taking over Nissa's view when she felt something on her hands and ankles and neck—the tickle of the rhizomes peeking out from the tentacles. An instant later the brood's hold loosened, and Nissa fell to the rock, gasping.

She looked up to see Sorin and Anowon fighting

the last two brood. As she watched, Sorin touched the blade of his sword. It pulsed black, and the Mortifier swung and swiped off one of the bifurcated arms reaching for him. The rot from the cut spread like a blue shadow through the rest of the brood's body. The creature's bony head, void of any semblance of a face, inclined sideways at an inquisitive angle as its body suddenly withered to the texture of an autumn leaf and fell to the ground with a dry crack.

Anowon had a bampha stick he had taken from the vampire Biss, and its obsidian edges whirred through the air in a sudden and complex array of attacks so fast that Nissa could not see it clearly.

Nissa turned and looked at the brood that had almost strangled her. The rhizomes from her stem sword had turned into thick roots and tunneled into the rocks. In rich soil those roots would keep growing, she knew, and eventually a blood briar would grow.

But blood briar or not, she had to get her sword out. Nissa searched until she found the stem sword, buried almost past the pommel. She grasped its slimy grip and pulled and pulled. Eventually she was able to rip the sword from the wet body of the dead brood. Thick roots extended off the stem like a brush; she would pare them off with a small knife later. She watched as Sorin assisted Anowon in destroying the last brood. After Sorin jabbed the creature and it lay still on the rock, she walked to them.

Nissa watched Sorin tuck his white hair back behind his ears and smile an impish smile at her. "Do you have any more shortcut ideas?" he said to Nissa, motioning to the smallest trail.

"We had better take it before more brood appear,"

Anowon said, out of breath. "I could not do that again if my very blood depended on it."

With her knife Nissa cut the roots off the stem before sliding it back into its sheath. She tapped her staff on the mountain and started walking down the small trail, which narrowed as they walked. Soon the rocks began to shut them in. They were walking through a deeply cloven gully, silent and dim, with high, ridged headwalls of red sandstone on either side. Crystals with bases as thick and as gnarled as old jaddi trees hung out over the cliffs above, and more crystals bunched into inclines of glinting tips. But Nissa's eyes were on the ground before them.

"What do you observe?" Sorin said.

"Nothing," Nissa said.

"Nothing?"

"No tracks or any sign of recent disturbance," Nissa said, trying to sound more positive than she felt. She wondered how a trail could have *no* sign of any kind, not even animal tracks. But her throat hurt from the brood's tentacle, and she did not want to explain to Sorin why a trail without *any* sign was more dangerous somehow than a trail with a sign. As it was, she was going to have a hard time convincing the ancient vampire to release the very creatures he was on Zendikar to imprison. She would save her breath for that debate.

Sorin looked up and around. "This place is familiar to me," he said. "We are closer."

They walked up the long gulley. Above their heads the high alpine wind howled through the crystals, which stood virtually shoulder to shoulder. But in the gulley there was no wind. *There had never been any,* Nissa thought as she ran her finger across the top of a nearby crystal and saw it covered with dust.

At the top of the gulley they stopped and surveyed.

Ahead the small canyon dipped and narrowed, so the talus and scree channeled down into the black maw of a large erosion hole.

"This is the very entrance," Sorin said. "This is where I stood long ago, dreaming this prison to life with the others."

Anowon spit into the rocks at his feet. "After you meted out pain and anguish to my people, abuse that has lasted for generations, then you imprisoned the very empire you helped?"

Sorin turned to Anowon. " I was charged with containing them. And I only gave your people what they deserved tenfold."

Anowon rose up, a snarl curling the corner of his lip. Sorin took a step back and dropped one hand to the pommel of his great sword, his own lips curled back off his fangs.

"Stop," Nissa said. Something about her voice stopped the two vampires in their places. She pointed upwards.

Anowon followed Nissa's line of sight. He whistled when his eyes fell on them. There were at least ten lava drakes, each perched on the tip of a huge crystal.

Sorin sniffed. "No," he whispered. "What energy I have left must be kept for the containment spell."

Nissa turned to Anowon.

"I cannot sup on a drake's blood," Anowon said. "Even if I was able to slay one of them."

"You were both more than ready to fight each other a moment ago," Nissa said.

Nissa looked back at the drakes. "We cannot match them," she conceded. "But we can run into the hole before they reach us." She turned to the others.

"We will drop the gear here and run for the hole," Nissa said.

"But they will reach us before we reach the hole," Anowon said.

Nissa cast the vampire a sidelong glace. "If we run like vampires they will reach us. Run like elves." Nissa turned back to the drakes and the hole. "Ready?" she called.

CHAPTER 21

The drakes saw them almost immediately, and they took to the air a second later. Nissa clutched her staff and ran as hard and as fast as she ever had, skipping between the larger boulders and trying not to slip on the gravel. She'd seen drakes before but always been careful to avoid them, knowing that in their way there were more dangerous that a dragon. A Zendikar dragon would not normally bother itself with two or three beings, but preferred lazy activities like sleeping in a deep hole or sitting in Glasspool soaking its scales.

Drakes were different. Aside from the obvious difference—drakes had no arms, only legs and wings—there was the large difference in bearing and disposition. Drakes were mean and dim. Their love of hunting in packs made them extremely difficult to fight, and their appetite was prodigious.

The drakes were on them before they reached the hill. Nissa had her stem sword out and managed to lop the leg off a drake that was extending its claw for her. She dodged another who had landed in her path and attempted to bite her.

A third drake swooped down and seized her in its claws and bore her up, at the same time it bit down at her head. But when it opened its mouth for the lethal bite, it received a thrust from Nissa's stem sword which traveled through the top of its palate and into its brain. Mana from the sword pulsed through the drake's body. Nissa had a flash image of rhizomes spreading out from the stem and constricting around the drake's brain and spine.

Nissa was able to land first with her feet and roll out with no injury, except for the deep gashes in her shoulder where the drake's claws had been.

A moment later she was charging over the rocks to the gaping maw of the cave. She reached the cave just as another drake was sweeping down on her. But the flying beast decided against following her into the darkness of the cave, preferring instead to land on the rocks outside and peer inside cautiously, screeching uneasily.

Nissa took a rock from her feet and threw it at the drake, hitting it in the eye and driving it away. Soon Anowon was in the cave having found a way to avoid attack completely. Sorin was soon to follow, with two drakes hounding his progress, and three bodies quivering on the rock, fallen to his sword.

Soon the drakes gave up and flew back to their perch, where they screeched and nipped at each other and began to fight.

Nissa turned and peered into the darkness of the cave. "Have we another tooth, Anowon?" she said.

The vampire pulled a tooth from his cloak. He whispered to it, and it burst to light. Outside the cave the drakes were screaming. Holding the tooth between his fingers, Anowon looked around the cave. Markings covered the walls, lines and lines of writing executed in a script so twisted and long that Nissa could not tell where one word stopped and the next began.

Anowon held out the tooth further and looked closely at the etchings. "These are utterly foreign to me," he said at last. "I cannot decipher even one word."

"We left these lines," Sorin said. "When we imprisoned the Eldrazi for the second time. They talk about the crimes committed against the planes."

Anowon blinked as he considered what Sorin had said. "The Eldrazi were imprisoned more than once?"

"They were imprisoned on another occasion, before my time," Sorin said. "Even I am not that old."

Anowon spit on the ground.

"And these are the titans?" Nissa said, pointing at the pictures in the rock. Three grotesque images looked hauntingly like the brood lineage, but different. She could not pull her eyes off the strange creatures, which looked a strange combination of insect, brain, and kraken. None had faces of any sort. And despite herself, Nissa shivered.

"They are—" Nissa began.

"Very terrible," said a screechy voice from behind. Mudheel stepped out of the shadows.

Nissa jumped. "Mudheel!" she said. It was all she could think to say, and she immediately regretted saying it as the word echoed down the cavern.

"Where is your kor mistress?" Sorin said.

The goblin's eyes cast down and then around the darkness. Mudheel shrugged his shoulders.

They stood in the near dark of the cave looking at one another. The drakes screamed outside as they fought over the meat still clinging to the bones of their fallen comrades.

"How did you get past the drakes?" Sorin asked, after a time.

"I crept through at night," the goblin said. "Little dragons see like humans in the dark."

"Well," Nissa said. "Should we continue to Ugin, whatever it is?"

The goblin stared at her.

"Which way is it?" Nissa said, finally.

"Oh," Mudheel said. "There." The goblin lifted one hand and pointed away, where the cave continued into blackness. "But we cannot go there."

"Why?" Anowon snapped. "Why not?"

"Because my mistress is surely there."

"That does not concern us," Sorin said, brushing past the goblin. "Even now I feel the containment spell weakening. I must reach it."

"She will be vexed," Mudheel said.

Nissa watched the goblin closely. "What is she like when she is vexed?"

"She is most cruel," Mudheel said. The words stuck to Nissa for some reason, and she looked around before following the others down into the darkest part of the cave. Nissa listened for Mudheel, who finally followed them.

They walked downward for many hours. Anowon was at the head with the glowing tooth pinched between his fingers. The cavern remained large. *Large enough for a full grown basalt crawler to move through without touching a scale,* Nissa thought.

Each of their footfalls bounced off the wet of the deep cavern and came echoing back to them as deep growls. The others seemed to make no notice of the noise.

But there was another sound, a far quieter but more persistent sound than their footfalls. Nissa stopped and turned her head, angling her long ear for better hearing. The sound was too irregular to be drips. It occurred in sudden bursts and then stopped for a time.

A bluish glow began to appear in the volcanic cavern ahead. As they walked the glow became stronger, until it was bright enough for Nissa to see her hand grasping her staff. The rock on either side of them began to slope downward, until they entered a huge carved cavern with no floor Nissa could see. Many thin causeways of chiseled basalt zigzagged at different levels across the deep chasm and trailed to a tunnel filled with blue light on the far side of the cavern. Multiple levels of stairs and paths joined the chiseled basalt causeways. The middle of the immense chamber was littered with debris, some of it scorched. But the lack of a floor was not the feature that caused Nissa's heart to start beating fast.

Hedrons floating in the air and pointing at skewed angles. In the middle of the chamber many hedron sat side to side and piled on one another, but they all seemed to be pointing loosely at the tunnel on the far side of the cavern. It was as if a great magnet had pulled them into place.

The cavern was so large that Nissa could see neither the floor nor the ceiling, and as she stepped out onto the causeway, the air seemed to ripple and refract.

"Wait," Sorin said. He put one cold hand on Nissa's shoulder and drew her back. "I will go first."

Nissa stepped out of the way and let the vampire pass. They followed him across the huge cavern and entered another after that and another after that. The light grew brighter and brighter until a glare caught Nissa's eye ahead. Sorin stopped and turned. The corner of his cloak swirled the foggy blackness under the causeway.

"Ahead is the entrance to the Eye of Ugin," Sorin said. "I will talk for us as it is I who will have to sing the containment back to fortitude," Sorin said. He fastened Nissa with a hard look. "Do not speak."

Nissa jerked her chin up. "Must you strengthen the prison?" she said.

Sorin turned his head. The most particular expression played across his face.

"Yes," he said. "I must. Otherwise the Eldrazi will scream free and eat your precious Zendikar in three bites. Do you not hear them? That far off sound? That is them clawing at the walls of their enclosure. They have been scratching for centuries. They never stop."

Nissa heard the same irregular sound she'd heard before, only now it was louder. A long, slow scraping.

"How are they unable to get out?" Nissa said.

"Keeping them contained is the job of Ugin," Sorin said. "The containment spell is one the ancients could never hope to break, without help from outside. To break the spell, the ancients would have to perform an action that is against their fundamental nature."

"They are their own prison?" Anowon said.

"Precisely," Sorin said.

"Yet the spell fails."

"Because of outside intervention," Sorin said.

They all stood listening to the Eldrazi scratching on the walls of their prison.

"We do not want them here," Anowon said.

"No," Nissa said, shaking her head. "We do not. They are the cause of Zendikar's Roils, her gravity wells . . . They are strangers here."

Sorin regarded them both for only a moment before speaking. "Zendikar is naturally dangerous. The mana existed here before the Eldrazi arrived and will remain here after they have rotted to dust. Zendikar is savage, and its most savage behavior is in its inhabitants, Ghet."

"Do not call me Ghet," Anowon said. "I will not have the slave masters of my people sucking the energy of Zendikar as they once sucked vampires dry."

"You *know* they would leave this place and travel to other planes," Nissa said.

"I do not know that," Sorin said. "There is mana in abundance here. That is what they lust for."

"They will leave," Anowon said.

"How do you know?"

"I know."

"How can you?"

Nissa turned to look at Anowon. It was a good question, she thought. *How could he know?*

Anowon snarled. "I have read it."

Sorin sighed. He looked at the bright light ahead of the causeway. "It is true that the magic we wrought to bind the Eldrazi in their prison has had some . . . undesired effects on this plane," he said. "But the prison is not the only reason this place is so wild.

"The hedron stones?" Anowon said.

"Are devices we made to condense mana and keep the containment spell strong."

Anowon's smile was unrestrained and large.

"Then you will cease this travesty," Anowon said. "By your own admission—"

"Enough!" Sorin boomed. Nissa staggered backward, pushed by the vampire's voice.

"I am Sorin Markov," the vampire boomed. Rock dust sifted down from the ceiling of the cavern as his words echoed. Sorin straightened his arms to each side. Blue-black energy snapped around his fists. "I will slay anyone attempting to stop me from performing the task given me."

Sorin's words were like weapons bludgeoning down on Nissa. She found it difficult to stand. The sound was in her, in her head echoing. Mudheel lay face down on the causeway next to her covering his head in an effort to escape the sonic assault.

Nissa squared her shoulders and stood despite her body's intense desire to fall to the ground. Years of Joraga training had given her the ability to ignore pain, but Sorin's voice was something else entirely—every part of her screamed in agony. Still, Nissa could tell by the shocked expression on the tall vampire's face that he was impressed she was still standing.

Blinking with effort, Nissa twisted her staff and drew the stem sword.

The words Sorin said were unknown to Nissa. But the pitch and timbre of Sorin's voice increased, and she felt those words ringing off the marrow of her bones. Yet still she stood.

Sorin winked at her before turning toward the light at the back of the chamber. He dropped his hands and the light brightened. Nissa could see the huge stone face of a dragon. Arc-shaped patterns filled the wall around the dragon's face and it was from these arcs that the glowing light emerged. The wall appeared slightly fluid. A huge stone hedron covered with markings writhed to the right of the dragon's eyes.

But the hedron was not writhing. Something *on* the hedron was writhing.

Nissa squinted for a better look, but in the low light it took more than the usual time to recognize the form of Smara. The kor had straddled the hedron and appeared to be pounding its pocked sides with her fists.

She moaned as she hammered. He body was smeared with dried mud and pebbles. Long, bloody abrasions where she'd torn her skin rubbing the mud onto her skin crisscrossed her arms and legs.

Mud had been smeared in circles around her eyes, as well. But her eyes—her strange, large eyes were unchanged. They stared unblinking as she raged with her fists against the stone.

"Why mud?" whispered Nissa.

"To bind the land," Mudheel said, his face still down. "The hedron is the key. It must be destroyed."

Sorin took a deep breath and straightened at the sound of the whispering. He looked out at the hedron, and a deep chuckle echoed from his throat when he saw Smara's sad form.

But the humor was gone as fast as it had appeared. Sorin closed his eyes and opened his mouth and began to sing. It wasn't a song like any that Nissa had heard before. She could not understand any of the words, and the melody was more of a dirge. Yet as soon as it began, a strange change occurred with the dragon's face. The dragon's eyes lit with the same blue glow that emanated from the arced patterns above its head. And the hedron's markings crackled with lightning fire.

Smara fell off the hedron. For a moment Nissa thought the lightning fire had struck her down. But after a second the kor struggled to her feet. Then she fell into a caterwauling run at Sorin, the rags of her clothes fluttering out behind as she gained speed.

It took the kor some time to make her way along the causeways and stairs, but soon she was near. Sorin did not see her. His eyes were closed as he sang. Smara charged across the space and crashed into Sorin, who let out a grunt and stumbled backwards. Nissa felt the force that had been holding her down release and she rose quickly to her feet, stem sword in hand. But Sorin did not notice her—he was too busy shielding himself from Smara's frenzied attack.

Nissa quietly raced to the hedron. It was large. Some of the white flame playing across its runic surface licked out toward her as she drew near.

From behind, There was a tremendous pop and singe and the air was filled with the smoke of charred meat. Nissa knew that Sorin had ended Smara's rebellion.

She had only moments. Only moments before Sorin dealt in a similar way with her. Looking down at her hands, Nissa realized she had only one option. She had never attempted to seed stone, and she was not at all convinced that it would work. But in a split breath she joined her staff and mouthed the familiar enchantment. She struck the end of it squarely on the hedron, and green fire funneled down its shaft. The fire snapped Nissa back and she found herself sprawled on the ground, half of her staff still clutched in her hand. The other half singed and lying under the hedron. It seemed as though the hedron had absorbed the spell without effect.

There was no familiar, glowing dent where her staff had struck the hedron, and Nissa began to despair her effort. From behind, Sorin sucked in air for an incantation that Nissa suspected would almost surely be his last, fatal strike against her. *All for Zendikar*, she thought as she sank back, expecting the blow from behind. *All for the forest. The brilliant stars and the face of the moon.*

When the blow did not come, Nissa turned. Sorin was standing with his eyes closed, still singing. A certain blackness emanated from his mouth like fine smoke as he sang.

Then a crack appeared in the hedron. Nissa turned in time to see. At first the crack was as thin as a spider's leg, then it widened, and a second later the tip of a bright, green leaf unfurled from within, and the crack widened. Nissa leaned forward just as a shoot, thick as her arm, uncoiled and rented the crack wide. The crack traveled up the hedron until it stopped at the tip, and the hedron broke cleanly into two pieces and tumbled with a tremendous crash onto the stone floor. Green arced from shard to shard, and then the fire blinked out altogether.

Sorin's voice boomed louder from behind. But clearly the vampire could not undo what had been done. Moments later his song took on a high, screeching sound, and then stopped abruptly. Nissa looked back at Sorin. His eyes popped open to reveal corneas the color of molten gold.

"Well," Sorin said, clapping his hands together. "This is my queue to leave. You, my dear fools, can deal with the consequences. They will be far worse than anything I can do to you." The vampire brushed a hand down his tunic, and Nissa turned her attention back to the broken hedron.

The hall echoed and shook as the hedron halves rocked in place. But instead of quieting when the halves came to rest, the cavern continued shaking, until large chunks fell from the darkness above and the cave floor began to pitch. The eyes of the stone dragon's face were still glowing. She smelled Anowon suddenly standing next to her.

"Well?" Nissa said to Anowon who said nothing, but stood at the edge of the causeway looking down into the darkness at the bottom of the cavern.

CHAPTER 22

As the cavern shook, small jags of lightening snapped between the hedron halves. Nissa closed her eyes and squared her shoulders as she waited for the last moment. Zendikar would flourish once again and the Eldrazi would be gone forever.

Mudheel was next to her retching—he wiped the corner of his mouth and looked up at the hedron with tears streaming down his face. "Mistress . . ." he said. "No."

The cavern started to shake. Three massive tremors shook the cavern sending more rocks showering down. And from somewhere deep in the mountain came a sound so ominous that Nissa turned away from the face of the dragon and started running. But the sound followed her, like the moan of ten thousand undead, and something else—a rushing roar.

"Out," Anowon yelled above the roar.

They ran. Twice Nissa almost slid off the causeway, catching herself at the last moment. Of Mudheel, there was no sign.

They crisscrossed over the causeways with rocks falling all around until they saw the light of the cave entrance ahead. The cavern shuttered again and Nissa turned back for a final look at the Eye or Ugin.

Something was rising out of the depression under the causeway. Shapes danced in the darkness. The shadow of a tentacle larger than any she'd ever seen flopped on the causeway behind, shattering it to pieces. She felt the stone around groan and buckle as it came undone and fell to bits.

The drakes were still perched atop the crystals when Anowon and Nissa burst out of the cave mouth. The small dragons surveyed them standing in the billows of dust issuing from the cave's mouth. Then they took off and flew away.

The ground began to shake more violently. The roar behind suddenly swelled to a deafening bellow and Anowon and Nissa leaped back against the rock next to the cave mouth.

And just in time. Moments later enormous tentacles snaked out of the cave mouth, followed by jagged, bony arms. The very mountain began to come down around the tentacles. What could only have been an Eldrazi titan glided out of the hole, its tentacles slathered in mucus.

Nissa began to run. The others followed. Whatever was coming out of the cave mouth was huge. The ground was fracturing under it. Nissa glanced back as she ran—the red tooth, the spire at the top of the mountain, cracked and tumbled down over the creature's bony neck. Nissa and Anowan ran as hard as they could until the ground was not shaking as much. Nissa stopped and turned.

As Nissa watched, the creature nuzzled its bulbous bone face into fine scree and rubble which was all that was left of the mountain. In appearance the beast looked much as a brood lineage, but larger by far. As tall as a turntimber tree. And the smell! The smell made her want to die. Rotting meat and mushrooms and sulfur from the very bowels of the rock.

But there were differences, aside from its immensity. The small plants eking out an existence in the scree withered to black smudges on the stones as the titan neared. A stone pig fled its burrow in terror, but fell to sludge as it passed near the titan's tentacles. Nissa felt the terrible power as well. She felt the force within her body pulling toward the tentacled menace, as iron to a magnet. It was hard for her to work her lungs at pulling air. Next to her, Anowon shuddered and slipped down the rock they were huddled against.

The next titan to emerge from the ruined mountain was nothing more than a mass of tentacles. The porous latticework structure floating above it scraped the top of the cave mouth as it was born from the cave mouth. Nissa blinked and found herself crumpled next to Anowon on the ground, she did not know she was holding her breath until she exhaled.

The last titan used its split arms to drag itself out of the mouth of the cave. It was a long creature, longer than the other titans . . . and more terrible somehow. Once it had pulled its rear tentacles out of the cave, this titan straightened itself. Its chitinous exoskeleton crackled as it stood taller than anything she'd ever seen. Nissa found herself cringing.

All standing together, the titans moved down the canyon. The very light around them bent as a desert mirage might, and the rock they moved over cracked to dust. As they neared the edges of the canyon, great chunks or red rock broke off and desiccated to dust filtering down to the canyon floor.

The last titan slithered to the middle of the canyon, and even its sound did not adhere to the normal rules of nature. Instead of the crushing sound that should have been heard as it made the rocks flat, Nissa heard a high-pitched squeak and low, moaning roll as the sound in the canyon bent and reverberated in the titan's dominion.

The terrible creatures moved close and as their tentacles wound together they began to make a sound that Nissa could not have imagined in her worst nightmare. At once it was the shriek of wounded warthogs mixed with the sharp cut of a gale wind. The titans raised their clinging arms and began to bellow at the sky.

Nissa glanced at Anowon, expecting to see the fear that she herself felt at seeing these massive creatures screaming at the sky. But the vampire would not meet her eyes, and when he did it was not fear of the Eldrazi that she saw. It was hunger. *He's hungry*, she thought with a dull dread.

Mudheel was gone. That left Nissa, alone with a vampire who had not eaten in days. Had not Sorin told her that Anowon was always trying to drain her? And that he, Sorin, kept this from happening? She did not doubt it seeing the hungry look in Anowon's eyes just now.

But by this time the titan's vocalizing had become deafening. Some of the canyon walls singed to vapor and the rest compressed to powder and blew away in the hot wind. Nissa watched as the creatures, their tentacles intertwined, moved down the canyon, knocking down walls. When they came to the mountain, they did not stop. The rock simply fell to pieces at their touch. And they stopped for a moment to nuzzle the rubble until it, too, was nothing more than powder sucked dry of any mana.

Nissa lay on the ground, exhausted. When she looked up Anowon was watching her, his chin resting on arms crossed over his knees. The pupils in his strange dark eyes were narrowed to points as he stared.

Rocks clattered and a form lurched out of the dust, dragging one leg. Nissa hopped to her feet and felt for the stem sword. But the figure turned to her and chuckled.

"Oh, this is rich," Sorin said. "You managed to break what could not be broken, and you almost did me to death in the process. Now *you* are responsible for what happens to your precious Zendikar."

Nissa's mouth must have gaped. "I did not know the seeding would undo such a desperate enchantment," she stammered.

Sorin took a deep breath and released it. "What is done is done."

Nissa looked to the path of destruction left by the titans.

With his most arrogant smile Sorin turned his eyes on the other vampire. "Anowon, come here."

Anowon did not move, did not even meet the vampire's eyes. "I do not serve you, Mortifier," Anowon said. "You should be dead now."

"I should," Sorin agreed. "But now that the elf has released the scourge, I will be needed elsewhere."

"First you will come with me to Guul Draz and answer for your crimes to the Septumvirate in Ib Nimana," Anowon said.

"Thank you for the invitation, but I will have to decline," Sorin hobbled over to a rock and sat down. His great sword clattered on the talus as he bent and sat down.

Nissa took a deep breath.

"You know what direction they are moving, don't you?" Sorin said.

Nissa imagined the titan's path and closed her eyes.

"Yes, you see," Sorin said. "Toward your jungles."

He looked from Nissa to Anowon, then back again. "What do you think will happen now?" he said. "Does your plane feel different now that the ancient enemy is released?"

"I will not even ask the Ghet," Sorin said. "I can tell the answer from his face."

Nissa glanced at Anowon. He was staring at Sorin with extreme distaste.

Sorin swept one arm out. "Zendikar is the same place as it always was. The brood still run rough-shod over your lands. The Roil will perservere . . . And elves will still bless the rest of us with their stunning opinions. But I," Sorin leaned foreword and stood. "I will have to let you see how this all turns out."

"You are not leaving," Anowon said. "You are coming with me to Guul Draz."

"Oh," Sorin said. "You were serious before about visiting the Septumvirate? Again, I am sorry."

Anowon stood.

Sorin was easily a head taller than the other vampire, and far more formidable, Nissa knew. He looked at Nissa. "Do not let him slake his disappointment-thirst on you," he said.

There was a sudden crash and one of the mountains in the direction that the titans had traveled began to teeter and crumble. Anowan turned to watch as the high mountain rocked far to the right and began to very slowly topple.

Sorin closed his eyes and sucked in a breath. Nissa stepped back involuntarily when the vampire's body tensed and began to shake. A deep growl emanated from his throat. Nissa could clearly see the veins standing out in Sorin's neck. *Is the planeswalking?* After a short time the growl became a whine and then Sorin's skin began to glow very slightly. He opened both eyes and winked one of them at Nissa. Then Sorin was gone, and the air which had surrounded his body rushed with a sudden pop.

Nissa's first inclination was to follow the vampire, to plead with him to come back to Zendikar and set things right—re-imprison the menace she had just released. But the moment passed and Nissa did not concentrate on moving through the Eternities.

Anowan had missed the whole event, but she felt he was meant to. He stood rapt, his eyes fixed on the crumbling mountain. Nissa did not want to explain what had just happened. It would be difficult to do so clearly, anyway. And there was something more important she had to make painfuly clear to the hungry vampire standing opposite her.

Nissa reached down and drew a long dirk from her boot and snapped it out so that the tip rested on the back of Anowon's neck. Sensing the danger, he turned and lunged. Nissa stepped to the side, caught the back of his neck with her left hand, and with the force of her backwards step, whipped him to the ground face first. Then she drew a length of rope from the pack and bound Anowon's hands behind his back.

Nissa yanked the vampire to his feet. "You will walk bound until Affa where we will part ways and I will travel to Bala Ged. My time trusting vampires has long since past," Nissa said, as she pushed Anowon before her along the trail. "I am going home."

EPILOGUE

Nissa Revine walked toe-to-heel along the rope that lead to the Joraga council sling. The other rope, the only other way to get to the council sling, the main meeting place of her tribe where the young elves were born and raised, was full of other Joraga walking easily to the meeting. Even though it took a bit more time to navigate the many trapeze ropes that joined her tribe's meeting slings and sleeping pods, Nissa knew that the advantages outweighed their inconveniences. They could be cut easily in a siege. And vampires, despite their stealthy quickness, had trouble with prolonged balance. Such knowledge, discovered by her Joraga forbearers, and paid for in blood, had saved her tribe more than once. So Nissa was glad to slow down and walk carefully along the rope to the meeting sling.

Of course, the trapeze lines would not hinder brood lineage or the Eldrazi titans in the least, Nissa thought as she watched the few remaining Joraga make their way to the meeting.

When she got to the sling, she followed the other Joraga inside and strode to the front bench. Unlike a Tajuru council meeting, the assembled Joraga did not speak. Outside council they were loud and vulgar, unless hunting. Strangely, she found herself missing the Tajuru prattle . . . the inane jokes and hushed giggles.

Nissa raised her hands and all eyes were on her. There were not that many eyes Nissa noticed with a sudden pang in her stomach. Most of the seats stood empty. *Was this really it, all the Joraga left?* They did not even fill half of the sling.

"It falls to me," Nissa said. "To tell you we have word of the scourge, at the Slim Blade."

Nissa imagined the Slim Blade, that tongue of land where two famous rivers met—a place at the western edge of Joraga territory. She listened for the response to this news. As usual there were no significant sounds. But that did not mean there was joy in the crowd. She heard a very slight intake of breath from two elves in the front row. That could only mean exasperation and fear—two emotions that were expressly forbidden in the sling or anywhere else in the Joraga rule.

"Half will go," Nissa said, simply. ". . . with the bags. As your leader, I will be one of those going." She lowered her arms, turned and walked out of the sling. The rest of the Joraga waited until she had left and then filed out without a sound. On the planks that encircled the sling Nissa broke their number to half and all made their way to the supply sling.

Soon her time as leader would be over, Nissa thought as she waited in line with the other Joraga, and she already knew what she would do.

Nissa took one of the bags from the supply chief. She slung it over her shoulder. It was not a heavy thing after all, and she and the twenty Joraga began their walk to the west. As she walked the contents of the bag shifted and jiggled. She liked that.

The trip took two days. Nissa could not help but notice that such a trip would have taken a Tajuru double the time as they walked along their foolish branches and took needless breaks. None of this was done by the Joraga. They walked on the ground, unafraid. And food was eaten once per day, before their short nap at daybreak.

At the head of her squad, Nissa's job was to notice everything in the jungle. She did this. But as her eyes flitted from movement to movement, she found herself seeing a certain humanoid shape in every shadow. They always dissipated after she blinked her eyes. But it was unmistakably the same form every time. *Anowon.* She'd left the vampire outside of Affa, tied up and buried to his neck in the sandy soil. She'd left him with a stern warning: follow and die. A new stem sword was being grown back at the sling, but until then Nissa kept an arrow nocked on her bow string at all times.

She wished she had to worry about Sorin visiting. Once Anowan was dealt with, she tried to follow Sorin, but his trail was too fragmented. She had planeswalked through the Eternities and found his first couple of stops on rocky, seemingly abandoned planes. On another plane where every surface was as the surface of a pristine pond, she found an old human who said he had seen a white-haired stranger. But that was all. The thin, trail left when individuals walked through the æther had dissipated too much to be followed, and Nissa eventually gave up her search.

She would try again.

She would ask Sorin to come back and re-imprison the menace she had unleashed on Zendikar. He had not told her what would happen if they were set free. She had not understood fully. Now Sorin simply *had* to come back and set things right. The outbreak was simply too large for her to deal with alone.

Suddenly Nissa stopped. A far off movement in the undergrowth made her drop into a crouch. After a second a bird flew out, and she straightened and started walking again.

Then the Joraga were at the site of devastation, which looked very much like all the others. The edge of the destruction started when Nissa began to notice the plants of the jungle looked sick, yellowish. As they walked further the plants withered to a dark brown, and the immense nula trees were seen toppled to the ground. Then it got bad. Nissa and the other Joraga found themselves walking through a land of almost total ruin extending on all sides for as far as they could see. Wide swaths of dirt were trenched and plowed up to reveal dead roots, which appeared to reach for the wrecked and brooding sky.

Nissa never understood how *they* got at the sky. But every new wasteland had the same orange and gray sky. And always the same plants, stamped to ooze. Only the bare tree trunks, dripping themselves away, stood as stark jags on the dark landscape.

What was left of the elf bodies was worse. Inevitably there were bodies, although they were hard to find. The Joraga who had tried to stop the desecration of the land had paid for their fidelity with their lives. Nissa stopped and looked down at one of the blackened husks that could have been a section of tree trunk. She knew it was the body of one of her kinsmen by the tarnished armband.

"Eldrazi scourge," the Joraga next to her hissed. Nissa jerked around and struck the male across the face, snapping his head sideways.

"No," she said. "Never *that* word." In the quiet that

followed, the waste seemed to echo with the word Eldrazi. Nissa turned her ear up to the wind, hoping not to hear movement. She could detect none, but that did not mean *they* were not hunching in some hole out there.

She slung the bag from her shoulder. "Let us start."

As she slit the threads to open the bag, she felt the total lack of life in the land. *The leach. They* had come and sucked every bit of mana out of the land, and they would come back. But in the meantime the Joraga could perhaps do something to heal the damage.

She spread the opening of the bag and felt the mana flood out and break over her face. It was such a welcome feeling in this wasteland. She reached in, took a handful of the seed, all of different sizes, textures, and colors. Enough variety of seed to make again the jungle forests of Bala Ged. In the palm of her hand she saw huge tramba seeds as large as her thumb, and the power-sized seeds of the creeping plants whose name she did not know. There were plenty of seeds she did not know. But she closed her fist around them all and waited.

Nissa knew that she was just the person to do the planting. Unlike the other Joraga, her magic was still strong, despite the Eldrazi. Her strong mana lines stretched to the different planes she'd visited, allowed her to grow these plants better than any in her tribe could.

As soon as the other Joraga had a similar handful of seed Nissa began the growth song. It was an old song, and she sang it as she had been singing it her whole life. *They* may come again, Nissa thought. Or *they* may flee Zendikar tomorrow, but right now the forest would be made anew.

Nissa drew her fist back.

She would travel the planes until she found Sorin and others who would help bind the Eldrazi once again. She alone among her people could do this, and save Zendikar from the gathering darkness. For the first time her planeswalking skill would help her people.

"I am of those that walk the Blind Eternities," Nissa said, throwing out the seed.

WALK THE BLIND ETERNITIES

They are the heroes of the Multiverse. United by their ability to bridge the chaotic gap between worlds, and set apart by that same unfathomable power, planeswalkers wander the Blind Eternities in an endless quest for knowledge and power.

TEST OF METAL

Matthew Stover

Tezzeret rises from the ashes of defeat, seeking that secret source of power he needs to reinvent himself.

OCTOBER 2010

Be there as destiny unfolds.

ALSO AVAILABLE AS E-BOOKS!